SHAKEN BLESSINGS

By

Celeste Charlene

This is a work of fiction, and is produced from the author's imagination. People, places and things mentioned in this novel are used in a fictional manner.

To Kathryn Page Camp, my faithful friend and critique partner. Thank you.

CHAPTER ONE

Sandra Calbrin slid out of the bush taxi and lifted her hand to shield the sun from her eyes. Her gaze wandered to the black goats that peppered the field. She took a deep breath before grabbing the medical basket with her backpack and walked to the mud-brick church.

A small man with tribal scars marched toward her. Dressed in filthy pants, he balanced an upside-down wooden table on his head and extended his calloused hand. "Welcome to Koala. I am Pastor Paul. I hope you brought lots of measles vaccinations."

"Yes, I have plenty."

"The sickness started in the northern villages. Many children died."

"I'm sorry to hear that."

"My brothers live there and lost some of their youngsters." Pastor Paul lifted the table off his head and set it on the ground. He picked up a large stone and put it under the shortest table leg to stop the wobble. "Put your medicines here."

Sandy opened her basket and set bottles of liquids and pills on the table. "I'd like to enroll all the children in the Under Fives Clinics that I'm starting and treat the ill ones. I'll give the injections and record them on the cards, plot weights on the graphs, and distribute the malaria prophylaxis."

"Did you bring the health cards?"

"Yes." A trickle of sweat slid down her spine. "I'm not the right person for this job. I offered to hire a local nurse who spoke the language, but she couldn't come."

"You are the best one for the work."

Many children had already died, and she couldn't refuse to vaccinate the others while she was in Africa, and so she volunteered. Mothers carrying infants arrived from every direction.

She shuddered. A deathly ill child had died in her arms while she worked in the Stateside hospital. Since then she'd not treated any children.

A large woman with black tattoos on her cheeks stopped in front of Sandy. The lady lifted a bucket of water off her head and set it on the ground.

"This is my wife." The pastor pointed to the woman. "She has given me four children in our five years of marriage."

Most likely the pastor meant it as a compliment, but Sandy's heart ached for the barefoot woman, who must work from sunup to sundown. Reproduction had to be her primary function.

"My wife goes with me to hoe the fields every day with the other villagers. And she sings like a dove."

The corners of Sandy's lips twitched. "I'm sure she's a good wife." Glancing at the dark water in the plastic bucket, Sandy cringed. Dust and maggots floated on top of the liquid. Who could keep clean and healthy in this environment?

"Pastor, where do people get their drinking water?"

"It comes from the river."

"Do you boil it?"

"We can't waste firewood boiling water for drinking."

She ran her fingers through her hair and flattened it behind her ears. What was the point of vaccinating babies if they could die from diarrhea, worms, and dysentery? Her chest tightened. She would do the best she could.

Sandy took out the baby scale and positioned it at eye level before tying it to a sturdy branch of the guava tree. A large pair of cotton pants, which accommodated the size of a newborn to that of a three-year-old child, dangled from the swinging balance.

She picked up a treatment card and squinted at the unique combination of letters. Opening and closing her mouth several times, she tried to form the words.

The pastor looked over her shoulder and shouted, *"Salubatu Hemouwa."*

A mother came forward with her infant. Sandy's gaze drifted over the soiled clothes as she reached for the sleeping boy. She lowered him into the hanging pants and slipped each leg inside the trouser openings.

The stench of amebic dysentery filled her nostrils. She leaned the infant back in the crotch of the dangling shorts as watery stools with blood ran out of the holes in the pants.

"Your baby is sick and needs treatment. This card says he is eight months old, but he only weighs seven pounds. He is malnourished and anemic." She calculated the number of worm tablets, antibiotics, and chloroquine pills based on his weight.

The clinic guidelines recommended patients pay a small fee. If the people invested in the medications it guaranteed they would take them.

"Thank you." The mother opened her bag and took out coins worth about twenty-five cents.

Throughout the day, Sandy worked quickly to treat and immunize as many children as possible. Cocoa-skinned babies in Africa were like American ones. Some were beautiful while others were cute, but they all clung to their mothers and wailed just as loudly when Sandy injected the vaccines.

Toward sundown the sky darkened. Thunder rumbled and lightning flashed.

She tried to continue when the pastor brought a bush lantern, but she couldn't examine the children well enough in the dim light. There wouldn't be enough time to weigh and inoculate all the infants.

A heavy downpour beat the ground as she tossed bottles of medications into her basket, picked it up, and dashed toward the house. She stopped at the door. Watching the pastor and his wife take off their shoes, she removed hers and followed them inside as rain hammered on the tin roof. Shivering in her wet clothes, she crossed her arms and rubbed them.

The pastor carried grass-woven mats and wooden benches from one room into another chamber. "I am preparing a place for you to sleep." He picked up a two-inch-thick piece of foam cushion and put it on top of a bamboo bedframe in a tiny room off the sitting room. "This will be your sleeping chamber."

"Can you close the wooden shutters to the windows and the door to keep the mosquitoes and other insects outside?"

The pastor banged them shut. "You will not get fresh air this way."

"I'd like privacy to take off these wet clothes and put on dry ones."

When the pastor left, Sandy changed and went into the sitting room.

His wife brought bowls of white rice with fish heads in tomato sauce and served a heaping plate to Sandy.

After eating her fill, she extended her dish to the pastor. "Your wife prepared too much food for me. Could someone finish this?"

The pastor took the plate. "Yes. Thank you. Feel free to go to bed now."

Hearing deafening screams, Sandy looked around. "What's happening?" More shrieks sent quivers up and down her spine.

"It is nothing. Go to bed." He took a towel, wrapped it around his head like a mummy, and positioned his petite body in the center, lengthwise on the eight-inch wide, wooden bench.

She couldn't find a match inside her room to light the bush lantern and went back into the sitting room, but the pastor was gone.

Bone-tingling cries came from outside and shook her from head to toe. Maybe the pastor left to rescue someone from being sacrificed. Blood pulsed in her temples as the piercing screams increased.

She stepped out the back door and peered into the dark, searching for witch doctors, headhunters, or cannibals. Hearing shrieks again, she dashed in their direction. She slid through mud puddles as she hurried toward the screeches.

Her heart pounded like thumping war drums.

CHAPTER TWO

The cries swelled as Sandy shivered under the cool rain, squinting at an old shed not far ahead. Her heart raced. She sprinted to the shelter, banged open the wooden door, and stepped inside.

Blinking several times to focus, she scowled. Wood smoke irritated her eyes as she moved closer to the screaming child on the woman's lap.

Sandy stroked the boy's hot face. "Unwrap these wool blankets, remove the flannel clothes, and bathe this child in cool water."

"He needs these covers because rain made my little boy cold." The mother clutched the baby to her chest.

The pastor came into the kitchen and glared at Sandy. "Go back to bed."

"If the child gets hotter, he will suffer a febrile convulsion." Sandy couldn't think fast enough to use local words for febrile convulsion, but fevers killed millions of babies. "It's over a hundred degrees in this kitchen. Take off the baby's clothes."

Why had she ever come to Africa? She wasn't the right person to carry out this job.

"Go back to sleep." The pastor moved closer to his wife and child as if protecting them from Sandy.

She clenched her jaws, dug her heels in the clay floor, and snapped, "Unwrap him and cool him off right now."

"You worked hard today." The pastor frowned. "Go back to bed."

With tears in her eyes, she left. She wanted to go to the airport and leave on the next plane, but she had a duty to vaccinate the children.

She mumbled, "God help us."

As she reached the house, hideous choking sounds shattered the night. Again she raced back toward the shed and slammed open the door. Stepping inside, she didn't understand what she saw.

The mother held her child on her lap with the baby's head dangling off her thigh. Strangling gasps came from the infant. The woman's thumb and index finger pinched off the baby's nose while the remaining fingers curled around the child's lower lip forming a container. With her other hand, the mother poured watery gruel down the child's throat.

Tears, kerosene fumes, and wood smoke filled Sandy's eyes. "Stop it right now."

The baby shrieked, thrashing his arms and legs. He looked like he was drowning.

"Stop." Wiping away a few tears, Sandy reached over to pull the mother's hands away from the child, but she couldn't free the baby from the woman's hold. "He is gasping for air because he can't breathe."

The mother jerked the child away from Sandy, who ran around to the other side of the woman and grabbed the baby. Sandy sat on a tiny stool and set the little boy on her lap. He leaned closer to her chest, as she picked up a spoon to feed him. The boy's weight and six front teeth suggested he was about a year old. He ate his food and fell asleep. Why had the woman been feeding her son in that barbaric fashion?

Sandy handed the child to his mother, returned to her room, and lay down on the bamboo bed. A few minutes later, intense screams jolted every sense in her body. She leaped off the bed and ran to the shed.

The mother was feeding a baby girl in the same manner as she had the boy.

"Please stop this." Sandy sniffed as more tears filled her eyes.

"Go to bed," The pastor declared. "Let my wife do her work. This is our way and culture. All mothers in our tribe feed children like this."

Sandy went to her room. Several minutes later, piercing shrieks prickled her skin. She wiped away her tears. Should she spend the night in the shed to save the children, but who would rescue them when Sandy wasn't there?

Sighing deeply, she opened the shed door again. "Why are you doing these terrible things to your children?"

"To make them strong and healthy. You white people waste time feeding babies with spoons. Pouring the food down the throat saves time."

Sandy threw her hands in the air. She didn't want to spend another minute with these people. She wiped the sweat from her forehead. "You could kill a child."

The pastor snarled, "It is forbidden to talk about death. Please do not speak of this."

The naked baby in the woman's lap soaked her skirt with loose, watery excreta. The woman grabbed the baby's arm, stood up, and dangled the child by its upper arm. The mother slapped the baby's face, backside, and legs.

Sandy's eyes blurred with tears. "Stop beating the baby!"

"My wife is not hurting him. She wants him to cry to make him stronger."

Tears ran down Sandy's cheeks. She snatched the infant away from the mother and picked up a cloth from a nearby wicker basket to wrap him. "Why do you strike a helpless baby? Beat the person who gave dirty food and water causing the diarrhea."

Sandy scowled at the ignorant mother and prepared to run away with the infant. Where could she go with a battered baby during a tropical storm?

Nowhere. Thunder roared. Torrents of rain beat the metal roof. The pastor's home sat several miles away from the center of Koala village, isolated in the middle of a cornfield. No taxis traveled in the night.

She couldn't escape with the infant, nor could she report them to the police for child abuse. If mothers practiced handed-down, dangerous traditions, local people would not see it as cruelty.

The rain stopped in the middle of the night. The house was hot and the pastor slammed open the wooden shutters in the sitting room. Lightning bolts flashed and illuminated the interior of the house. "Please do not be angry." He found the box of matches and struck one. He lifted the glass globe and lit the wick of the lantern. "Please do not be annoyed we have no electricity."

"I am not annoyed there is no electricity."

11

"Do not be annoyed we have no toilet."

"I am not annoyed there is no toilet."

"Do not be annoyed there is no running water."

She grimaced. "I am not annoyed there isn't electricity, water, or a toilet. I am annoyed because your wife is going to kill the children."

"She will not kill the children."

The pastor's wife pulled a baby bottle out of a basket. She sat down on a stool and stuffed the bottle in a child's mouth.

Sandy flinched at the little black exclamation points slithering inside the filthy bottle. Worms? Maggots? Bugs? The jug's sour odor caused bile to rise in her throat.

Sandy looked from the woman to the pastor and then yanked the repulsive container away from the mother. "Look at this. Black mold and squiggly worms are in this plastic. It is dangerous and will make your child sick."

Did Sandy have the right to take the infected bottle away? If a woman held a gun to a child's head, Sandy would have snatched it away. "I'll keep this for now."

She had all she could handle of Africa and its deep-rooted customs. Tears ran down her face as she went into her room. Control, like the slippery flies she tried to kill, slid out of her fingers. She wished she had stayed in a logical world where she had authority. She lay on the bed but couldn't sleep.

At five in the morning a crowd of villagers arrived for prayer meeting.

"Please build us a hospital," said an elderly gentleman.

How dare the people make such a request of her? "If you had a hospital, but kept urinating in front of the house and passed excreta in the back, the environment would be filled with dangerous germs which could bring diseases to your children." Sandy swept her arms up and down and whispered through her scratchy throat. "You need a pit latrine and clean water more than you need a medical facility. Dig a well and boil the drinking water from the dirty streams."

Terrifying screams filled the air, and Sandy rushed outside to the kitchen shed again. Her eyes widened at the shrieking child in the pot of hot water as steam rose from it. "Take that baby out of the boiling water!"

"I am making my children strong." Built like a lumberjack, most likely from chopping firewood and carrying one hundred-pound loads on her head, the tall, muscled mother blocked Sandy from touching the baby.

Sandy wanted to bash the woman on the side of the head, strangle her, or toss her into the pot of boiling water, but she couldn't fight a woman three times her size. She ducked around the mother and lifted the screaming baby out of the cooking vessel.

After the child was out, Sandy stared at the pot. The bubbles Sandy had taken for boiling stopped. It was then she saw there was no fire under the pot. The child's frantic kicking to get out of the liquid caused the bubbles. Sandy plunged her hand and arm into the water. Her limb turned red. "The water is too hot."

The mother yelled, "It is not too hot. I added a little river water and black soap to the boiling water before I bathed the baby."

"Please stop cooking your child."

Villagers crept into the kitchen.

"I am not boiling my baby."

An elderly man came forward. "Madam, these are our traditions. We've had them hundreds of years, and they will not hurt anyone. We all bathe our children in the hottest water possible."

"You are burning the child."

"Hot water will kill the sicknesses." The gentleman sighed. "The child will be very clean."

Sandy shouted back, "The child will be very dead!"

A moment of silence, and then several men in the crowd let out a loud gasp. They filled their lungs and growled. Other men shook their fists. Some women shed tears while others jabbered. The pastor's wife moaned and buried her face in her hands.

CHAPTER THREE

Sandy turned away from their horror-stricken faces, but there was no place to look. Angry people filled the tiny shed. She breathed in and out to suppress the quivers running up and down her spine.

The elderly gentleman yelled, "Why have you cursed this baby?"

Blood pulsed in her ears. Cursed a baby? She squared her shoulders so her five-foot frame appeared more impressive. "I haven't cursed the child. I'm trying to save him."

"You proclaimed his death. It is taboo to mention death, most especially on a baby. You spoke the words of death out loud in the same breath as a person. The evil spirits heard those words. You are responsible if anything happens to him."

Sandy stiffened and dug her heels deeper into the earth-packed floor. "I'm not to blame for this child's suffering. Speaking a few words cannot curse a baby."

The pastor lifted his hands in supplication. "Our white sister does not want to harm anyone. She came here to vaccinate our children against diseases so they won't die."

Men shook their fists. Women wiped their tear-streaked faces, and the pastor's wife sobbed. Sandy needed to diffuse the hostile situation.

She'd read every book and magazine about different tribes and their diverse beliefs before her arrival but knew little of these isolated people and their strange ways. She was drowning in the ocean of ebony-skinned people surrounding her. She wanted to close her eyes and wake up from the nightmare.

As the manager of a fitness center, she could talk her way out or suggest a compromise in the most disagreeable circumstances. She calmed the ruffled exercise outfits and agitated temperaments of her clients with ease. Smoothing out wrinkled conditions came naturally, but she could think of nothing in that bleak situation of cursed and abused babies.

God help.

She had never prayed out loud but it was worth a try. She shuddered at their livid stares before lowering her head to her chest. "We must pray for this baby. His life is in danger from his fever." Sandy knelt on the clay floor and put her hands on the child sitting on the mother's lap. Sandy prayed a loud prayer of distress.

At the end of her short request to God, the hostile crowd turned silent, and people smiled again. Was it a miracle?

The pastor left and returned with a half-filled bucket of water. "This is for your little bath."

Eager to leave the mob, Sandy took the bucket from him. She strolled behind the shed to the three-sided, bamboo booth. After flicking open the giant cloth the pastor's wife loaned her, she draped it over the pole joining the top of the walls. The fabric shifted in the breeze. After she undressed, the wind blew the makeshift curtain and lifted it up.

She twisted away from the opening and squeezed into the corner, hoping no one had been watching. She washed, dried, and dressed in record time.

When she returned to the sitting room the pastor offered her a covered tray. "Here are bean cakes for your breakfast."

Sandy picked up a deep-fried round and bit into it. "These are delicious. How do they make them?" Listening to cooking instructions would take her mind off tortured babies.

"My wife takes black-eyed peas, soaks them overnight, and skins them. She crushes them on her grinding stone, adds pepper, salt, onion, and chopped tomato. She drops spoons of it into hot oil." The pastor bit into one.

His wife came into the room. "Here is a flask filled with boiling water for your tea."

Sandy's tongue tangled in her mouth. "Aaah. Aaah. Thank you." She had yelled at the pastor's wife for mistreating her children, but the woman cooked breakfast and boiled water for tea. Sandy cared about the minister and his family, but at the same time she wanted to strangle the parents for harming their children.

Her conflicted heart pounded as she battled love and disgust. Cultural traditions and taboos controlled their lives and actions. The people couldn't help what they did, but she couldn't stand by and watch a mother, even in her ignorance, kill her children.

Sandy took out a tea bag from her backpack, put it in the cup, and poured water from the thermos over it.

The pastor turned to her. "Do you want sugar and milk for your tea?"

"No, thank you. I prefer it black."

The pastor stared at Sandy. "Are you normal to drink tea without sugar or milk?"

She wasn't normal. No woman in her right mind would be found in the situation she was in that morning.

Several minutes later, screams erupted outside. Sandy set the bean cake and teacup down on the lopsided table.

"Pastor, I've had enough." She didn't just mean enough bean cakes. She had enough of everything. Enough child abuse, enough ignorance, enough noncompliance, enough hopelessness, and learned helplessness. She wouldn't stay another minute and listen to the screams of mistreated children.

Then she remembered the wife's hospitality and the pastor who had given Sandy a mattress. "Pastor, do you always sleep on a wooden bench?"

"No, I wanted you to have the bed in my bedroom, so you would be comfortable. My wife kept the children with her in her bed."

Sandy couldn't stay angry with them. "Thank you. I am grateful." She loved and hated them at the same time. Their gracious, accommodating behavior tugged at her heart, while their treatment of children distressed her.

The pastor accompanied her outside. "I am sorry that the mosquitoes were so many last night."

"What mosquitoes? There were none in my room. Do you remember we closed the door and wooden shutters so they wouldn't come inside?"

He sighed. "I thank God for that."

"I can see you do the best you can, but please don't let your wife kill the children. Feed them upright with a cup and spoon, and don't bathe them in hot water." Sandy moved away from him.

Like a warrior defending his family, he drew his short skinny body up to his full height, making him eye-level with Sandy. He puffed out his chest. "I will never allow my wife to hurt the children."

Sandy narrowed her brows and crossed her arms. "It could happen at any time, in just a moment."

With a screaming baby in her arms, the wife came to Sandy. "You don't know anything about black babies. Our children are different from your white ones."

Sandy's eyes watered. "All babies, African or American, are little children who need proper care."

The pastor's wife scowled. "But our babies are tough."

Sandy stiffened. "Most babies, when given the best food and care, will be strong and healthy."

She thrived on challenges, but teaching health to them felt like a lost cause. If she was going to save the children by training parents how to care for them, she needed to show them.

But where could she get an African baby to teach the people children's health?

CHAPTER FOUR

A horn blasted, and Sandy jumped as a car engine roared toward her on the dusty cow path. The vehicle stopped in front of her.

David Jubilee, the chauffeur from the church headquarters, climbed out. "Good morning. My father sent me to bring you back to Hose to settle an immigration problem."

"I can leave now." She wanted to go as far away as possible and never return to the village of Koala but had promised to finish the vaccinations. She slid into the vehicle, slumped back against the cushion, and slept.

She woke up as David pulled into the headquarters and parked in front of his father's office.

Sandy stepped out, walked to Mr. Jubilee's office, and knocked.

The medical director called, "Come in."

As she went into the pea-green room, she caught a musty odor. One of the four windows was broken, and all the screens were ripped, which accounted for the flies that flew straight toward her.

Mr. Jubilee, a heavyset man in a business suit, stood behind a desk. He came forward and pushed a chair toward her. "I hope you had a pleasant trip. I apologize for bringing you back before you've completed the vaccinations, but I learned that foreigners without visas must leave the country immediately."

She'd be glad to leave and be free of the filth and disease, but her heart plummeted. What about all the innocent children who might die without the vaccinations?

"We must settle the problem with your visa. The immigration officer lost the stamp to put it in your passport."

Sandy cocked an eyebrow. "How can we solve that problem? Are we going to the office to help search for the stamp?"

"Yes, we will both go down there together."

David drove Sandy and Mr. Jubilee to the immigration office, and Sandy followed Mr. Jubilee inside.

He shook hands with an official. "Where is Colonel Tsaou, the officer in charge?"

An officer, whose badge read, 'Lieutenant Coutene,' stepped out from behind a desk. "Colonel Tsaou has not returned from siesta. You can come back in an hour or wait."

African names were difficult to pronounce. To keep Lieutenant Coutene separate from the others, Sandy mentally nicknamed the tall, well-mannered officer with one stripe, 'Lieutenant Courteous.' She shook hands with him. "I'll wait here."

"Please sit down."

She lifted her chin. "Can I help you look for the lost visa stamp?"

"Stay seated, Miss Calbrin. This is a government office."

Mr. Jubilee turned to Sandy. "Would you mind waiting while I go and speak to someone?"

"No, that's fine."

"David and I will be back soon." They left.

Sandy turned to Lieutenant Courteous. "My temporary visa expires in three days."

"No worry. We will find the stamp before three days." Lieutenant Courteous opened drawers and pulled out a small box. "I found the stamp for a five-day visa and can put this in your passport."

"A five-day visa will not give me enough time to finish the vaccinations."

"This is the only visa stamp we have, so you must take it." Lieutenant Courteous glared.

"If the choice is leaving in three days when my visa expires, or five days with this new one, it would be easier to leave today since I'm here in the city and close to the international airport."

An officer with two stripes and no nametag stepped into the office and approached her. "Have you been to the American Embassy?"

"Yes." She stared at the officer's blood-shot eyes and nicknamed him, 'Lieutenant Red Eye.'

"Why did you go there?" Lieutenant Red Eye thrust his head to within six inches of her nose.

"I went to register as an American citizen which is a requirement."

20

Another officer stepped up to Sandy. She tried not to grimace at the thirty odd, deep scars marring his face. His name tag said, 'Lieutenant Bemouta.' She nicknamed him 'Lieutenant Scarface.'

He raised his hand like he was halting traffic. "When did you go to the US Embassy?"

"I went there after I arrived." Her heart pounded.

"Do you have a return ticket to the U.S.?" Lieutenant Scarface moved his head in even closer.

Sandy trembled. "Yes, because that is the law, too."

Lieutenant Scarface looked chiseled from stone. "Show it to us."

"It is at the mission guesthouse with my luggage."

"Go and get it." Lieutenant Scarface raised his voice. "We demand to see it right now."

She was grateful for the chance to get away from the hostile, obnoxious officers. She stood and went to the desk. "It might be easier to collect my passport, get my ticket, and leave your country now." She didn't want to stay in that awful place any longer.

The word "leave" shot out of her mouth like a cheetah sprinting across the plains. What would be the point of delaying a couple of days if they intended to force her to leave after that?

Why hadn't Mr. Jubilee asked to see her return ticket? It would be best to show it to everyone. The officers surrounded her and closed ranks. She gasped for air. Her pulse quickened.

Lieutenant Red Eye's mouth twisted into a sneer. "We will not give you your passport, unless you show us your return ticket. Go and get it."

Eager to escape the office, she went outside and hailed a taxi to her room at the guesthouse. After collecting the ticket, she returned to the office a few minutes later.

A giant official screamed, "We have impounded your passport and will escort you out of the country." His nametag said 'Colonel Tsaou.'

He was built like a football player with lots of insignias and stripes and appeared to be the highest-ranking officer there. She nicknamed him 'Colonel Big' due to his position and size.

Her heart banged like an empty bucket falling to the bottom of a dry well. She collapsed in the nearest chair. Pressing her hand to her chest, she stared at their cold, black eyes. She would prefer to leave voluntarily before anyone accompanied her in disgrace out of the country. Holding out her ticket, she blinked rapidly and sniffed back a few threatening tears.

Lieutenant Scarface didn't take the travel document but nodded. "Come with me."

She followed him into a tiny room. He pointed to a metal chair. "Sit down."

He left. A key turned and clicked in the lock. Even in Africa there had to be a law against securing her in a room. Cobwebs dangled from the immobile fan. The light was off and the room dark, and hot as an oven. The cracked glass in the window of the door let in the only light, but it was still too dark to see properly. Was it a type of cell?

She'd brought her airline ticket to them as they asked. With her fingertips, she flicked the drops of sweat off her forehead. She wiped her wet palms on her skirt and looked around and began shaking.

If she managed to escape from the room, at least ten officers on the opposite side of the door would stop her from leaving. She lifted her face toward the ceiling. The water spots looked like they moved in circles making her dizzy. Spiders and layers of dust indicated the cell hadn't been used in a long time. She examined the chair she sat in more closely. It looked like an old electric chair. Was it the first electric chair ever built? Her limbs shook. Were they planning to electrocute her? She couldn't breathe.

Sandy hadn't been to church in a long, long time, but she believed on Jesus and asked Him to come into her life and forgive her of her sins when she was eleven years old. It would be wise to make certain of her salvation now if she was about to die.

Lord Jesus, forgive me for all of my sins. Come into my heart and save me.

Maybe she wasn't in danger. Without electricity she couldn't be electrocuted, but the officers might molest her, beat her, or worse. She needed to get out of there, right away.

God, help. She was talking to the Lord a lot for someone who hadn't spoken to Him in years.

Colonel Tsaou unlocked the room. "Come with me."

She stood and followed him. The colonel pushed a chair forward and pointed to it. She sat down and shivered at the enraged faces of the beasts that surrounded her.

"We think you are lying." Colonel Tsaou sat on top of the desk and faced her.

She spoke with a shaky voice. "I'm not lying." Tears filled her eyes.

"We believe you are carrying out illegal business in our country. You are not with any organization. Why did you come here?"

"I came to collect nuts from the Shea tree for a beauty cream I'm working on for the fitness center. I wrote Mr. Jubilee who offered to help me. After I arrived, he asked me to vaccinate the children."

Colonel Big crossed his arms and nodded. "So that is your ticket as you said. May I see it?"

She extended a shaking hand to the officer. The soldiers' dark, hard eyes shot daggers through her. Angry faces riveted her to the seat. To stop her hands from trembling, she clutched the edges of the chair. Her knuckles turned white. Raw terror iced her limbs causing every bone to quiver. She would never leave unharmed, unless God delivered her.

Colonel Big lowered his face until it was eight inches from her. He raised his voice. "You seem annoyed with us. This is not good. We are in charge. You are a stranger in our country. You must never get angry with us. We can do whatever we want with you."

Her throat constricted. Trapped, surrounded by ten men who might carry out their threats. Her chest tightened. She couldn't escape the group of military officers.

Please, please help me, God.

Colonel Big scowled. "I can give you a three-month visa. You will need to leave Norgia when the visa expires."

She wanted to leave immediately and never return so she wouldn't see the officers again, but visions of the dying children ran through her mind. The room spun around her.

Had they seen she was innocent, or were they trying to confuse her, torment her, or prepare her for worse?

CHAPTER FIVE

Prayer had worked and it should help again. Sandy closed her eyes. *Lord, help me.*

When she opened her eyes, Mr. Jubilee was strolling into the office. He chatted with the soldiers in the local language. The men shook their heads and pointed to her. Colonel Big opened his desk, stamped Sandy's passport, and handed it to her.

The medical director shook the officers' hands and thanked each one. Sandy had learned the local word for thank you and used it. Mr. Jubilee and Sandy headed toward the door.

Colonel Big raised his voice. "Miss Calbrin, all of us will be watching you."

She trembled from head to toe. Why would the military officers observe her? Her tortured mind flashed back to the locked room, the electric chair, and screaming officers. She didn't want to stay in Norgia, but she had to finish the job. Maybe, it wouldn't be so bad. Sweat dripped down her neck and chest. Her heart pounded as she walked beside Mr. Jubilee to the car.

Inside the vehicle, she handed her passport to him. "Would you check if everything is in order?"

He flipped through the pages. "They gave you a four-month visa of regularization, much better than I hoped, considering the political problems. I asked them for this preliminary visa. This one is necessary to secure a residence visa to live here." He handed the passport back to her.

"Live here?" She gasped and put her fingers to her lips. "I didn't come here to live."

"The longest visa is a three-month one. It may take six months to vaccinate all the children."

"Six months!"

"Yes, the Health Organization of the World estimated the time. You will need two of those visas and many more trips to the

25

immigration." Mr. Jubilee sighed as if explaining an incomprehensible concept to a small child. "With this visa you will not need to come back here. I can take your passport to the headquarters for the residence visa."

Sandy only heard, "never come back to the office again." Was it another miracle?

"You can leave Norgia whenever you want." Mr. Jubilee handed the passport back to her. "God did this for you. No one has ever received a four-month preliminary visa for residency."

"They scared me." Sandy wiped the sweat from her forehead. "Why will they be watching me?"

"Don't mind them. That is their way. The government has been unstable since before the *coups d'état*. The military officers are worried that foreigners will provide arms for another takeover."

"Do they suspect me of passing out guns?"

"No, but they like to intimidate people to keep everyone in line. It's all normal."

"None of it appeared normal to me." Sandy raised her brow. "They stared at me."

"Naturally. The officers saw a single, beautiful lady. It would be best for you to go right back to Koala and finish vaccinating the children and establish all the Under Fives Clinics. The village leaders should provide housing for you. When can you be ready to leave?"

"I'm ready now. I'll go anywhere to distance myself from those officers."

Did she say she'd go anywhere? That wasn't true. She wouldn't travel anywhere. She didn't want to return to Koala where the people harmed their children through dangerous customs. But she had a job to do.

"David will drive you tomorrow."

"Thank you. That will be fine."

"We should set up our first Under Fives Clinic as soon as possible and send the official report. Can you organize it and prepare the document?" Mr. Jubilee asked.

"I will get it done for you." She'd do anything and go any place to escape the officers, even live in a mud house in the bush without electricity and plumbing.

***

At six the next morning, David loaded Sandy's bags into the trunk. After she was seated in the back, he drove out of the guesthouse and onto the street.

Syrupy fragrances wafted through the air and teased her nose. Heaps of bananas, pineapples, oranges, and papayas lined the road, so she asked, "Can you stop to buy some fruit?"

"It is cheaper in Koala and best to purchase it from the local people to give them business."

Piles of flat stones, firewood, and charcoal filled spaces among the mounds of fruit. Sandy clenched her jaws at the young girls who bent under the weight of huge sacks of charcoal. The girls stumbled along the road single-file. More children shoved heavy bags off their heads and wiped the sweat from their brows with the backs of their hands. Black dust floated through the air and covered their bodies. Sandy pounded her fists into her thighs as other youngsters carried stacks of firewood on their heads. They dropped them on the side of the road next to fuel vendors.

"Why aren't these children in school?"

"Many parents don't send their girls to school."

"Why?"

"There's a limited amount of funds for uniforms and books, so boys are sent to school first. Some girls are given out as servants to large families. Each month the head of the family sends money to the girl's parents."

"That is terrible. I read about those little slaves."

"They are not slaves."

"Maybe not legally, but they are forced to work from sunup until they go to bed."

"That is true if they get an evil family. Most parents try to find good families for their daughters to serve."

Sandy's mind ran through options of how to help the little girls. What could she do? She was a stranger in a foreign land.

At noon David pulled into an eating place. "This is a good food restaurant. We will get some lunch."

She followed David to several wooden planks balanced on stacks of cement bricks that served as benches and tables. Walking past large kettles, Sandy choked on the frying pieces of black meat covered in hair. The annoying stench of burning fur gagged her. She'd never put that in her mouth.

Sandy stopped in front of the women, dressed in blue and white skirts, blouses, and headscarves, who sat on tiny logs in front of campfires. She peeked into the steaming cast-iron pots, as women with giant metal spoons stirred fish heads and tails in tomato sauce.

"Where are all the fish bodies?" Sandy asked.

David pointed to an iron pot. "I do not know, but we believe eating the fish heads will make us intelligent."

The woman picked up half of a broken plastic bowl and dipped it into a substance that resembled white play dough. She heaped a glob of clay onto a tin plate and handed it to David.

He turned to Sandy. "What do you want to eat?"

She grimaced at the furry dark pieces of meat and fish heads. Her choices included hairy globs and skulls with eyes. She was afraid to ask about the white clay that looked like glue. With these selections she'd never need to worry about gaining weight there.

A young woman shuffled past her with a tray of small bottles of Coca Cola, orange soda, and Sprite. Sandy never drank Coke because of the calories but it would fill her. "I'm not too hungry but would like a bottle of Coke, thank you."

David bought Sandy's beverage, opened it, and handed the bottle to her.

"Thank you." She sipped the sugary drink. The warm liquid cooled her parched throat, and the caffeine revived her.

He purchased a bowl of red sauce with a fish head and tail. Then he carried that and his plate of white dough to a plank serving as a table. A small girl, about waist high, dragged her feet to him, lifted a plastic pan of water from her head, and handed it to David.

Sandy frowned. "Look at this girl. She's about six years old. Why isn't she in school?"

"She is too young."

"Maybe you're right. It looks like there's no kindergarten in Norgia."

David dipped his right hand in the water container, then lowered his hand to the plate and broke off a mouth-sized bite of white glob with his fingers. After dunking it in the sauce, he popped it into his mouth.

"This is corn meal mush, our favorite food. You should eat some."

"Maybe next time, I can try it."

She maintained a pleasant expression as she drank. Mush was the last thing she'd eat. Trying to find decent food and surviving without electricity and plumbing would be challenging.

CHAPTER SIX

After lunch, David drove another two hours to Koala and parked in front of the church. "The pastor's house is barred and locked. It looks like he's not at home."

Sandy was grateful she wouldn't need to spend more time with the pastor and his family.

David walked into the church and carried a bench outside. He set it under the shade of a baobab tree. "My father said you should stay here in the village until you finish vaccinating the children."

She stared at the mud huts behind the smoking campfires. Wide-open pastoral lands with grazing animals brought her peace after the noise and congestion of the big city.

A distinguished gentleman dressed in blue and gold matching shirt and pants headed toward them.

"Here comes the chief." David stood. "He is carrying his official staff."

The village leader stopped in front of Sandy, who had also stood. He extended his hand to greet her. "I am sorry I did not come when you first arrived. I should have escorted you to your lodging, but the storm held me captive in my home."

She chuckled at his use of the English language. Norgia had been a British colony. Their spoken words sounded stiff and formal. Without the use of contractions the everyday phrases came out stilted.

The chief grinned. "I have a two-room house with an aluminum roof. Follow me, and I will show it to you. I hope you can live in it while you are in our village."

David opened the car doors. "I will drive you."

Sandy and the village leader climbed into the vehicle. The chief directed David onto a wide cow path, which opened into a harvested cornfield where the stalks had been clipped close to the ground.

"Stop here. We must walk the rest of the way." The chief opened the car door and led the way through the narrow rows. He stopped in front of an isolated mud building. He inserted a miniature key in an equally small padlock, an inch wide and twice as long. With both hands the chief pushed the door open and entered the room. He went to the window and banged on the wooden shutter with his fist. The swinging door popped open with a loud groan, letting in a brilliant ray of sunshine.

David carried Sandy's bags inside. "I hope you will enjoy it here. I need to be on the road. I'll see you in Hose after you have finished." He left.

Sandy went inside and swept away dangling cobwebs that hung from the rafters. Several cockroaches scurried toward her, and she jumped. In the far corner she spied an ancient two-burner gas stove. Her gaze went to a couple mice that darted behind three sacks of rice.

She pointed. "What about those?"

"I'll take the rice to my brother's house."

She was talking about the mice, not the bags of rice. She ran her fingers over the mud walls. Its primitive chill made her shiver. Straw and stones stuck out of the bricks. The aluminum roofing would endure a storm but held the heat, so it would stifle her. A thatch roof would have been cooler in the hot weather, but according to her research, it invited insects and rodents. She slipped out of her shoes and let the coldness of the packed earth floor flow through her feet.

The chief pointed to the open doorway. "Go look at bedroom."

A narrow homemade cupboard stood against one wall. A broken, bamboo bedframe filled a corner. Only a single bed and tiny table would fit in the small room.

"How do you like it?" The chief puffed out his chest and beamed.

It was the worst accommodation she'd ever seen. What had she gotten herself into by coming to Africa? She'd left her elegant, apartment in Florida for a mud dwelling in the bush.

She couldn't tell the truth to the elderly gentleman for it would hurt his feelings. The building was most likely the best he had to offer.

"Thank you so much for your generous hospitality. You are kind to allow me to live in one of your own houses."

32

"You wait here. I will call my son to fix the bed, and I have a mattress for you." The chief stepped briskly down the trail.

Sandy collapsed on the boulder in front of the door. How had coming to Africa to collect nuts from Shea trees, and agreeing to vaccinate thousands of children progress to living in a mud house in the isolated bush?

She peered through the open door and winced at the square that resembled a window. It needed a screen so insects and rodents wouldn't crawl into the room. Where would she get wire netting in the boonies? And if the gas burner didn't work, she'd have no way to boil drinking water or cook food.

A few minutes later a young man arrived. He gripped a cement brick in each of his hands with another brick balanced on his head.

Sandy stood. "You must be the chief's son."

"Yes. I've come to fix the bed." He went inside and stacked the bricks on top of each other. "I need three more blocks. Wait here."

Five minutes later, he returned with more bricks, went into the inner room, and stacked them in a pyramid. He shifted the bed in every direction and at last had the broken corner of it resting on the blocks with the damaged end of the bamboo frame higher.

"I can bring the mattress now. Here is the key to the padlock."

Several minutes later, an old Peugeot stopped in front of her.

A short man, dressed in a business suit, climbed out of the car. "Good morning, I'm Dr. Pelougu from the Christian hospital in Maliblitta. Mr. Jubilee sent word you were coming. I want to welcome you to the area. I hope you will enjoy Koala."

"Thank you." She pointed to the giant log under the mango tree. "I'm sorry I have no chair to offer you." She bit her lower lip at the tribal scars that ran vertical from the corners of his eyes. The big black teardrops were similar tattoos to those of the pastor and his wife.

Dr. Pelougu glanced at the log. "Thank you, but I will stand."

"I appreciate your visit. What kind of medical cases come to the hospital for treatment?"

"I see patients with malnutrition, malaria, typhoid, dysentery, broken bones, ulcers, and goiters. Right now I have a rather interesting case."

"What is it?"

"A woman had already given birth fourteen times over the years. After the delivery of her fifteenth baby, she died of postpartum hemorrhage. The father left his newborn at the hospital because he has nine daughters and doesn't want another baby girl."

"Are many infants abandoned?"

"It happens if the people believe the baby is cursed."

Sandy gasped and put her hand to her mouth. "How could an innocent child be cursed?"

"People in some tribes believe if a healthy baby survives delivery while the mother dies, the infant has a powerful spell to kill the mother."

Sandy's heart went out for that poor, innocent child. Did people truly believe a tiny, vulnerable baby was evil? She wanted to help the infant. "What happens to these children?"

"Sometimes an old granny will care for the baby, but most of the time no one will take the child, so it dies. Before the political problems, they were sent to the orphanages, but they were all destroyed during the military coup. This child has nowhere to go, which is why she is still at the hospital. Ugly rumors circulated that this infant has a more powerful curse on her." The doctor pulled a cotton handkerchief out of his back pocket and wiped his brow. "I'm reluctant to hand this baby over to anyone. Someone might want to hurt her."

Sandy wanted the baby, but could she care for a newborn? Her career hadn't allowed her to spend any time with infants. And what would she do with the baby when she returned to the States? She'd deal with that situation when the time came.

"May I have her?"

The doctor raised his eyebrows. "Why do you want a baby?"

"If I had an infant to love and care for I could teach good child care."

The doctor stared into Sandy's eyes as if testing her. "I studied medicine in England. Unfortunately my people are uneducated and backward, but I promised them I'd return to my village and help. Maybe your care of this child will show my people the best child care." His wide, thick lips moved. "My people, the Nunaa, find change difficult and prefer their traditions."

"Many people, even Americans, find change hard. Since the orphanages were destroyed here, could I take her?"

The doctor shrugged. "She'd be far better off with you than any other person I know."

"Will you give me the child?"

"If you took the baby, it would be a great help to all of us." He folded his handkerchief and put it back in his pocket, as if considering his response. "You can have her."

"Thank you." Sandy's heart swelled with pleasure. "When can I have her?"

"You can have her soon. I must go now. I only stopped by for a moment to welcome you." The doctor slid into his car and drove away.

She sat back on the boulder, thinking about that baby.

The chief's son brought a thin piece of foam. "I've brought your mattress."

She stepped across the threshold of her new home and stiffened. There was no electricity, running water, plumbing, bathroom, kitchen, or furniture. She rubbed her temple as more thoughts raced through her mind. She didn't have any bottles, formula, or diapers.

How could she care for a baby?

***

The old chief returned. "I want to show you our dispensary. It has been vacant for many years and is in need of repair, but you could use it."

She raised her brows. "Use it for what?"

"To treat sick patients."

What was the chief talking about? She followed him down a dirt trail to an abandoned building located on the opposite side of the village.

A tall, slender young man rushed up to them. The chief put his hand on the boy's shoulder. "This is Adam, the son of a village elder. He brought the key for the dispensary."

Adam brushed cobwebs away from the door's lock. "The pastor asked me to translate and assist you with the patients."

Did they expect her to treat patients, establish the Under Fives clinic, and vaccinate all the babies? And soon she'd have a newborn child to care for.

She followed Adam into the small room. "Are you in the university?"

"I failed my entrance examinations."

"Will you take them again next year?"

"No. I need to work on my father's farm."

She stepped gingerly around the clumps of animal droppings that spotted the floor and shuddered at streams of ants and roaches crawling across the mounds of garbage. Sweat broke out on her brow as mice leaped around piles of firewood, smelly papers, and soiled plastic bags.

"Would you please bring me a bucket of water, lots of soap, bleach, and a broom? Thank you."

Adam departed with the chief to collect the supplies.

Walking through the trash stirred up an obnoxious, moldy odor. She gagged and choked back bile. She blew the dust off a fifty-year-old notebook of patients' names and dates and then picked up several open bottles of old drugs to read the British labels and instructions.

Sandy went outside to take a break from the filth. How had she walked into another messy problem?

Adam returned with a stuffed bag and a bucket of water. He pulled a short broom out of the sack. "My parents were the first converts to Christianity among our people. My father washed all the clothes for Rev. Boyden, his wife, and their children. My mother learned to cook American food. She made bread, oatmeal, spaghetti, peanut butter cookies, and custard. So I know a little about white people."

An elderly African gentleman approached them. He pulled up his trouser leg revealing a tropical skin ulcer and handed Sandy his government-issued health card.

She was grateful she'd studied African diseases before coming and turned to Adam. "We need to wash this wound with soap and water and dress it."

Adam translated.

Sandy had already picked up some of the words in the local language. "Adam, please pour several cups of water over this sore." She scrubbed the patient's wound and patted the skin ulcer with a clean cloth. "Adam, are there any dressings?"

"A few."

She picked up a three-inch wide reel of cotton bandaging fastened with a rusty safety pin. Pressing open the pin, she unwound the strip of bed sheet, and wrapped it around the ulcer. She pulled it smooth and snug. Then she ripped the end down the middle, knotted it, and flipped each half around the backside and tied it.

"You're fee is a hundred francs." She collected the coin from the gentleman before he left the clinic.

"I need to sweep the big dirt out of the dispensary." Adam turned away.

She sat down on large rock and removed the rusted pins and the dirty ends of the rolled-up dressings.

Trash flew out of the open door. Dust filled the building and fluttered out of the windows. Adam coughed and choked.

After the dirt settled, Sandy went inside. "This is a mess. Were the clinics destroyed during the military troubles?"

"No. They've been going downhill for years."

"What happened to the equipment and supplies? In Hose the screening is ripped off the windows in the church and there are no desks or chairs in the classrooms of the school."

There were many broken-down churches, schools, and clinics. Where did one start to fix them or how without supplies?

CHAPTER SEVEN

The rumble of a car engine woke Sandy the next morning. She dressed quickly and looked out the window. The hospital doctor parked his car and stepped out of it. She was disappointed he didn't carry a baby.

When she saw his grim expression, Sandy's heart plummeted to the pit of her stomach and landed with a bang. She wanted that infant, but life in Africa was fragile. Maybe the baby had died?

She took a couple of deep breaths and walked to the doctor. Stopping in front of him, she swiped her clammy hands on her skirt before shaking his hand. "Good morning."

"I talked to the father. He changed his mind."

"What happened?" She blinked several times to suppress the threatening tears.

"The father wants someone to care for his child but just until he decides what to do with her. Would you still want her if you can only keep her temporarily?"

Yes. It was the perfect solution. God had worked in her favor, even though she'd left the Lord out of her life for so many years.

Thank you Lord.

Her hands stopped shaking. "Yes, even if it is for a little while I still want that child."

"Go to the hospital and see her. You may change your mind." Dr. Pelougu shrugged. "I'm on my way to Hose to collect medical supplies. I hope to see you at the hospital later. Goodbye for now."

She'd never change her mind, even if the baby was blind or paralyzed. If the child had a cleft lip, club foot, or seven fingers on each hand, she still wanted the baby.

When she returned home after treating patients, Sandy trekked to the junction, hailed a taxi going to the hospital, and joined the other passengers. As the vehicle bounced up and down over the rough, dirt roads, she gripped the door handle so she wouldn't slide into the woman next to her. She choked and sneezed on the black dust that flew in the open windows. Would she ever get used to the dirt that covered her skin and clothes?

She descended at the hospital road and walked down the lane to the main entrance. Going through the main door, she searched for the doctor.

A few minutes later Dr. Pelougu approached her. "Come down this hall with me. We keep the baby outside the tuberculosis ward, since there is no room for her in the nursery."

Her mouth fell open. "Isn't the tuberculosis ward dangerous? Couldn't she get that disease?"

"The hospital is full of sick people. She might get anything. We do the best we can."

Once again, Sandy clamped her mouth closed. Everyone did the best they could.

He stopped at a baby bed. "Here she is."

Sandy's jaw fell open. "What a beautiful baby. She is adorable with perfect little features, but she is not a newborn." Sandy's heart raced faster as she smiled at the baby.

Dr. Pelougu furrowed his brows.

She picked up the baby. "Look, she grinned at me." The infant clutched Sandy's finger. "You will be my baby, my blessing, and I will call you Blessing. You are not cursed as everyone says. You are blessed. You will bless thousands of mothers when I teach child care."

Blessing grinned, and her expressive, happy eyes sealed the relationship. Sandy wanted to walk out of the hospital with the baby. She wrapped her arms around the child and clutched her tighter. The baby's heart pounded against Sandy's chest. Her biological clock ticked loudly. The alarm was about to ring.

The doctor plucked the child from Sandy's arms and put her back in the bed. "I see you still want the baby. After I finish her tests and paperwork, a nurse will bring her to you in Koala."

Sandy took in a lungful of air and let it out slowly. With the promise of a baby, she returned home, but she kept thinking about

Blessing. The idea of having a baby seized her heart like an African wildcat gripping a rat and wouldn't let go.

***

At the Koala clinic the next day, Sandy finished the Under Fives Clinic and treated adults.

A male patient handed Sandy his card. "Doctor, I have pain all over my body, and my head is very hot."

"It sounds like you have malarial fever." Sandy counted out pills and handed the patient his treatment.

He opened his bag, bowed, and presented her with a bunch of bananas. "Thank you for coming. These are to welcome you."

Sandy's heart caught in her throat as the barefoot man beamed at her. He was dressed in old, tattered clothes. His generosity reminded her of her selfishness over the years. She had built her own comfortable world and forgotten about those in need around her. Maybe God was transforming her self-centered heart into an organ of love for others.

As she dressed wounds, diagnosed diseases, and treated patients, an overwhelming love for Africa and its people took root in Sandy's heart. There were no complaining patients, screaming supervisors, and bureaucracy. Essentially no stress, just patient care. In the American hospital, she had mountains of paperwork, long hours, and ungrateful patients. She'd had enough of everything one night and left to take a job in the fitness center.

The African authorities required simple statistics, just the patient's name, sex, and village. She completed the report for the Under Fives Clinic in a few minutes.

"Adam, why do all the people call me doctor? I keep telling them I'm not one."

"We have witch doctors and traditional healers. We have one word in our language for healer which is doctor. We do not have health people like nurses, medical assistants, and technicians. Everyone in the medical profession is addressed as doctor."

A mother brought her toddler into the clinic. "My child has diarrhea and is weak. Do you have medicine?"

41

Sandy cleared her throat. "It sounds like he has parasites. Worm treatments are recommended every three months, so I'll give him these pills."

After the mother and her child left, a man with pus-filled, watery eyes handed Sandy his treatment card. "I have eye disease."

"How long have you had it?"

"A month or more."

After examining his eyes and referring to an old medical book, Sandy jotted the diagnosis. "You have trachoma, and it can lead to blindness. Why haven't you seen a doctor before this?"

"I was financially handicapped."

"You must start taking this medicine today, if not, you can go blind. Lean your head back." Using her thumb and index finger, Sandy held his eye lids open as she squeezed two drops into each eye. Then she handed him the small bottle. "Take this home and put these drops in every day."

Adam called, "Teepola Beeri."

A young man dressed in a shirt and tie sat down facing her. "Last week someone sneezed in my face. I have had a headache as a direct result of that sneeze. If a drug does not work on the first day, I try a different pill the second day. I have taken amoxicillin, metronidazole, penicillin, vermox, and Valium, but I am still sick."

She took a deep breath and let it out slowly trying not to wrinkle her nose at the young man's odor. Why would he dress in a business suit without taking a bath? He had money for pills but not soap.

"Take no medicines except two Tylenol pills every day for a week and come back to see me."

An older African woman with a chicken in her arms came into the clinic. "My hens are lazy. They have diarrhea and refuse to lay eggs. Can you give me medicine for them?"

Adam scowled at the woman. "Sister Sandy is a people doctor, not an animal doctor."

"Why do some people think I can treat animals?"

"Our local healers and witch doctors treat animals and people, so they think you do, too."

42

"I understand now." Sandy checked the time. "Since there are no more patients, let's break for lunch."

She stared out the window as she ate her peanut butter sandwich and hoped Blessing arrived soon. By the time she'd finished eating, no patients had arrived. So she strolled to the open village market. Acting in faith, she searched for diapers, but only found medicine sellers.

Women dressed in gold and purple headscarves with matching, striped blouses and skirts yelled, "Codeine. Valium. Morphine."

The ladies paraded down the passageway with tin trays of pills balanced on their heads. Could everyone buy narcotics without a prescription? Innocent people might become addicts or resistant to certain drugs.

Stepping into a pile of excreta, she scrunched up her face and picked up a rock to scrape the smelly clump off her shoes. They allowed local people to practice dangerous customs that hurt babies but had no laws for trash regulation, sanitation, and drug control.

Empty-handed, Sandy returned to the clinic. "Adam, I could not find any diapers at the market."

Adam stopped wiping the counter. "What is a diaper?"

"It is a cloth you put on a baby's bottom so he can urinate in it."

"People call them napkins. Only rich people put them on babies." Adam shook his head. "Do you think the father will be pleased to have a white, American lady caring for his child?"

"The father should be happy I will feed, clothe, and care for his daughter."

"You people have strange customs. The father might be scared you will teach his child unusual ways."

"What tradition is strange?"

"You believe men and women are equal and should eat at the same table together. This is one of the many reasons the old people in our village would not become Christians."

"How could I teach a tiny baby, who can't even talk, that she is equal to a man?" Sandy teased. "I'll feed her, bathe her, dress her, and care for her."

43

David shook his head. "You are the strangest white lady, and most bizarre doctor I have ever seen."

That evening after Sandy returned home from work, a woman knocked on the door. She carried bowls on a tin tray. "I am Adam's mother. You can call me Phoebe, the name I took from the Bible when I was baptized. I brought food from your country."

What special food had the woman brought? Sandy looked out the window expecting to see a car, truck, or even a plane from the States.

For years Sandy maintained a strict diet of fruits, vegetables, and broiled meat to keep her weight down. She took the platter, set it down, and peeked under the covers. The American-style spaghetti and bread made her mouth water, and she was hungry. For the few months she lived in Africa, she would abandon her strict diet.

"Thank you so much. This is kind of you."

The woman didn't ask for anything in return for preparing the food. Her generous hospitality brought tears to Sandy's eyes. The local people had so little but freely shared what they had.

She thought of her own selfishness and business plans to make more money with ingredients from Africa for beauty creams. She was ashamed of her complaints and having so many possessions.

Lord forgive me.

"White people are hard to understand so I hope you like the food."

Sandy asked, "Why are we hard to understand?"

"Americans have lots of furniture, dishes, and appliances that they never use or need." Phoebe took a deep breath. "We thought they brought them for us."

"Why did you think they would give you the things?"

"They kept talking about free gifts. They spoke of the gift of Jesus Christ, the gift of the Son of God, the gift of eternal life, and the gifts of the Holy Spirit."

Sandy giggled. "So you thought white people came to give you gifts."

"My son said that Jesus paid for the gift of eternal life, so everlasting life wasn't free. Christ gave his life and died for us to be

44

saved." Phoebe shrugged and lifted the plastic covers off the food. "Americans are rich."

"Not all of them are rich."

"That's what they keep telling us."

"We have a hard time giving up things." Sandy paused. "So many people must have brought their personal belongings with them."

Sandy hadn't given up her designer clothes, expensive shoes, and cosmetics which she'd stuffed in her over-packed and excess luggage. She hadn't brought furniture and appliances with her but lugged around far too many items for a week's visit, which was turning into a stay of several months.

"A long time ago many of us saw Jesus, as a white man, a white God for the white people. We had our gods, and they were ebony like us. We never asked outsiders to accept our gods and couldn't understand why they wanted us to accept their white god."

"There is only one Almighty God, the Lord of all."

A lady's voice interrupted them. "Sister Sandy."

Sandy and Phoebe glanced out the window. A woman walked to the house. She had a cloth knotted at her waist, which indicated a baby was secured to her back. Sandy went outside and Phoebe followed.

The stranger had no tribal scars. Most likely she had been raised as a Christian. She handed Sandy some documents. "Here is the health card, birth certificate, and letter from the baby's father."

Sandy glanced at the papers. "Blessing is three and a half months old."

Phoebe took the documents from Sandy. The nurse untied the knot at her waist and reached around her back for the baby. She handed Sandy the naked infant, and then the worker retied the cloth around her. Sandy looked more closely and saw the nurse had only re-claimed her wrap-around skirt that matched the blouse she wore under her white uniform.

Sandy carried Blessing into the house. "This baby is beautiful."

She hadn't found any baby clothes or tiny blankets in the village market, so she ripped up several cotton blouses to serve as diapers.

After pinning one on Blessing, she wrapped the baby in her red, satin lounging pajamas which Sandy would never wear in Africa.

"Lord, thank you for my baby. She looks like a little black angel, with perfect features sent from Heaven."

"She is no angel." Phoebe shrugged. "Remember. She is a cursed child."

CHAPTER EIGHT

With the baby in her arms, happiness filled Sandy's heart. She stroked the child's cheek and lifted Blessing's tiny hands to tickle her.

Handing the baby to Phoebe, Sandy pulled an empty cardboard box from her closet. She spread her denim skirt in the bottom of it and took the giggling child from Phoebe to try out the new bed. Sandy pulled out her red satin pajamas and covered the child. Blessing kicked her legs, so the cloth rose and fell above her.

Sandy patted Blessing's stomach. "I love you."

Phoebe rolled her eyes.

Holding the tiny miracle had felt so right and perfect. Panic rang over and over in her soul. She was already thirty. Would she ever enjoy the miracle of giving birth? She loved Blessing. Would she ever be able to let her baby go when the time came?

She had put off marriage and a family to work long hours and pay bills for things she never needed, just wanted. Would Blessing be the only baby she'd ever have? Tears ran down Sandy's face.

"What is wrong? Are you sick? I knew this baby was cursed and made people ill."

Sandy sniffed. "No. I'm happy."

Then the perfect baby bawled. Tears wet her face and the red satin pajamas.

"I think she is hungry."

Phoebe picked up the child and paced. "Give me the food, and I will feed her."

"I don't have any baby food."

"What is baby food?"

"It is special food for infants."

"We do not give our babies peculiar food."

Sandy didn't have any powdered or evaporated milk in her house because she drank her tea black. There was no refrigerator or fresh milk. She had assumed the hospital would send Blessing's food, but the worker had handed her only three documents and a naked baby.

"Why didn't the nurse bring her food?"

"The hospital does not give anyone food. When a patient is admitted he is responsible to find his own meals."

Hearing another worthless law, Sandy raised her voice. "How can a sick patient find food if he is in the hospital?"

"His family members cook and bring it to him. Several staff members must have bought food for this baby. What do you want to give her?" Phoebe lifted Blessing to her shoulder and patted the baby's back.

"Could you please go to the market and buy powdered milk?" Sandy snatched her coin purse from the table.

Phoebe handed Blessing to Sandy. "What about corn porridge? All babies eat that."

"Yes, please buy ground corn for porridge."

It sounded like something from the dark ages. She didn't know how to make porridge but could ask someone. She handed the money to Phoebe, who folded it in the corner of her wrap-around skirt and knotted it.

Sandy wrinkled her brow. "The nurses fed Blessing with a small cup and spoon. Buy those too."

Someone outside called, "Hello. Hello." Sandy went to the door.

A young woman, dressed in a red blouse and long, purple skirt greeted Phoebe in the doorway. Phoebe put her hand on the girl's arm but spoke to Sandy. "This is Eve, my daughter."

Eve looked like her mother with her square dark face, large nose, full lips, and straight, white teeth. Her red-painted fingernails shimmered as she used them to push her jet-black hair under her yellow headscarf.

Phoebe departed for the market, and Eve came into the house. "Where did you get a baby?"

"The doctor at the Christian hospital gave her to me. I'm taking care of her for a while."

"What are you going to do with her?" Eve reached out for the child.

"How did you know the baby was a girl?"

"Didn't you see her ears?"

"Yes, she has tiny, gold earrings in her pierced ears."

"At birth if the child is a boy the midwife circumcises him. She pierces the ears of all the female babies and puts in earrings."

"That is a clever idea. So when the baby's head peeks out of the mother's covering on her back every one knows if it is a boy or girl."

"Give me the baby feeder."

"What's that?"

"You Americans call it a baby bottle."

"I don't plan on using one to feed Blessing. Baby bottles killed a million babies in Africa last year according to world statistics on infant mortality. Every bottle I've seen since I arrived in Africa was contaminated with black mold. Rubber nipples and plastic containers take in smells and tastes, but most of all they absorb germs that cause sickness."

"Mothers in the bush have never gone to school and cannot read. They don't know how to take care of a baby feeder."

"Who sells these bottles?"

"You and your people do. We saw the pictures of white women giving the baby bottles."

Sandy fumed. "Did they teach the mothers how to sanitize the bottles?"

"No, they did not. Mothers use bottles to be modern."

"You may think bottles are modern, but breast-feeding is more sanitary."

"Yes, you are right. Mothers buy baby bottles after giving birth. They use them over and over again without cleaning them. Women can't afford the soap to wash them properly." Eve lowered Blessing face down to her waist. She lifted her right arm, and slid the baby under her arm onto her back. She bent forward, untied her wraparound skirt and placed it on top of Blessing. Then she tied the child to her back.

49

Sandy's mouth fell open. She would learn to tie Blessing to her back like Eve did. Sandy put her hands on her hips. "One day I saw several babies drinking from filthy bottles. The diarrhea ran out of their sick, lean bodies. I haven't seen a fat, healthy baby in Africa drinking from a baby bottle."

"Most mothers cannot afford the expensive, imported formulas or powdered milk. They use corn porridge and add lots of water to it, so it flows through the nipple." Eve sat down with her upper body leaning forward so the baby on her back would not be pressed into the chair. "Our people love to economize. We dilute everything to make it last longer. Women put dirty river water in the baby bottle, but I know that is bad."

Phoebe returned twenty minutes later from the market and handed Sandy the change from the groceries and a sack of purchases.

Sandy emptied the light-blue, plastic bag the groceries came in and pressed it flat on the table. "This can serve as plastic pants."

Phoebe stared at the bag. "Are you going to dress your baby in a plastic sack?"

"It's the perfect size to cover her diaper."

"Adam told me what a diaper was, but why must you cover it?"

"I want to stop urine from soaking through on people." Sandy held the bag up to the light.

Phoebe scowled. "We do not mind if a baby urinates on us, but white people do not like this."

Sandy pulled a can from her backpack. "How can I change milliliters to ounces to measure the milk powder?"

"Why must you be so accurate and measure it?" Phoebe rolled her eyes. "We add a few sprinkles of powder until it is white."

That was why there were so many lean, malnourished babies. Mothers diluted milk and cereals to save money, but in doing so starved their children.

Sandy stared at the label of the tin. "This tuna fish can is six ounces."

Eve's jaw dropped. "Please don't give the baby tuna fish."

"No, I won't, but the can is six ounces. I could empty it and use it as a measuring cup."

"I do not think it is necessary to measure everything." Eve frowned.

"Could you fill this big pot with water, please?" Sandy held out the gallon pan.

Phoebe's eyes widened. "This will be too much milk for that baby."

Sandy emptied the tuna fish into a small bowl. "I must boil the cups, spoons, and the empty tuna fish can. One ounce is 30 milliliters. This can holds 180 milliliters."

Eve took the empty tuna fish can outside and washed it with soap and water and Sandy put it in the pot with the rest. Eve lifted the sleeping baby off her back and put her on Sandy's narrow foam cushion mattress. Sandy covered the temporary diaper with the plastic bag and pinned it in place.

Phoebe pointed to Blessing's new plastic pants. "I have never in my life seen a baby wearing a plastic bag. You do strange things, Sister Sandy. None of the white people I've ever met dressed their children in plastic bags."

Sandy picked up Blessing. "Phoebe, would you like to come every day to wash clothes by hand and sweep the floor?"

"Yes, I will be glad to do that, but you will need a house girl to take care of the baby at night so you can sleep."

"No, thank you. I want to care for Blessing day and night."

Eve raised her eyebrows. "Who will take care of this child when you are at the clinic all day?"

"I'm taking this baby to work with me."

"You can't take a baby everywhere you go." Eve shook her head.

"Why not? Is it against the law?"

Eve shrugged. "No, but we leave our babies with servant girls."

"Blessing comes with me wherever I go. I will never leave her."

"You can try it, but it will not be convenient." Phoebe grimaced. "The people will not like it if you take a cursed baby into the clinic with you."

"Blessing is not cursed." Sandy sighed. "I didn't ask God for a baby so I can leave her in the house all day or give her to other people to watch for me. The Lord gave me a child so I could love her and take care of her. She will always be with me."

"We must go home now. It will soon be dark, and we have to prepare supper." Phoebe shook her head as she walked out the door with Eve.

Four hours later, Blessing woke up and screamed. Sandy boiled the cups, spoons, and the tuna fish can again to assure herself they were clean. Blessing clutched the satin pajama top in her tiny hands and chomped on the cloth. By the time the utensils cooled, and Sandy had calculated, measured, mixed, and poured, Blessing had cried herself back to sleep.

Sandy returned to bed. At three in the morning a cry woke her. She mumbled. "Too bad I don't have breast milk, so I could feed and rest in bed."

She would need to get up several times a night, make baby food, feed Blessing, and take her child to work, but she could do it with God's help.

CHAPTER NINE

Blessing wailed as Sandy set the pot of water on the stove to boil the utensils. She calculated, mixed milk powder, and positioned the baby upright in the crook of her arm. Sandy reached for the cup of prepared drink and dipped the spoon in the cup. She held it to Blessing's lips.

The baby shrieked between sips on the tiny spoon. Tears coursed down the infant's face. It had been over twelve hours since Blessing had eaten, but sipping a few drops from a little spoon wasn't satisfying the child, so Sandy lifted the tiny cup and put it to the baby's lips. Blessing gulped down the milk like she'd been drinking from a cup all her life. Her eyelids fell shut a few minutes later.

That was easy. Sandy slumped back in the chair and clutched her sleeping child. Mothering skills weren't hard. The most difficult part was boiling the utensils and keeping them clean. She was a professional career woman and could learn everything necessary to be a good mother, too.

She carried Blessing to the bedroom and put her in the cardboard box. If Sandy wanted a crib she'd have to ask a carpenter to build one, and not many woodworkers in the bush had ever seen a crib. All newborn babies and those up to two years old slept next to their mothers to nurse on demand through the night.

Sandy had wanted to take Blessing to sleep with her, but her bed was the narrowest one she'd ever slept in. She wouldn't take the chance of rolling on the baby. It didn't seem right that Blessing slept in a cardboard box. But it was better than Blessing being crushed in the night.

***

Chomping noises woke Sandy at seven in the morning. She looked over at Blessing who gnawed on the red satin pajamas. Sandy boiled water and mixed powder. Preparing the milk took time without a sink and running water.

When Phoebe arrived, Sandy carried her dirty clothes outside and tossed them in a rounded metal tub. Phoebe fetched a bucket of water from the well, poured it over the clothes and pitched in a giant bar of soap. She bent over the tub and used her knuckles and hands as a washboard to scrub the clothes.

Sandy sat on a rock in front of the door to listen for her sleeping baby. Sipping on a cup of tea, Sandy enjoyed the tropical birds serenading her. She caught a whiff of the orange-scented fragrance and let the rural country air refresh her. The blue sky and puffed-cotton clouds were peaceful.

The crunching steps on the trail sounded like someone who wore boots. She glanced toward the foot path. Colonel Big, the officer from the immigration office in Hose, headed straight to Sandy.

Her heart plummeted to the pit of her stomach. She stood on trembling limbs. Why had the obnoxious officer traveled the long distance to Koala?

Colonel Tsaou glowered. "Good morning."

Sandy nodded. "Good morning."

He pointed to the building. "Is this your house, Miss Calbrin?"

"Yes. I'll be right back. I need to check inside."

Phoebe stopped washing clothes and followed Sandy into the house. She checked on Blessing, who still slept. Phoebe carried a wooden chair outside and set it under the shade of the mango tree.

Sandy brought a second chair to the tree. "Please be seated, Colonel Tsaou."

Colonel Big nodded and sat down. "How are you, Miss Calbrin?"

Sandy angled the chair away from the sun, but also farther from him. "I'm fine. Thank you, and how about yourself?"

"I am well."

"May I offer you a cup of tea?"

"No, thank you. I came on business. You are under investigation."

Sandy's hand fluttered to her lips. "Why am I being investigated?"

"We believe you are carrying on illegal business in our country." He opened a file and flipped through hand-written pages.

54

She wrinkled her forehead. To her knowledge she had done nothing illegal. "I'm under the official authority of the Evangelical Independent Church of Africa. It is a legal position under the laws of your country."

"Maybe so, but tell me what is the real reason you came to Norgia?"

"I want to use the Shea nut in my beauty creams. When I arrived here, Mr. Jubilee, who knew I was a nurse, told me about the measles epidemic that had taken children's lives in the northwest. He asked me to vaccinate the youngsters and establish Under Fives Clinics."

"Mr. Jubilee explained all of that, but I want to know the real reason you came here."

She had just told him. What more could she say? Since Mr. Jubilee was the medical director of the church perhaps Colonel Big expected her to talk about God. "I'm a Christian. Have you heard about Jesus?"

"Yes, he is the white man's god."

"He is God Almighty, the Lord God of all."

"I did not come here to talk about God. I came to talk about you. I can make all your problems go away."

"How is that?" She turned away a little to avoid his glare.

The colonel lifted one of his polished boots and placed it on the highest tree root. As he unbuttoned the top brass clasp of his shirt, he puffed out his chest. Footsteps trudged on the opposite trail. They both turned to the sound. Eve walked toward her mother still washing the clothes.

Colonel Big grimaced at Phoebe and Eve. "Miss Calbrin, I will not trouble you anymore today. Think about what I said. Goodbye and good day." He turned and headed down the cow path.

Phoebe and Eve left the washing. They picked up the chairs, turned them upside down, and set them on their heads.

Eve led the way into the house. "Why is the immigration officer coming to you?"

"He is investigating me, but I don't know why."

"There is no reason to check you out, even though you are quite different from the other Americans." Phoebe put her chair down.

"Why do you think he is doing this?" Sandy asked the ladies.

Eve set her chair on the floor. "He wants to sleep with you."

Sandy's flesh crawled. "Why do you say that?"

"I had a teacher in high school who behaved like him. He said if I did not sleep with him he would give me a zero."

"What happened?"

"I told him I would never sleep with him, and he could give me the zero. But if I got a zero I would report him to my uncle, the chief of the village. He never bothered me again. That officer is making threats to frighten you and force you to do what he wants."

If he only wanted to terrorize her, why did he hint at so much more? Sandy's heart thumped faster. Sweat dripped down her face.

Eve frowned. "Do not allow him to scare you."

"I need a drink." Sandy moved to the stove and put water on to boil. "Let's sit down. I have water and hot tea. What would you like?"

"Tea please, if you have sugar and milk." Phoebe smiled.

"I do not want to frighten you, but you must never go anyplace alone. If you were by yourself and that officer showed up, it would be his word against yours if anything happened. In Africa, men, especially military men, are always right. They are in charge. Even a strong woman like you could never win against him. I saw his badges. He is a very important government official. Stay in a public place with other people." Eve set three ceramic cups on the table.

"So if he comes to the house, it's best if I step outside like we did today."

"Yes." Phoebe sat down. "That is why I went in the house to bring a chair outside. You must always offer him a seat, for it is very rude not to do this. Never stand over him. Always be on his level or lower than his eyes. Many people in our tribe kneel down in front of a senior or a superior."

Eve opened the box of sugar cubes. "Do you have a fiancé?"

"No, I don't. Would having a fiancé help me?"

"Yes it would. In Africa being engaged is almost as good as being married. Men, like the colonel, never trouble married women or engaged ones. He would be afraid of what your fiancé or husband would do to him."

Sandy had broken up with her boyfriend six months earlier because they had drifted apart during their three years of dating.

"I don't know any American men here." Sandy poured boiling water into the cups

"You won't even find a European husband here." Phoebe scowled. "I've never seen or met any single white men in our region."

Eve put a teabag in her cup. "I am 19 and spent the last year at the university in the national capital. I never saw any white men by themselves, only married couples. You must go back to the States if you want an American husband. But if you want an African husband, there are many good Christian men here who have not married because they have no money."

"Do you have a fiancé?" Sandy set the jar of peanut butter on the table.

"No, I do not. Not one of the Christian men in our church has any money." Eve stirred her drink.

"Why is having money so important for a future husband?"

Once the words were out there, Sandy couldn't take them back. Most women throughout the world preferred rich husbands or at least ones who had stable jobs and could provide for their families. It had to be the same in Africa.

With a trembling hand, Eve straightened some of her tiny braids. "Our parents must approve of our fiancé."

"Surely, they would endorse someone who was a good Christian and worked hard to provide for his wife and family." Sandy sipped her tea.

"If a man does not have enough money to pay the bride price of three goats, two chickens, one fifty-pound bag of rice, two fifty-pound bags of corn, twenty yards of cloth, and whatever else her family demands, how could a young man ever hope to support a wife and family?"

Sandy wrinkled her brow. It sounded expensive. The cost of a bride shouldn't be so high it discouraged young people from marrying.

Sexual promiscuity would increase if young people were forced to wait many years until they could afford to marry.

Phoebe picked up a tablespoon. "May I have more than six sugar cubes?"

Sandy nodded and handed her the box of sugar.

"Thank you." Phoebe tossed in twelve cubes, stirred her tea, and sipped it from the spoon as if it were soup.

Sandy sliced the bread and opened the evaporated milk with her machete. She missed her beautiful china dishes. Each month at the fitness center she sponsored a tea with Earl Grey, Chinese blend, and proper English scones served on silver plates. But the friendship of Phoebe and Eve meant more to her than high teas. God must be changing her inside out for she no longer desired the expensive furnishings and entertainment she used to enjoy.

"Would you like peanut butter for your bread?" Sandy offered the jar.

"Peanut butter is too hard for us to eat. We make peanut butter gravy, a spicy sauce with hot peppers. We cannot eat simple peanut butter on bread."

"It's hard for me to eat a crust of plain dry bread, which is why I spread peanut butter on it." Sandy grinned.

"I talked to someone who saw your baby in the hospital." Eve picked up her hot mug. "Your baby has been drinking from a cup since she was two months old. That is not normal. Blessing must have a very powerful curse on her to do something so bizarre."

"Drinking from a cup isn't strange."

"It is for a two-month-old baby." Phoebe stood and took her cup and spoon to the plastic basin filled with soapy water. "I will finish washing the clothes."

"I need help with water." Sandy pointed to the bucket.

Phoebe glanced at the pail in the corner. "What kind of help?"

"I have no water filter and must boil all my drinking water. The heat makes me thirsty all the time, so I drink all the hot, boiled water before I can prepare more water. It takes time. I cannot prepare enough drinking water, and now I need more clean water to mix with milk powder for the baby."

"I can fetch water from the well for you every day. I have a fifty-five-gallon drum at my house that Mrs. Boyden gave me for water, but I never use it and can let you have it."

"I would appreciate that." Sandy stood. "It would be a great help."

"Eve and I will go home and bring the drum now. You will need lots of water with the baby."

Thirty minutes later, laughter interrupted Sandy's reading. She went to the door. Adam carried a giant steel container on his head.

"Where would you like this barrel?" Phoebe asked.

Sandy pointed. "Next to the door."

Phoebe and Eve lifted the large cylinder off Adam's head.

Eve reached out to steady it. "If we move it here a little to the right it can catch rain water from the roof."

Carrying water inside the house from the drum to cook and clean would be easier than hiking to the well or river. Better still, she wouldn't need to tote it from a faucet three hundred yards away like the one they had at the guesthouse. Life in the village seemed easier and more hygienic than in the city.

Phoebe picked up several stones, positioned them under the drum, and leveled it on the uneven ground. "I can fill this with water, sweep, and hand wash all the clothes. You will have to bathe, dress, and carry Blessing."

"Thank you, Phoebe."

Adam and Eve departed. Phoebe stayed and finished the washing while Sandy unpacked the rest of her clothes. The majority were designer jeans, which she hung in the tiny closet in the cramped bedroom.

Phoebe brought the empty tubs and pails into the house and picked up the broom. She went into the bedroom to clean. A moment later the woman shrieked, "Sister Sandy, how could you do such a wicked thing?" She raced out of the chamber. "Why have you deceived us? We thought you were a Christian, but it looks like you are a prostitute."

Sandy jumped up. Her chair crashed to the floor. The book and pages of notes scattered.

Why did the woman think Sandy was a prostitute?

CHAPTER TEN

Sandy dashed into the bedroom. Her gaze clouded as she peered around the tiny space. There had to be a mistake.

Phoebe's black eyes widened. "Why do you have men's trousers?"

"Where?" Sandy's heart pounded.

Anguish covered her face as Phoebe pointed at the jeans dangling from hangers.

Many Christian churches and some people isolated in the bush forbid women from wearing pants, but Sandy had seen photos of women wearing pants in large cities like Logatti, the national capital. She didn't think there would be harm in bringing them and wearing them in the city when she wasn't on duty.

"I'm so sorry." Looking away from the woman, Sandy rubbed the back of her neck.

She turned to the jeans and pulled the first pair from the hanger and extended them toward Phoebe. The woman jumped away as if it were a puff adder, one of Africa's most deadly snakes, responsible for many human fatalities.

Phoebe wrinkled her nose. "A prostitute came to our village. She wore trousers to attract men. Any woman who wears pants is a prostitute. No proper Christian lady wears them."

The jeans had offended the African lady. A verse in the Bible talked about not offending others, and Sandy had to do something about the garments.

"These must go." She tugged them off hangers and hurled them onto the bed. The pile grew higher and higher as she tossed all the pairs of her expensive jeans onto the mattress.

Phoebe's eyeballs rolled left and right. "How could one prostitute have so many pants?"

Sandy could hide them away until she returned to States, but where? She scowled at the small room.

Phoebe with her arms crossed stood like Mr. Clean in front of her. "This is very bad." Then she wrung her hands.

"I'm sorry." Sandy pasted an expression of extreme remorse on her face.

She wouldn't offend the poor woman and her family. They'd been kind and hospitable by cooking, carrying water, washing clothes, and cleaning. Most of all Phoebe and her children offered Sandy friendship which she appreciated and needed.

Phoebe's mouth tightened. "What have you been doing with these trousers? Everyone believed you were a Christian lady."

Sandy closed her eyes and put her hands on her temples to suppress a headache coming on. The situation was more serious than she first thought. Either the pants were hers, and she wore them to parade around the village like a prostitute, or the pants were not hers and belonged to men who visited her at night. Either way, she was condemned.

Lord, I need your help.

How could Sandy redeem herself?

"Help me carry these to the trash pit." Sandy picked up half the pile of jeans.

Phoebe gathered up the rest of them. "Do you have matches?"

Sandy halted in her tracks. She didn't want to burn her clothes for they hadn't hurt anyone. Why destroy her favorite jeans? She shouldn't let anyone force her to do something she didn't want to do. Glancing again at the woman's shocked expression, Sandy knew it was best to get rid of them.

Maybe the match wouldn't light and the jeans would stay in the garbage pit. Later she could rescue them. But if she did that, they might be found again. With a shaking hand, Sandy picked up the matches from the top of the gas stove and followed Phoebe outside. Sandy stopped for a moment and looked at the tiny matchbox. Could she destroy all her favorite clothes just to make another woman happy? Sandy trudged to the garbage pit, about thirty yards from the back of her mud house.

Phoebe picked up small twigs and papers for kindling. She took the matchbox from Sandy and struck one. It lit. Within a minute, Phoebe had a bon fire with flames higher than she was.

Sandy stepped back to avoid the heat. She stiffened as the flames rose higher and higher, and she breathed faster and faster. Red and gold fire consumed her treasured possessions. Tears filled her eyes.

She wasn't crying over her destroyed jeans, but that a worldly possession had come between her and another person. If only her sins could disappear with the strike of a match. But they could, by asking forgiveness. She picked up stray papers and tossed them on the flames so the pants would be completely gone.

Lord, I accepted you as my Savior when I was a child. But I've forgotten you and lived as if you don't exist. I love you, Jesus, and acknowledge your Lordship. Forgive me for all my sins. I surrender all to you. Take my life and use it.

Phoebe looked at Sandy. "Your tears tell me you are sorry for this evil. Now that you have repented of your sins we can put this behind us."

Sandy cried and laughed at the same time. She wanted expensive clothes, and they were gone. She'd lost all her cosmetics when they'd tumbled out of her overstuffed bags during the trip. Sandy had sacrificed her designer shoes by slicing off the heels so she could walk on the uneven rocky trails. What more would she need to surrender? Was the Christian life one of constantly making sacrifices?

Phoebe stirred the fire. "Now that we are burning the pants, everything will be fine."

With the Lord's help, Sandy would follow Him. Asking forgiveness and rededicating her life to the Lord put her back on God's path.

Sandy tossed the rest of the papers onto the fire and whirled away. "Blessing is alone in the house. Someone may take her."

"Take her? No one wants a cursed baby." Phoebe threw more rubbish into the flames.

Sandy ran toward the house. "Blessing is not cursed."

Phoebe raised her voice. "You will find out. Lots of bad things will happen to you."

Sandy jogged faster. She went inside and checked the sleeping baby who was fine.

Why had Sandy wasted years building up her personal kingdom, when God's realm was for eternity? She ran her fingers over the three business suits left hanging in the closet. A deep sigh of surrender escaped her mouth. Picking up scissors for trimming her hair, she snipped at one of the jackets and sliced off most of the sleeves. The short sleeves would be better for hot weather. After cutting out the linings, she pulled the thread from the seams and pressed open the cloth on her little table. Within a few minutes, Sandy had cut out and basted a tiny garment. She held up the dress and sighed in contentment. The little dress for Blessing matched her own short-sleeved jacket.

The baby woke from her nap and giggled. Sandy tickled the child's stomach to hear her laugh again. Sandy adored Blessing.

Her old life had been so empty, unsatisfying. In Africa Sandy had no home, no clothes, car, or other amenities, but she had Blessing and deep joy. Sandy had never loved anyone as much as she loved her baby.

Phoebe knocked on the door before stepping inside. "You will never get any work done if you waste your life playing with a baby."

Blessing didn't cry or fuss, like other babies. The child always grinned and gurgled at Sandy, who couldn't resist the urge to pick her up and cuddle her.

"I finished burning all the trousers." Phoebe stepped closer and handed Sandy the matches. "I have a hand crank sewing machine. Would you like to use it?"

"Thank you. I cut off the sleeves of the navy jacket to make this dress for Blessing." Sandy lifted the tiny garment. "I want to cut these two straight skirts, the navy blue and the black pin-striped, alternate strips of cloth and turn it into a full skirt. The lining will make a good trim for Blessing's dresses and a hat to shade her head from the sun."

"You are a clever woman. None of our ladies can do all that you do. I will go home and bring the machine. It will be much faster than sewing by hand." Phoebe turned to go.

Sandy tried to put the baby on her back but couldn't do it. She wasn't used to tying an infant to her. She needed a reliable, secure method. Picking up the third business suit of heavy linen and wool, she scowled. Why did she bring it? It was much too hot to wear in Africa. Reaching for the scissors, she cut, measured, calculated, and then basted the seams.

Phoebe returned carrying the sewing machine on her head. She set it on the small table. "You may borrow this as long as you need it."

"I appreciate this." Sandy slid the cloth under the pressure foot and turned the crank by hand. It felt awkward at first not having two hands to guide the cloth, but Phoebe helped her get the hang of it.

After Phoebe left, Sandy kept sewing. Thirty minutes later she completed her handiwork. Lifting the project, she beamed. It wasn't bad, for a baby carrier.

"Excuse, Sister Sandy."

It sounded like the pastor. Sandy opened the door and offered him a seat.

"How are you?" The pastor looked at the machine. "Our church prays that God will bless you for coming to our village."

"God has blessed me. This is Blessing." Sandy nodded toward the giggling child.

The pastor frowned. "I heard about her but didn't expect her to be so black-skinned. You are white-skinned, but she still has much in common with you. She is happy, talks all the time, and laughs. I never saw such a cheerful baby, but she must have learned it from you." The pastor picked up the red satin pajama top, turned it around several times, and shrugged before covering the baby again with it.

"You Americans have bizarre clothes. I heard about the men's trousers in your closet. Phoebe said you burned all of them. We are glad you repented of your sins."

Sandy lowered her head so the pastor couldn't see her amusement. "God showed me my sins, and I asked His forgiveness."

"I am pleased to hear that." The pastor picked up the little dress for Blessing. "What is this?"

"I'm making baby dresses. I've already finished this one."

"This is a lot of work for a baby who will be small for just a short time."

"That's true."

"Why is she in a cardboard carton?"

"My mattress is quite narrow, and I don't have a bed for Blessing, so she sleeps in the box."

The pastor scowled. "I saw a baby bed in a white man's house a long time ago. They called it a crib, like a corncrib. It looked like the baby slept in a little prison."

Thank God she hadn't found a crib for her baby. That would have been another offense.

Blessing giggled and kicked the pajama top off her legs again.

The pastor bent over and covered her once more. "I wanted to remind you about the health lecture you are teaching in church." He stood to leave. "I will see you there."

Sandy put on her short-sleeved jacket. She dressed Blessing in the matching blue dress and bonnet. Picking up her baby, she carried Blessing to the church for the lecture, but first she greeted the pastor, elders, and women.

One of the elders' wives extended her arms toward Blessing. "I will hold your daughter while you give the speech. She is so beautiful, and you dress her so smartly." The woman carried Blessing to a pew close to the back.

Sandy stood in front of the congregation. "There are tiny creatures called germs, which cause sickness. One germ causes malarial fever, another causes typhoid, and another dysentery."

Blessing howled. Sandy stopped speaking and glanced at her daughter. The elder's wife handed the baby to another woman.

Sandy looked down at her notes. "You cannot see these germs with your eyes, but you can see them at the hospital if you look into powerful glasses called a microscope."

Blessing wailed louder. Sandy halted mid-sentence as the woman handed the child to a younger lady. Blessing screamed as if being tortured. Sandy's heart caught in her throat, and she took a deep breath. "If we keep our food clean, wash our hands with soap and water after using the toilet, before cooking, and before eating we can get rid of most of these germs."

Sandy stopped for a few seconds as Blessing shrieked louder. Her baby was passed to another female. Tears streamed down the baby's face and glistened on her cheeks. The woman handed the child to an older woman, but Blessing kept howling.

"In conclusion, there are many sicknesses we can prevent by eating the right food and being clean." Sandy collected her notes and trotted to her child.

Blessing reached out for Sandy who took her. The baby smiled at Sandy and fell asleep a moment later.

The older woman grinned. "The baby only wanted her mother. She would not be quiet with any of us."

The pastor's wife pulled Sandy aside. "I thank God you repented of your sin."

Sandy pressed her lips together and let out a deep breath through her nostrils. If burning her jeans showed her sincerity in repenting, it was worth it.

But what if the church leaders in the headquarters didn't believe she'd repented and took Blessing away?

CHAPTER ELEVEN

Sandy looked over the twenty patients who waited for treatment in the Koala clinic. She shifted her child to her right arm and picked up a pen to write with her left.

Eve arrived, took Blessing, and tied the baby to her back. "Are you sure you want to bring her to work every day? You should get a house servant. Taking care of a child is not as simple as you think."

Caring for the baby was easy. When Blessing was awake, Sandy played with her or put her in the carrier on her back. After Blessing ate, Sandy washed the cup and turned it upside down so it was clean for the next meal. She washed the diaper and hung it in the sun to dry. Not having toys, dolls, rattles, and blocks meant less work and no picking up.

An immigration officer stepped into the clinic. "Excuse me."

He stomped closer and straightened his wrinkled uniform. After removing his dust-covered hat, he snapped it against his hand. The officer pulled out a handkerchief from his back pocket and wiped the sweat from his face. He raised one of his boot-clad feet to a chair and flicked the cloth across the soiled boot. Then he lifted the other foot to the chair to swat away the dirt.

"Sir, please sit down." Sandy pointed to the chair. "How can I help you?"

The officer sat on the wooden bench and pulled out an official file from an ancient briefcase. "Are you Sandra Calbrin, from the United States of America?"

"Yes." Sandy's heart thumped faster. What could he want from her? Had he come all that way to the village to ask what her name was or to haul her back to Hose? Maybe he came to threaten her.

"May I see your passport, please?"

"It's in the house."

"You and I can walk to the house together and get it."

Sandy glanced over at Eve who shook her head ever so slightly before nodding toward her brother Adam.

"I need to prepare medications." Sandy stood and walked to Adam. "Would you please go to my house? Here is the key. Bring the backpack on the table. Thank you."

Eve whispered in her brother's ear as she escorted him outside.

Sandy opened a container of one-thousand Tylenol pills. She counted out twenty tablets and slid them into a little packet. By the time Adam returned, she had filled thirty envelopes.

She opened the backpack and took out the passport, which she handed to the officer. He flipped through the pages. Scowling, he pulled a pair of reading glasses out of his breast pocket. He put them on to write information from the passport into his ledger.

He closed the passport and handed the document to her. "I have all the facts and figures for the investigation. Good day." He stood and left.

Sandy cocked an eyebrow. "Do you think he was a genuine military officer?"

Adam glowered. "What do you mean?"

"Could he have been an imposter who stole a uniform pretending to be an officer to collect information on me?"

"No, he was an officer."

"I was going to ask him for his credentials."

Adam paced the small room before raising his voice. "You must never ask any officers for identification. It is a terrible insult. It would look like you doubted their authority."

"But I did."

"You have no right to doubt their power. You should be able to see their domineering ways and know they are in charge."

Every officer she'd met had been dictatorial. Some were more overbearing than others. If Adam were right, an average man couldn't impersonate such an officious manner. Thank God she'd kept her mouth shut and didn't ask to see the officer's badge.

Adam frowned. "He would have carried you off to prison for insulting him, or you might simply disappear."

She stared straight ahead. Shivering, she rubbed her forearms and sat on the wooden chair.

Eve removed the sleeping baby from her back. "I can help with Blessing until I return to the university. If you want to bring the baby with you to this clinic I will carry her for you, since there is no place to lay her. I cannot travel to the villages with you."

"I should get another cardboard box for her to sleep at work."

"When a woman in our family has a child, the woman's mother or mother-in-law and female relatives come to the house to care for the child. They fetch and boil water, wash clothes, bathe the baby, cook meals, and clean the house for at least a month."

"Blessing is not a newborn baby, and I didn't give birth."

"After the female relatives depart they send a young girl, maybe ten years old to stay with the new mother. The child jumps up and gets whatever the mother needs or wants, carries the baby on her back, takes care of the other children, cooks, and cleans."

"It is wrong for this young girl to be denied school to do this. It hurts my heart to see these females working all day like slaves."

"It is our culture. No one can afford a nanny. This is the only way we can manage to have all our children. Besides, most of these house girls cannot pass the examination for school."

"Is it because they were never given the opportunity to learn? Everyone should have a chance to go to school, even girls."

Eve nodded. "I agree with you that girls should be allowed to go to school."

"Maybe these girls are intelligent, but are forced to work all day and don't know how to study."

"What you say is true."

The elderly man with leg ulcers came into the clinic.

Sandy smiled at him. "Have a seat and I will check your wound."

The ancient man unwound the dressing.

Sandy examined the ulcer. "This is healing well."

"Thank you. Thank you." The patient grinned.

Her lips twitched. Sandy turned away to suppress a giggle. Surely the patient didn't believe he was responsible for his healing.

She washed and dressed the sore. "Your fee is fifteen naros."

"Thank you, sister." The patient handed her the coins.

"Can you bring a papaya tomorrow?" Sandy wrote the treatment on the health card.

The elderly gentleman stood. "Would you like to eat one?"

"I want to use it as a medicine. This ulcer is deeper than most and although there is no infection the hospital record shows you have had it over a year. According to this, the doctors tried all the medications. The peeling of a papaya, placed face down on the wound every morning and evening should speed the recovery."

"I will bring the fruit, but I prefer the medicine you give."

"Our treatments have not helped it." Sandy handed the man his card. "Maybe the papaya will heal the ulcer."

A male voice from outside shouted, "Sister Sandy, come help."

Sandy glanced out the window. Five farmers dressed in dirt-stained clothes escorted a limping man. A pool of blood oozed from the injured man's lower leg where filthy rags covered the wound.

She picked up a bar of soap and some dressings. "Adam, please bring a bucket of water." Sandy went outside to the bench under a colossal baobab tree. "Put the injured man here."

Sandy sat next to the patient and lifted his bleeding leg to her lap. The people in the crowd gasped. Men shook their fists and women covered their faces. Sandy's eyes moved slowly left to right at their shocked faces. What had she done wrong? She must have broken another taboo.

Lord, please help me.

She pointed to one of the farmers dressed in dirt-soiled clothes. "You there. Come here and hold this leg up like this. The foot must be elevated to stop the bleeding."

The young farmer gripped the man's injured leg and took Sandy's place when she stood putting the leg on his lap.

"Would someone else like to keep this man's leg elevated to stop the flow of blood?"

The villagers gasped, shook their heads, and jumped back several more paces.

Sandy bent over the injured man and with her fingertips lifted the dirty rags covering the wound. After scrubbing it with soap and water, she let it bleed several seconds to flush out dirt and germs. Blood dripped on the ground forming a puddle. She picked up a clean dressing and applied pressure with her right palm to halt the flow. Peeking under the cloth, she was pleased to see the bleeding had stopped. The six-inch gash had closed, and she set the injured man's leg back on the other man's lap.

"He needs sutures, but there are none here. Can you take him to the hospital?"

A farmer leaning on his hoe turned to Sandy. "The taxi has already left for the hospital."

"And it takes six hours for a vehicle to reach the medical facility." A man wiped the sweat from his brow with the back of his hand.

"Can't you treat our brother?" another farmer asked.

"I'll do my best." She found yellowed, surgical tape in the box of dressings. Using scissors she cut out butterfly sutures and applied the sticky strips. She covered the wound with several cloth dressings.

Sandy pointed to the injury. "You need antibiotics and a tetanus shot. Can you go to the hospital tomorrow to get them?"

The patient and his brothers nodded agreement.

A gray-haired man approached Sandy. "How much is the charge?"

"Thirty naros." Sandy picked up the remaining bandages and bar of soap.

The youngest farmer tilted his head. "They charge one hundred and twenty naros at the hospital to treat and dress a wound. Why do you only charge thirty naros?"

"I'd like everyone to afford it."

The farmer handed Sandy the coins.

She wrote on the card and gave the document back to him. "Take this treatment record to the hospital so the doctor is aware of my care of the wound."

With the help of his brothers, the injured man hobbled away.

And then Blessing wailed. Eve handed the baby to Sandy. "I think she is hungry."

Sandy sat down on the bench under the baobab tree and held Blessing on her lap. All eyes in the crowd turned to watch her and the baby. The men squatted while women spread their skirts in the dirt and sat on the cloth as if watching a sideshow. It looked like everyone in the village was there.

"I'll bring her food." Eve went into the clinic and returned with the jar. She handed it to Sandy who mixed the corn porridge into the milk. Then she poured it into Blessing's tiny metal cup and held it to her mouth to drink.

A farmer shook his head. "She's drinking from a cup like a person. It is not normal."

More people approached from every direction. Some sat on the ground. Others brought flat rocks to sit on, while some stood.

One farmer stared at Sandy. "We came to see the leg that was cut off, and you put back together again."

"No leg was cut off. I did not put a leg back together. Only God can do that."

The roar of a car engine caused everyone to twist their heads toward the cow path. The driver stopped the car in front of the Koala clinic. David climbed out and approached Sandy. "Good morning. I see you have been well and treating many patients. My father heard about the baby and thought it best that you come back to Hose now."

"Right now? This minute?" Her heart beat faster. Only trouble or a major crisis would make Mr. Jubilee send his son, the chauffeur, to take her back to Hose. "Is there a problem?"

"No problem."

There had to be a major problem. The medical director told her she'd stay until she'd finished vaccinating all the children.

"I don't have much to pack and can be ready to leave in thirty minutes."

"I will help you." Eve went into the clinic and pulled the wooden shutters closed. She stepped outside and locked the door.

David, Adam, Eve, and Sandy with Blessing climbed into the vehicle for the short ride to Sandy's little home. After he parked there, everyone marched into her small mud house.

The driver went to the stove. "Should I put all the food in this carton?"

"Yes, please." Sandy turned to Eve. "Pack all of Blessing's belongings in her cardboard bed and take it to the car. Adam, please put all the household supplies in the empty bucket."

Sandy tossed all her personal effects and meager clothes into her suitcases. Everyone lugged a suitcase or carton to the car. In less than ten minutes the vehicle was loaded and ready to depart.

"Goodbye." Sandy turned to get in the car. "Thank you for your help. Please tell your mother I am leaving, so it won't be necessary for her to come to my house and clean. Please give this key to the chief."

Her heart beat a little faster. Maybe the immigration officers wanted to ask more questions. Perhaps the church leaders disapproved of her taking an abandoned child. Or worse, Mr. Jubilee heard about the pants and was sending her back to the States. She couldn't work under the church if they believed she was a prostitute, or could she?

CHAPTER TWELVE

Sandy ran her fingers through her hair and flattened it behind her ears. Why was the medical director's son hauling her back to the headquarters before the vaccinations were completed?

When they reached Hose, David took Sandy, Blessing, and the baggage to the guesthouse. "You should rest this afternoon. Tomorrow morning I will pick you up and take you to my father. Should I bring a girl to take care of the baby for you?"

"No thank you. The baby comes with me every day."

Shaking his head, David frowned and left.

Sandy put Blessing in her cloth carrier, tied her to her back, and walked to the guesthouse kitchen.

The cook, an older gentleman, Mr. Godo, stared at Blessing. "Where you get baby?"

"She was left at the hospital because the people believed she was cursed." Sandy set her bag on the floor. "May I come early in the mornings to use your stove to boil a big pot of water? I need to fill my thermos to make the baby's food."

"I will boil water each morning before I prepare breakfast for the guests. I will be happy to fill your flask, since you are helping with this poor baby." The toothless cook grinned. "Would you like tea? I can boil water now."

"Yes, please." Sandy sat on the stool he offered her.

The African people always accommodated her. Even the poorest person would offer her a drink of water.

Mr. Godo prepared a cup of tea for her and filled her flask.

She asked, "Would you hold my baby so I can go to the restroom, please?"

"What kind of curse is on this child?"

"She's not cursed. Her name is Blessing."

"Why do the people believe she is cursed?"

"She didn't do anything. She survived birth, but her mother died."

Mr. Godo gasped. "She killed her mother."

"She didn't kill her mother."

"Take her to my wife next door. Maybe she will hold her for you."

"Couldn't you take her for five minutes?"

"No. I do not want to take chances. Suppose something happened. Who would cook food for all the guests?"

Sandy carried Blessing into the lounge and found a cleaning lady. "Would you hold my baby for a moment while I use the restroom?"

The worker reached for the child. "She's a beautiful baby."

Sandy returned a few minutes later, took Blessing, and went back to the kitchen. If she couldn't persuade an educated cook to abandon superstitious beliefs, how could she ever convince illiterate people in the bush that Blessing wasn't cursed?

"Thank you for the tea, Mr. Godo." She sipped the hot drink. "Ever since I arrived I've seen so many different scars on people's faces. Most of the folks who live here have cuts like yours. Could you explain the marks to me?"

"There are three hundred and sixty different tribes in our country. When we had wars many years ago we cut our faces with scars to distinguish our neighbors from our enemies." Mr. Godo tossed some chopped onions into a large cooking pot.

Sandy set her teacup down. "I saw one man who had three, long scars on the outer corners of his lips. He reminded me of a cat because the marks resembled an animal's whiskers."

The cook stirred the ingredients in the kettle. "Those people had a local god who resembled the cat, so they cut themselves to look like that animal. They will not eat cats like the rest of us."

Sandy swallowed and took a breath.

He stopped stirring and looked at Blessing. "Your baby is a pleasant child. She smiles and laughs, but you will not change people's minds. They will always see her as cursed."

Did Sandy fight a losing battle? After finishing her tea, she returned to her room at the guesthouse and fed her baby.

That night, Sandy tossed and turned. She tried sleeping on the outer edge of the mattress to avoid the lumps but kept rolling into them. At sunrise she was exhausted. She stood and stretched to relieve her aching back.

David knocked. "Good morning. Did you sleep well?"

She hadn't had much sleep, but she didn't want to complain about the conditions. She said nothing as she lifted Blessing, grabbed her backpack, and followed him to the car. With Blessing in her arms, Sandy slid onto the seat.

David maintained his distance in a professional manner. He seemed about ten years junior to her but mature and a cautious driver. He braked for people, pigs, and goats running into the road. As he turned into the back gate of the church headquarters, he said. "There are two entrances. The official one is in front for dignitaries. This is rough as you can see."

It looked like folks tossed their garbage out the back door. The stench of trash infected the air. She wrinkled her nose. It appeared no one wanted to take care of anything, but maybe it was the only way of life they knew.

Sandy and David stepped out of the car and went to Mr. Jubilee's office. The medical director opened his door and looked at the baby in Sandy's arms. "I heard about the abandoned child from Dr. Pelougu."

"I will keep her until the father decides what to do with her."

"Our people believe this child is cursed."

"Blessing is not cursed."

"Christians do not believe she is cursed, but there are many superstitious beliefs among our people in the rural areas." His facial expression turned serious. "Now tell me about the men's trousers you had in your room."

"In my country, many ladies wear pants."

"In England, Christian women wear trousers, but the prostitutes in our country were the first to wear them, signaling who they were. Some people believe all women who dress in trousers are prostitutes."

"I'm so sorry. After Phoebe and I burned all the pants, I hoped word would spread I no longer had trousers in my possession."

"Word spread that you were entertaining men at night, but repented of your evil ways when you burned the pants. Are you a born-again Christian?"

"Yes, I accepted Jesus as my Savior."

"Promise me you will never wear pants and do such a wicked thing ever again."

Having pants wasn't evil to her, but she nodded. "I promise I won't."

"The white people who established our church asked me to send you back to America. The immigration officers are searching for any indiscretion to harass you." Mr. Jubilee scowled. "Why did you anger the medical people by charging thirty naros for a dressing, when the hospitals charge one hundred and twenty naros? That action made the Christians at the hospital look greedy."

"In the bush there is no overhead like rent, electricity, and water. I only asked for money to replace the supplies. Am I in a lot of trouble?"

"You are a courageous woman to stand up for what you believe and follow through on your principles, but as Christians we must keep peace with everyone."

"What do you want me to do?"

"Set up the Under Fives Clinics and vaccinate the children. All the people in Koala love you. I would like you to stay here in Hose for two weeks, but if you want to go back right away to escape the people who want you to leave, that would be fine."

"If I leave immediately it will appear I'm running away."

"Of course, you are right."

"What do you want me to do while I'm here?"

"Would you be willing to help in our employee clinic?"

Every time she caught her breath, she was given another request to work in a clinic or treat patients. She had only intended to stay two weeks to collect the Shea tree nuts, but she agreed to vaccinate children and establish the Under Fives Clinics. After that, the chief of Koala wanted her to set up the clinic.

Maybe she should do as much as she could while she was there. "Yes, I can do it."

"Thank you. Here is the key. My son will take you to the clinic. I am late for a meeting, but I wanted to speak to you before I left. I think bringing you back to Hose now will show everyone, including the immigration officers, that you are under our authority." He laughed. "It looks like you are making a lot of enemies. When I first met you, I never imagined you would do that."

"I spent most of my career in public relations and never had any troubles with anyone."

For the first time in her life people said awful things about her. Up until then no one had ever criticized her or spoken negatively of her. What if she couldn't prove everyone wrong?

CHAPTER THIRTEEN

Sandy found it easy to go back to nursing in Koala. Treating African patients was fun. Without the stress of completing reports, obeying the time schedule, and listening to demanding patients, she enjoyed the job.

The Africans claimed it was the will of Allah if they didn't get better by the time Sandy saw them again and no one blamed her for anything.

In the States, she'd worked twelve-hour shifts in the hospital, running from one end of a long hall to the other, giving medicines, checking IV fluid lines, and adjusting oxygen levels to grumbling patients. She'd had enough of nursing and the disrespect that came with it, so she'd left it.

As David parked on the busy street, she glanced at the cement building, nestled in a cluster of papaya trees at the far back corner of a colossal church. Would working there be easy and free of stress? He opened the car door and accompanied Sandy to the small dwelling covered with a tin roof. He unlocked the wooden door, and Sandy went inside. Dust fluttered from above and covered Blessing's hair. Sandy sneezed as she brushed off the dirt. Something landed on her head and she shivered. What was it?

"David, get this off me."

He pushed something off her head. "It's just a piece of the cardboard ceiling."

Grimacing, she pulled strands of cobwebs from her hair. She jumped away from the cockroaches and spiders that skittered across the floor. "This clinic looks like it hasn't been cleaned in a year."

David reached out and batted away wayward spider strings. "Can I be your first patient?"

He hadn't acted ill while driving. So she didn't take him seriously, but she asked, "Are you sick?"

"I have a hot head, and it has pained me for days."

She held up a hand indicating he should wait a moment. Trying not to laugh at David's description of his symptoms, she went to the cabinets and opened the doors in search of medicines. She needed that moment to control the giggles that threatened.

Sandy found one bottle labeled Tylenol with a few tablets in it. "Here are two pills for fever and pain, but where are the other treatments?"

"I will speak to my father about it." David reached out for the tablets.

Sandy hunted in the closet, under the small table, and behind the door.

"What are you looking for?" David frowned.

"A broom to sweep."

He pointed to several reed brushes in front of her on the floor. "These are brooms." David bent down and picked one up. A strip of cloth held the ends of the dried palm-leaves together. He tapped the thick end of the short broom in his palm to level out the bristles, flipped it over, and bent down to sweep. Dust filled the clinic.

She pinched her nose. "Thank you for showing me." With Blessing on her back, Sandy bent over and picked up another broom.

David stopped sweeping. "Take my broom. It is better than the one in your hand."

"What?" Sandy stopped sweeping.

"My broom is sturdier. See it has more bristles." David handed his broom to her and left.

Sandy kept sweeping until she saw a pair of white cotton socks peeking out of black, laced up boots. She lifted her head and stared at the stranger.

"Hello, I'm Helen Swallow." The voice sounded American.

The old woman had combed her gray hair into a lopsided bun, which stuck out of the back of her pith helmet, similar to the one Dr. Livingston had worn in many pictures. Her ancient glasses balanced halfway down her nose. A mosquito net dangled in the breeze from the visor of her head covering. Her blue and white checked gingham housedress swayed six inches lower than her knees.

Sandy stared at the old Caucasian female in the doorway. Had she gone back in time a hundred years? "Good morning. I'm Sandra Calbrin, but everyone calls me Sandy."

"I'm a very curious woman. Why are you bending over to sweep with that useless broom?"

"David gave it to me." Sandy pushed a chair toward the visitor. "Please sit down."

After the woman sat, Sandy smiled. "This is a great form of exercise. I manage a fitness center and help women stay in shape." She bent at the waist, up and down, as if teaching exercises, and counted out loud, "One, two, one, two, I try to incorporate activities into every day chores."

"I can see that, but you won't need much of a workout here in Africa."

Sandy stood her broom up in the corner. "Why not?"

"Most of us walk places." Helen removed her helmet and put the straps inside of it. "By the way, they sell imported American brooms at the European store."

"Thank you for telling me. I planned on purchasing a transformer, too, at the European shop." Maybe then, she could use her hair dryer.

"I'm sorry to tell you." Helen heaved a sigh. "During the military problems all the electrical transformers, voltage regulators, and adaptors were confiscated and the foreign businessmen who brought them left the country."

Sandy shook her head. "That's a big disappointment."

The older woman's gaze swept over Sandy's clothes and her face. "I'm kind of snoopy, which is why I came to visit you myself. Excuse me for asking, but do you always put on so much make-up, even when it's one hundred degrees?"

"I'm afraid it's a habit. I'm too proud to go in public without it. For nearly a decade I've had to appear picture-perfect at the fitness center."

"It gets even hotter here, and none of us working in the Christian hospital wear makeup. You should think about abandoning it. How did you find your way here to Hose?"

85

Sandy tried not to stare at the deep wrinkles on the taller woman's face. "I needed to collect some nuts from the Shea tree to prepare beauty creams. So I wrote the church medical director and he invited me."

"But why now? The country is recovering from a *coups d'état*."

"The people at the Norgian embassy told me it was quite safe to travel at this time and the political problems were settled."

"They say that to encourage tourists."

"When they announced on the news that the borders were open, I secured a seat on the first plane coming to Norgia."

Sandy's friends advised her not to travel to Africa. No pampered career woman could survive in a third world country even for a few days, but so far she'd managed without plumbing and electricity.

Helen seemed a little upset with her, but Sandy's diplomacy was her greatest asset. As the manager of a fitness center, she had talked her way out of many disagreeable situations.

The older woman shook her head. "I'd have never attempted to travel at a dangerous time."

"It was terrifying. Every uniformed man carried a rifle, pistol, or revolver and a baton for beating folks. On the night I arrived, three different groups of armed soldiers stopped the taxi and threatened me."

"You should have waited longer before coming. None of the people who were evacuated have returned yet." Helen shrugged. "But you traveled through the worst and arrived in good condition."

"I saw the tribal conflicts televised on the news. Opposition forces slaughtered thousands. Their corpses lined the city streets. Bodies covered with black flies were left to rot. I assumed when the borders opened that everything would be back to normal."

"Logatti is the national capital city where the resistance party fought and gained most of the control. You can see devastation everywhere left from the military conflicts." She took out a handkerchief and wiped her face. "You don't look like the kind of girl who fits here in the African bush." Helen looked down and stared at Sandy's broken fingernails. "And it's hard to maintain a good manicure here."

Sandy glanced at her hands and bit her lower lip. "I should cut my nails."

The older woman sat primly in her seat with her hands clasped and back straight. Would Sandy look like her visitor if she stayed in Africa for any length of time? The poor woman probably didn't have a good wrinkle cream or face foundation. If most of Sandy's cosmetics hadn't fallen out of the bag and disappeared on her way there, she would have shared some with Helen. Without beauty creams, Sandy might look like poor Helen with leathery, wrinkled skin. Thank God she wasn't staying for a long time and wouldn't have skin damage.

Helen stood up and put her helmet on her head. "I must get back to work, but I'll come another day to finish this talk of ours."

"I look forward to it." Sandy walked Helen to the door. "It was so nice to meet you. Thank you for coming to visit. Goodbye." She pasted her very best smile on her face, the one that calmed everyone.

Helen never mentioned Blessing, but the baby would probably be Helen's next topic of conversation.

After sweeping the clinic from top to bottom, Sandy picked up a dusty rag and tossed it into the bucket she retrieved from the closet. She'd seen a tap outside before entering the clinic and carried her pail to it. She filled it with water, lugged it inside, and washed the cupboards and counter tops. She hoped no patients arrived until she had medicines.

When Blessing woke, Sandy fed her and put the baby in the carrier on her back.

Sometime later, David returned with a tray of food. "Excuse me, Sister Sandy. My father asked me to bring you lunch from the guest house every day, since you will be volunteering in the clinic."

Her mouth watered. "Thank you so much." She hadn't eaten since lunch the previous day. Thank God she was accustomed to fasting. She'd maintained her petite size by rigid diets and exercising with her female clients.

"I will return at five this evening and drive you back to your room." David departed.

Sandy folded the pink-knitted shawl that covered the hot bowls and lifted the largest metal lid to take a peek. Steam rose from the white boiled rice. Her face contorted at the fish head floating in tomato sauce in another bowl. Two old-fashioned glass bottles, one of Coca Cola and the other of orange soda lay on the tray. She picked up the bottle opener and removed the cap from the Coke and drank the entire warm contents. The drink tasted overly sweet to her. In the States she always drank club soda or seltzer water to avoid weight gain.

Wrinkling her nose, she transferred the fish head to the upside-down lid. With the spoon still in her hand, she put a dab of tomato sauce into her mouth. Pursing her lips, she blew air out while fanning her mouth with her hand. Tears filled her eyes. She grabbed the bottle of orange soda, opened it, and drank half to relieve the burning. Her mouth was still on fire, so she ate a couple bites of the boiled white rice. She mixed a few drops of sauce into the rice and added a few pinches of salt from the tiny cup. She ate all the reddened rice but put the fish head back into the remaining sauce and covered it with the lid.

A woman's cough startled her. Sandy glanced toward the door. Her mouth fell open. A lady in a pink-striped polyester dress with a giant butting goat at her side marched into the clinic. The beast clomped toward Sandy who backed away from the creature. With Blessing still sleeping on her back, Sandy clambered onto the wooden chair. She didn't want to offend the woman by pinching her nose, so she tried to hold her breath from the stench of the goat as she stood rigid on top of the seat.

"Excuse me. My goat suffers the plague. Do you have medicine?"

"I'm sorry. This is a clinic for humans, not animals."

"Do you know someone who can help me?" The woman ignored her goat as it headed closer to Sandy.

"I'm sorry. I know no one." Sandy stared straight ahead at the goat.

"You must be a stranger among us. Welcome." The woman opened her red purse, pulled out a blue-plastic rope, tied it around the animal's neck, and tugged it out of the clinic.

At five, David came and picked up the tray from lunch. "It's time to go home."

As he drove her to the guesthouse, Sandy thought about her elegant apartment in the States.

She was exhausted from scrubbing the dispensary but still needed to clean her room. So she lugged buckets of water from the outside tap to scour the chamber. After washing the window, walls, and floor, she secured some clean folded sheets from the housekeeper.

The mattress on the floor was the only piece of furniture in Sandy's room. After bathing and feeding Blessing, Sandy washed and put on her blue satin lounging pajamas. She pulled half of the mattress so it leaned against the wall. Relaxing on her makeshift couch, Sandy played with Blessing until it was time to sleep. Then she tugged the mattress so all of it was flat on the floor and in a corner where she put her baby. Sandy slept on the outside of it.

She mixed a spoon of peanut butter into some milk when Blessing woke her. That was the only food she could give the baby without a stove to cook corn porridge and beans.

She was grateful she'd only need to stay in these conditions for a few weeks.

CHAPTER FOURTEEN

The following morning David drove Sandy to the clinic and asked, "Why did you not eat your red sauce and your fish head? We are giving you our best food. You insulted the cook by returning them."

Sandy hadn't heard any taboos about leaving fish heads and didn't know it was an offense to return uneaten food. "The red sauce was so hot, it made my eyes water and burned my mouth."

"I am sorry and will tell cook. Can you eat peanut gravy?"

She'd never eaten peanut sauce in her life. Would she even like it? "Please do not put any hot, spicy pepper in it."

After David left her, Helen arrived. "I stopped yesterday to see your baby. I was so caught up in talking to you that I forgot to ask about the child."

Sandy shifted her position on the chair and crossed her legs.

"I'd suggest you not cross your legs in front of any Africans. It's taboo."

Sandy had only been there a few weeks but was already tired of all the taboos.

"In this culture it's forbidden to show anyone the bottom of your foot. It gives the impression you are kicking the person." Helen scowled.

"Thank you for telling me." In slow motion Sandy uncrossed her legs.

A smile creased Helen's face. "You may cross your legs at the ankles like this." The older woman planted her feet on the floor, slid her right foot above her left, and slipped it down the left side of her left foot, all the while keeping her feet on the floor.

"Thank you for showing me."

"The Americans and Canadians are talking about the illegitimate baby you had."

Sandy's mouth fell open but she snapped it closed. "I didn't have a baby."

How had everyone, hundreds of miles away, heard about the baby and the men's pants without any means of communication? She thanked God none of the church leaders believed the stories.

"I was given this baby girl from the hospital to care for until her father is able."

"I didn't believe you had a baby. Your figure is perfect and your stomach is flat."

"Why do others think I had a baby?"

Helen heaved a deep sigh. "Why else would you run away to the bush after arriving?"

"I wanted to get started on the job I promised to do."

"The Africans didn't think you had a baby, and they seem to love you. I can see for myself that the baby is not yours."

"I thank God for that."

"The baby's skin is much blacker than a child of yours would have."

"Her mother died delivering her. The local people believe she killed her mother and is cursed. The father left her at the hospital."

"I'm glad you're helping the father." Helen sighed deeply again. "Everyone heard about the pants in your closet, but we'll discuss that next time I visit."

I can hardly wait.

"I'm working in the pharmacy today and only have a short break."

"I appreciate your visit."

Sandy had studied different cultures, but all the little offenses she'd been learning each day weren't written in any books. She'd crossed her legs in front of Mr. Jubilee, not knowing it was a taboo, and she insulted the African cook. Would she unknowingly break other bans?

Sandy picked up a pen and scrap paper to jot a list of supplies and medications for the clinic. By the time she had finished, David arrived and escorted Sandy to the car. He opened the back door of the shiny Mercedes, and she slid onto the seat.

She glanced across the street at a naked child. The boy poured dirt from a tin can with his right hand while extending his empty palm under the falling grime as if washing it. Plopping down in the garbage heap, he filled the little can again. Her eyes moistened at the child's misery. Wiping a tear off her face, she clutched Blessing tighter and darted across the street.

The little boy lifted his head, looked at her, and shrieked. As he ran away, his screech sent chills down her spine.

Sandy turned to David who had followed. "What happened?"

"The boy is from an isolated village in the bush. He has never seen anyone with white skin. He was terrified of you."

"I didn't mean to frighten the child. I wanted to help him."

"Sister Sandy, there are thousands of little children like him, and others worse off. You will find many in the rural areas that you can help."

They returned to the luxury vehicle. She didn't need a fancy car with a chauffeur to pick her up in the mornings, take her to work, and drive her home each evening. But refusing it would probably offend Mr. Jubilee. She had already upset enough people, so she kept her mouth closed.

David took her to the guesthouse, and Sandy went to her room. After she had fed Blessing, she opened her daily planner to check her calendar. Flipping through the pages, she found a farewell card from her assistant at the fitness center. Sandy opened the card and fifty dollars fluttered to the floor. Picking up the bills, she slipped the card back into the book.

Under the new military regime, no foreigners were permitted bank accounts. Without financial credit there appeared to be no legitimate way to exchange money. She had researched black market moneychangers, in case she had to use one, but where were they? Mr. Jubilee was a busy man, and she wouldn't waste his valuable time to exchange fifty dollars. Better still, she wouldn't bother him over twenty dollars. She slid thirty dollars back in the book. Tomorrow she'd search for a money man. If it went well, she'd deal with the rest of the funds later.

Since it wasn't late, she tied Blessing to her back and approached the guesthouse manager. "What is the exchange rate for twenty dollars?"

The manager pulled a small calculator out of his breast pocket and tapped in numbers. "It is between 1150 and 1240 naros."

"Where is a local money changer to exchange funds?"

"The foreign exchange fellows sit at the end of dead man's alley. As you face the city market, it is on the far left-hand side. Walk under the large Coca Cola sign and head down the passageway."

"Is it safe?"

The manager nodded.

"Thank you. Did you know that the electrical outlet in my room is broken?" Sandy cocked an eyebrow. Should she mention the broken faucets and cracked windows? No, she didn't want to appear like a demanding, rich lady, but the outlet was the most important. Best not to mention the other needed repairs.

"I would appreciate it if someone will fix it."

She turned and walked back to her room. The money wasn't enough, but how would she get more African currency? The church leaders had encouraged her to come. They had told her she could obtain funds, buy necessary supplies, and appliances, and it was safe. Nothing they said was true.

***

Sandy waved Helen into the clinic.

Helen sat down and pulled out her knitting. "I wanted to talk to you about the pants that were found in your closet in Koala."

News traveled fast without telephones.

"I burned all the pants."

"Yes, I heard about it. But Sandy, you should be more careful of your reputation."

She tried to make light of the matter and teased. "Do you think they will lynch me, burn me at the stake, or stone me?"

"You shouldn't joke about this." Helen stopped to count the stitches. "You laugh far too much."

94

"Me? You think I laugh too much? Are you serious or are you joking?"

"I never joke." Helen scowled. "I'm always serious."

Sandy believed that as she glanced at Helen's laced up black boots and old-fashioned house dress. She liked Helen and she pressed her lips together to suppress another smile, but the gray-haired woman was the most solemn person Sandy had ever encountered.

"You're in deep trouble. How do you get into these predicaments?"

"I walk right into them." The corners of her lips twitched. "Would you like peanut butter and bread?"

"Yes, thank you."

Sandy mixed a large spoon of peanut butter into Blessing's porridge, which she was able to get from the cook that morning, and then spread another spoon on a piece of bread. She put the slice of peanut butter bread on top of a piece of toilet tissue, since there weren't any Kleenex or napkins, and handed it to Helen.

Without hesitating, the older woman reached out for the snack. "Thank you."

Blessing was fidgeting and Sandy changed the baby's diaper.

"Is that a plastic bag covering the diaper?" Helen asked

"Yes, there are no plastic pants here in Africa."

"You're quite clever at making do with little. I would have never thought that of a high-class girl like you."

She accepted the compliment and grinned. With Blessing in the crook of Sandy's arms, she held the cup of thick fluid to the baby's mouth. Blessing slurped and beamed at Helen between gulps.

"She's a happy little baby, and quite stunning, isn't she? She seems to enjoy that corn and peanut butter milkshake." Helen crossed her legs at the ankles the correct way. "My colleagues believe you had men in your room at night."

"You don't believe that story, do you?"

"It sounded pretty convincing." A sly grin crept across Helen's face. "But no, I don't believe it. Some people claimed you wore men's trousers and paraded the village as a prostitute."

95

"I brought my jeans, but I've never worn them. I had read many rural people frowned upon it, but in large cities, pants were acceptable for ladies. When I arrived in Logatti, I wanted to wear them but didn't see any others wearing them." Sandy sighed. "The woman who swept my bedroom found the jeans in the closet. We burned all of them right away."

"That was wise. It caused the Africans to believe you repented of your sins." Helen swallowed the last bite of bread. "You should think about returning to the United States. The rumors about you are nasty."

"It's a little too late now. I agreed to vaccinate all the village children. I went to Koala to check out the village, and I like it. I have Blessing and want to show these people how to care for children. Maybe they will accept health teaching and practice it."

"They do need an education in that area." Helen picked up her knitting. "We wanted to teach them in healthy ways but couldn't speak the language."

"How long have you been here?"

"Fifty years."

"That's a long time." Sandy looked at Helen's two-foot-long scarf. The woman must have the patience of Job. "How did you learn the language?"

"Language specialists and translators came. They studied it and taught us." Helen stopped to count more stitches.

"If the people don't learn basic health and sanitation principles, they will fall sick with the same preventable diseases again and again."

"That is exactly what has happened." Helen lifted the orange scarf.

Sandy smiled. "That is pretty. Will you wear it this winter?"

"Rainy season is from April to October, and there's no winter. The weather is seventy to eighty Fahrenheit, wet, and humid."

Sandy puckered her brow. "I thought they measure in centigrade."

"They do, but we Americans brought our own thermometers."

"I read the dry season starts November and lasts until the rainy season. In January the temperature can drop to sixty Fahrenheit when the thick Harmattan winds block the hot African sun. After the heavy dust storms depart, the sun is bright and the temperature rises to one hundred-twenty degrees Fahrenheit."

"That's true." Helen nodded. "We are a little north of the equator."

"How do you cope in the hot season?"

"We have fans. By the way, this scarf is a Christmas present for the hospital director. The chilly, damp weather during the rains bothers the Africans more than it does us." Helen put the knitting in her bag. "By the time we learned the language, the educated Africans in the church wanted responsibility. We taught math skills and how to balance a budget, but the culture took precedence over Biblical principles."

"How can culture take precedence over the Bible?"

"If we gave them money for a new microscope, they used it to send their children to school. At first we didn't mind that, but we became annoyed when it looked like they were having more and more children for us to educate."

"They have many more children than they can afford."

"Their parents are the second priority. They care for their folks in their old age. The church leader took the money designated for the hospital generator and used it to build a home for his elderly parents, so the mission doctors couldn't do lab tests or perform surgeries."

"What did you do?"

"We stopped giving them money. If the hospital needed equipment, we bought it."

"I've seen strange things myself."

"Like what?"

"Mr. Jubilee has a chauffeur for his Mercedes Benz. He could sell the car and buy medicines for this clinic."

"He did not buy that vehicle. A local rich man attending the church, who became a Christian, gave the vehicle to Mr. Jubilee. If he or his son doesn't drive it, the man will be insulted."

"Does the local church pay for his son to drive him?"

"Yes. David failed his university examinations and it was decided to hire him to be a chauffeur to build up his confidence." Helen picked up her helmet. "I like you. I hope you get to stay, and I enjoy watching you treat patients."

The elderly woman's out-of-style clothes and laced-up boots with white cotton ankle socks fascinated Sandy. Helen was her exact opposite, but Sandy was fond of Helen and partial to her company.

Sandy didn't ask Helen why she tickled Blessing and examined her feet because the older woman was accepting Sandy and Blessing.

Sandy's chest tightened, and she exhaled deeply. Maybe her situation wasn't as serious as Helen implied.

But it might be even worse.

CHAPTER FIFTEEN

Sandy picked up Blessing and walked out of her room early the next morning. She waited on the bench in front for David. When he arrived she went to the vehicle. "On the way home this evening, can you take me to the city market?"

"Yes, I can drive you after work."

At two that afternoon, David brought her lunch tray.

She lifted the covers and breathed in the scent of roasted peanuts. The aroma of the steaming brown sauce made her mouth water. "Please tell the cook, thank you. This looks delicious."

Sandy stuffed one of the three bites of brown meat into her mouth and chewed several minutes. Grimacing, she spit the morsel into a tissue. She tried the other two bites, but they were tougher. A soupspoon was the only utensil on the tray, and she used it to taste the peanut sauce and white rice. The unique flavored gravy with a little touch of red pepper and ginger tasted like something from a gourmet restaurant, and she ate all the scrumptious sauce and rice. She was full and the bananas would make a delicious breakfast, so she slipped them into her sack. This time she wouldn't insult the cook by leaving any food.

An ancient gentleman entered the clinic. "I have a fever and my chest hurts. I have a persistent cough and spit out yellow stuff. Can you write a prescription?"

"What did you say?"

"Write the name of the medicine and sign your name." The patient handed her a sheet of paper. "I will take it to a pharmacy. I heard there were no medications here, which is why only a few people are coming to you."

Was writing a prescription legal? There was no one to ask, but what harm could it do? Not thinking about the consequences and wanting to help the gentleman, she picked up the pen and jotted.

"Bronchial pneumonia. Prescription of Amoxicillin 250 mg, two capsules three times a day for ten days." She signed, Sandra Calbrin, RN, USA.

Thirty minutes later the grinning patient returned and handed her a small box. "Please look at this medicine and see if the pharmacy sold me the right one."

She took the little package, read the label, and handed it to him. "This is the correct one."

If she wrote prescriptions like a doctor, patients could go to pharmacies to purchase medicines, but would they have enough money? What if it was illegal and she was in trouble for doing it? Without anyone to ask, she wrote prescriptions the rest of the afternoon.

David arrived after work that evening and drove her to the market.

"Is it okay if I write prescriptions?"

"Yes, you are the doctor."

"That is why I'm asking. I'm not a doctor, only a nurse."

"In the clinic you are the only medical worker and therefore the doctor."

They went to the car, and he drove about two miles. He parked in front of the huge open-air market. "Let me go with you to help buy what you want. Many sellers are not honest. They cheat white people. I can get a good price for you."

"Thank you, but I'd like to look around at everything. Besides, you need to pick up your father. Please do not wait for me. I'll walk home. The exercise will be good for me." She recalled the directions and searched for the large Coca Cola sign. With Blessing on her back, she walked toward the large billboard and headed down the passageway. It looked like all the other aisles she passed.

Halfway down the lane, a seller held up a picture of a naked African man. "Hey, there. I know what you want."

"I got what you need, girl." A filthy man reeking of alcohol held his hands open to her.

She glanced at the posters of naked women and pornographic books. Was she in the right place? Sweat trickled down her neck and back. She stumbled down the lane, clutched her bag tighter, and reached behind her to pat the baby on her back.

A trader urinated in front of his vulgar bookstall. "Hey, little lady, come here."

"Marry me. I'll give you everything." Another vendor wiggled his backside and started to lower his pants.

Sandy turned to the opposite side of booths.

An unshaven man with brown-stained teeth made a lewd gesture. "Come over here. I have what you are looking for."

More sweat dripped down her face. Her stomach fluttered. She needed to turn back but didn't want to face those vendors again. Were more lewd men farther down the alley?

Lord Jesus, please help.

She twisted around, but three men blocked her way. She twirled around again and faced more men. The scoundrels surrounded her. Terror weighed down and tightened her chest. Her breathing grew ragged as the seven loathsome creatures circled in closer. Her eyes moved left and right seeking an escape, but there was none. Up ahead she saw only a dead end.

"Hey, let the lady go." David, six foot tall and built like a football player, approached the group of traders.

She looked up and in slow motion let the air out of her lungs. With trembling limbs, she moved through the widest gap in the circle of rogues and headed toward her rescuer. Unsteady beats pounded in her chest. Thank God David came when he did.

He escorted her to the end of the passageway. "No one in our church is allowed to come down dead man's alley. Even white folks never enter this lane. Why are you here?"

"I wanted to buy a few personal items, but I needed to exchange this twenty-dollar bill." She opened her palm to show him.

"One of the moneychangers became a Christian during the political problems. He attends our church. I will take you to him. My father wrote you about him."

"I never received that letter."

"He sent it about the time of the military coup. We later heard for security reasons the post office burned mail." David pointed to a narrow opening. They slipped through to the outside of the market. "Why didn't you tell me you needed to exchange money?"

"I didn't want to trouble anyone. You and your father have been kind to bring me food and drive me to work."

"No trouble." Reaching the car, David opened the back door. "I will take you to the Christian moneychanger right now." After adjusting the rearview mirror, he caught her attention. "Your baby would not have been able to save you in there."

"What do you mean?"

"Among some tribes a woman who has a baby will never be molested by anyone. But the black-market money changers are from tribes who do not respect a mother and child."

She glanced at her reflection. "How did you know I went to dead man's alley?"

"I saw you enter the lane. So I drove around to the other side and came looking for you."

"Thank you for helping me."

He drove Sandy to a two-story stone mansion, set fifty yards away from the road with a twelve-foot-high electric fence surrounding it. David stopped at an iron gate and rolled his window down to address the guard.

"I am David Jubilee and have a customer for Mr. Funo."

The gatehouse guard jabbered into the phone and then said, "Come in."

Sandy peeked out of the window at the gigantic video camera on top of the gate. It buzzed as its long, slender lens zoomed in toward the car.

When the iron gate swung open, David drove to the side of the house, parked, and opened her door.

A guard approached, escorted them to the back door of the building, and punched in the security code. When it buzzed, David followed the guard inside. She and David faced a uniformed man with a pistol, who shook David's hand. The security officer looked Sandy

102

over from head to toe and nodded toward Blessing before motioning Sandy forward. The iron door of the mansion clicked shut behind her.

She clutched Blessing tighter to her chest. Her stomach fluttered as she peered around at the locked doors, windows with steel grids covering them, and armed guards at every door.

"Come this way." The guard led them to an inner chamber.

They entered an office, where a small, nondescript man pointed at two colossal, purple chairs in front of a six-foot-by-six-foot mahogany desk. "Please sit down."

David shook Mr. Funo's hand. "This is Miss Sandra Calbrin. She is helping at the employee clinic. Sister Sandy, meet Mr. Funo."

"What can I do for you?" The bald moneychanger rubbed his hands together.

"I have twenty dollars and would like to exchange it for Norgian naros." Sandy handed the bill to him.

"The exchange rate is 52 so that means you should receive 1040 naros." He opened his desk drawer, lifted out a pile of money, and counted out the currency. Then he handed it to Sandy.

She smiled. "Thank you."

"I'd like to see you back soon with more funds."

She and David stood and shook his hand. They were escorted to the car.

"I'm a little confused, David. The guesthouse manager told me the money changers would give me one thousand and two hundred naros."

"It is safer to come to Mr. Funo because he is a Christian. He keeps his house secure. If you go to one of the moneychangers in the alley someone will hurt you and steal your money before you leave. Besides, Mr. Funo gives a lower exchange rate so he can give more money to the church."

She looked at her bills and shook her head. What if Mr. Funo wasn't at home when she needed money?

"Would you please drop me at the European store before picking up your father?" Sandy turned to David. "Is it safe to walk home in the dark?"

103

"No one will bother you. Do you know the way to the guesthouse?"

"Yes, I do. Thank you." Sandy stepped out of the car and entered the European boutique. She stopped in front of a man with facial scars. "Excuse me, sir, when will you have transformers?"

"Under the new military regime we are no longer permitted to sell them."

She couldn't use her hair dryer and curling iron but had already managed without them. She was glad she kept her toothbrush from the plane because her electric toothbrush was useless without electricity or a transformer.

She sorted through ceramic coffee mugs until she found several that weren't cracked. As she rummaged through imported Chinese bowls, drinking glasses, plastic plates, and utensils, she found several knives, forks, and spoons. She held each one to the light and examined it like a health inspector, keeping several sets that were not used and free of tarnish.

"Excuse me, where are your teabags?"

The clerk pointed. "Over there with the sugar cubes, jars of instant Nescafe coffee, and Ovaltine on the opposite shelf."

She picked up a tin of margarine, read the ingredients on the label, and shoved it back on the shelf. Sandy didn't need all those chemical preservatives and went toward the basket of bread. Mold tinged most of the loaves, but she found one free of blemishes. After reading the ingredients of flour, sugar, salt, and yeast from the list on the package, she took it and reached for a jar of peanut butter. She picked up a small iron coil with an electrical cord and examined the plug with three rounded prongs. It might work in her room, if the manager repaired the outlet. The emersion heater was priced at sixty naros, about one dollar. She collected a pair of flip-flops, a bar of soap, and a towel from the crates on the floor and placed her items on the splintered, wooden counter.

The clerk wrote the name and price of each item on the page of his ledger. After adding the figures, he tore off the sheet and handed it to Sandy. "This is your receipt with the amount you must pay."

She paid him and strolled down the road under the few streetlights. The light breeze lifted the bangs off her forehead. Her heel-less shoes squished on the pavement. She loved walking, her favorite exercise, and could hike for hours. At the junction, she turned toward several wooden stalls to look through the leather sandals.

Having no idea of the price, and with just a little money left, she offered a hundred naros. Then she laughed along with the traders. She shrugged and kept walking.

A seller dressed in Muslim garb with matching skullcap picked up the pair of sandals she admired. He followed her and raised his voice. "Bring money."

She stopped and turned to him. "A hundred naros for this pair of sandals?" she doubted it costs two dollars.

"No, pay six hundred naros. Good price."

She shook her head and kept walking.

He followed her. "Buy sandals."

"I do not have six hundred naros. I only have one hundred." She walked down the road.

"Give me six hundred." He yelled and went after her.

Two more men joined him. Each held a different style and color of sandal as they shouted in unison. "Buy mine. Buy mine. Buy mine."

The three merchants circled her. One hand reached out to grab her arm. She ducked and slipped between two of the men and started running. Without thinking she dashed across the road under a streetlight, turned around, and hailed a taxi. It stopped. She opened the back door and slid onto the seat.

"Please take me to the mission guesthouse."

The driver adjusted his mirror.

She caught him eyeing her in the mirror, but then he glanced away.

As he pulled into the driveway she searched through her purse for coins to pay him. She gave him the money and turned to open the door. There were no handles and the lock buttons were pressed lower than the height of the door making it impossible for her to lift one. She stared ahead at the guesthouse signboard. Tears filled her eyes. What was going on?

She snapped, "Why is this car door locked?"

If he were kidnapping her, he wouldn't have driven her there. Her heart landed like a rock in the pit of her stomach. Strange lecherous men pursued her down alleys and in taxis. Threats almost as dangerous as cannibals, headhunters, and wild animals lurked everywhere. Koala had seemed so much safer compared to the dangers in the city.

And why was she still locked inside the car?

CHAPTER SIXTEEN

Sandy scowled at the driver. "Unlock the door."

"No problem." He handed her an iron lever.

She examined the door handle. "What is this?"

He beamed. "It opens all the doors to the vehicle."

With Blessing in one arm, she opened the door next to her with her free hand. Grabbing her bags, she left the taxi. She went into her room.

She glanced around and saw the electrical outlet was reattached to the wall. She filled a ceramic cup with water and set the mug on the floor. Carefully, she fixed the emersion heater to the cup and pushed the plug into the three-holed outlet. She needed a cup of tea but didn't want to start an electrical fire or blow up the room. So she didn't take her eyes off the mug. When tiny bubbles flowed near the edge of the cup, her heart burst with pleasure. If she could boil water in a mug she could prepare the instant food she'd bought Blessing and have hot tea each morning.

The water simmered. It should have boiled for five minutes to kill all the microbes, but half the water boiled away after one minute. Nothing would be left if she kept cooking it.

Early the following morning, she jumped up, eager to make Blessing's breakfast and prepare hot tea for herself. After feeding the baby, she sliced a banana to top her peanut butter bread. Sandy carried the food to the mattress. She hadn't eaten such a heavy breakfast since she was in nursing school.

She fetched a bucket of water and bathed and fed and dressed Blessing. A few minutes later David picked them up.

Inside the clinic, she checked the cupboards, but they were still bare. She shook her head. "I don't understand why your father wants me to work in this clinic when there are no medicines to treat patients."

Footsteps crunched on the gravel outside the clinic. A gentleman with deep tribal scars under his eyes that ran down his cheeks knocked and entered the clinic. "Excuse me."

Sandy faced him. "May I help you?"

He handed her the treatment card. "Yes, I came for you to test my disease."

She glanced at the previous recording on the card and picked up the blood pressure apparatus Mr. Jubilee had given her. She wrapped the cuff around the man's arm before pumping. "Your blood pressure is higher than last month." She removed the cuff and folded it.

"It is the will of Allah." He bowed his head.

"What is the will of Allah?"

"It is the will of Allah that my blood pressure is higher than last month." The gentleman fidgeted in the chair.

"We have no blood pressure medicine in the clinic. Here is a prescription for it at the local pharmacy. Please come back next week for a check-up."

She wondered what kind of trouble she'd be in if she wrote the wrong prescription. Would the authorities detain and threaten her or put her in prison?

An elderly woman interrupted her thoughts and handed Sandy a stuffed, plastic bag. "Here are some bananas to thank you for curing me of fever."

"God cured you, not me."

Another man with only two tribal scars on his face came into the clinic. He handed a woman's treatment card to her. "My wife has hypertension, and she is very old. She has had many children, and I do not want her jumping and running around with hypertension."

"How old is your wife?" Sandy rocked Blessing with her right arm as she wrote with her left hand.

"She is 30 years old." The man shook his head. "That is too old to be jumping."

Sandy choked on a giggle. "Why didn't your wife come so I can check her blood pressure?"

"She is too busy at home caring for our eight children."

"I must examine your wife who is ill." Sandy handed the card back to the man.

"I can explain all the sicknesses that worry my wife, and you can give me medicine for her."

"I must see your wife to understand the disease."

"The traditional healers and witch doctors give us herbs for our family members."

"I'm not a traditional healer or witch doctor. I'm an American nurse and need to examine the sick person." Sandy stood indicating the interview ended.

"Do you want my wife to leave all the children and come here?"

Sandy took a deep breath and filled her chest. "If you want me to give your wife medicine or even a prescription, I must examine her."

She didn't like the harsh-speaking man or the way he stormed out of the clinic.

Without time cards, reports, and forms to fill, she looked forward to treating people each morning. Every day she learned new words from the members of the Houlu tribe.

Mr. Jubilee arrived. "Good morning."

Sandy smiled. "Good morning, and how are you today?"

"I have a headache." Mr. Jubilee put a hand to his head.

"Will you be sending medications? There are no pills in the clinic."

"Our supporting agency told us we must charge and collect fees, save the money, and start buying our own medicines."

"That sounds reasonable."

"We do not want to do it, so they stopped sending medications. In our culture we must never charge anyone who is senior to us or of a higher title than we are. No one charges my father because he is my senior. When the president of the Evangelical Independent Church arrives for treatment, he is not expected to pay because it would not honor him as our leader."

"If all the people, who have the highest salaries, do not pay, you will never be able to collect enough money to replace the medications." Sandy furrowed her brows. "What will you do?"

"We will ask the agency for mercy." Mr. Jubilee changed the subject. "Do you have tea?"

"No. I don't even have drinking water because the water filter is broken." Sandy pointed to the ruptured pipe fixture.

Mr. Jubilee glanced at it and shook his head.

David arrived with the lunch tray, and she took it. "Lunch is early today, only eleven o'clock."

"I need to drive my father to a meeting at noon. You ate everything yesterday. Here is a bigger bowl of rice with peanut sauce, six pieces of meat and six bananas. The cook is so happy you enjoyed all his food."

Returning full bowls upset the cook. Empty bowls informed the chef to give her more food. Perhaps she should leave a few bites on the plate to indicate she had enough to eat, but that, too, might be forbidden.

How could she stay out of trouble not knowing all the cultural taboos?

CHAPTER SEVENTEEN

Sandy was feeding Blessing when Mr. Jubilee came into the clinic the next morning.

"Would you like some peanut butter on bread?" she asked.

"No, thank you." Mr. Jubilee sat in the vacant chair.

Sandy pointed to the jar. "African peanut butter is so delicious I eat it every day. How do they make it?"

"The women roast the peanuts and put them through a local machine to grind it into a paste. A lady in the city makes pure peanut butter without red peppers for Americans."

"Is it without salt, sugar, and preservatives?"

"Yes, it is all natural. We cannot eat peanut butter like you eat it."

"I'm sorry I have nothing else to give you until David brings lunch from the guest house. He often brings it at two and I get hungry before then, which is why I bring peanut butter and bread."

"On those days he must pick up the children from school." He took a deep breath. "I came to offer you something to show our appreciation for working here in the clinic. The church will pay all your expenses at the guesthouse. A nurse will start work here in two weeks, so you can move to Koala permanently."

Permanently? The medical director calculated it would take six month for the vaccination of the children. Maybe she would stay that long but not forever.

After Mr. Jubilee left, David arrived. "Excuse, Sister Sandy. I brought your lunch."

"What did the cook prepare today?" Sandy lifted the knit shawl to peek into the bowls. "Rice and peanut sauce, how delicious."

David turned to her. "The hospital administrator is selling a motorcycle. Would you like to buy it?"

"I'd like to see it, first."

David turned to leave. "I will go to the hospital and ask the administrator to drive it here for you to check out."

By the time Sandy had eaten, David returned with two men dressed in business suits, and he introduced the tall man as the hospital administrator and the other as his brother.

The administrator shook Sandy's hand. "I drove the bike here. Come outside and see it."

Sandy followed the men to the motorcycle. She ran her fingers over the handlebars. "It looks like it is high quality."

"I need to sell it to buy a car because I now have six children."

"May I drive it?" Sandy stepped closer to it.

The administrator loosened his necktie and hesitated before giving her the key.

Sandy mounted the seat, started the engine, and drove around the yard.

When she stopped, the administrator wiped the sweat from his face. "I have never seen a lady drive a bike."

David's mouth fell open and his eyes grew large. "You ride a motorcycle like a man. Do you know how to drive a car too?"

Sandy nodded and handed him the bike keys.

"We assumed you wanted to buy the motorcycle to give an African pastor. Surely, you will not drive it yourself? I am not sure I can let you purchase it if it is for you."

"Why can't I buy it and drive it myself?"

"You are a white lady, and no proper ones ride motorcycles."

Sandy put her hand to her forehead and rubbed it. Was this another African taboo that prevented her from doing something she wanted to do?

She spoke through clenched teeth. "Do African ladies drive motorcycles?"

"A few rich African ladies ride motorcycles in large cities." David scowled. "Not here."

"I have never seen any white folks driving one." The administrator scowled. "If you bought the motorcycle from us and had an accident, people would blame us for selling the motorcycle to you."

It made no sense. Why would people blame them if she had an accident? She ran her fingers through her hair as if straightening it

112

would smooth out the situation. She scrunched up her face and then relaxed her expression. "I don't understand. Is it against any laws in your country for a lady to ride a motorcycle?"

The administrator grimaced. "We do not know."

David jiggled his keys and looked at the two men. "Perhaps, we should ask my father. We'll go over to his office."

"That is good." The administrator wiped the sweat off his face. "If your father thinks Sister Sandy should drive a motorcycle, I will be glad to sell it to her for twelve thousand naros."

The three men departed.

Thirty minutes later David, Mr. Jubilee, and the men returned.

With sober expressions, they marched into the clinic. David said, "Let's go outside."

Sandy followed them to the yard.

Mr. Jubilee pointed to the bike. "Sister Sandy, do you know how to properly drive a motorcycle?"

She had shown them she could ride a motorcycle, but how did a lady ride a motorcycle properly? Every scenario she could think of ran through her confused mind. Was she supposed to ride side saddle? Should she wear a long skirt or a special dress for riding? Should she drive slowly, little by little to make certain her dress was down?

"I will try my best to ride a motorcycle properly with the most suitable dress."

"Who taught you how to drive a motorcycle?" Mr. Jubilee asked.

"My boy...oh boy oh." Sandy started and stopped. "I meant to say a friend taught me how to ride a motorcycle."

She didn't want them to know she had a boyfriend, who taught her how to ride. Boyfriends, who were not fiancés, might not be culturally acceptable.

It would be best to show Mr. Jubilee her most proper driving behavior. So she remounted the seat and in an unhurried manner tucked her skirt in all around her legs in what she hoped was proper. Surely, Mr. Jubilee would tell her if she was improper. After starting the engine, she took a slow drive around the compound as properly as she could.

She pulled to a complete stop. "The motorcycle is a high-quality machine, not many miles. It feels lighter to drive than my friend's bike. It's easy to turn."

Sandy didn't tell them her father was a mechanic and taught her how to repair motorcycles, too. For surely that wouldn't be at all proper.

Mr. Jubilee frowned. "If I give you my consent to buy it, you cannot drive it here in town. You must take it to Koala in the bush and ride it there."

"Yes, that is fine. I will take it with me."

"David will drive you to dead man's market to buy proper clothes."

Sandy shuddered. What was dead man's market? And why must David go with her to buy clothes? That just didn't seem at all proper, but she'd agree to do whatever they suggested.

"After that, he can take you to Mr. Funo to exchange money. All of us trade with him." Mr. Jubilee nodded. "You'll need the money before you go to the market."

Miss Sandra Calbrin, with a masters degree in nursing and manager of a fitness center had lost all her independence. She hadn't been able to exchange funds at dead man's alley without a man to rescue her. She needed David to take her to the moneychanger for local currency. She couldn't buy a motorcycle without the approval of the men. The males told her where and when to ride her new motorcycle. She couldn't buy clothes without the assistance of a man. Control was slipping away like the buzzing mosquitoes that slipped through the rips in the screen.

After the men left, she wrote a few prescriptions for some patients.

"Well, Blessing, here in Africa we might need those men to protect us from the corrupt officers and unscrupulous money changers. But you and I will visit every village, vaccinate every child, establish Baby Clinics, and teach mothers how to care for their children. That's something I can't see any man doing." She tickled her baby. "No man can mother you as well as I can."

Did she need a man to keep her out of trouble?

CHAPTER EIGHTEEN

After work that evening, David returned and drove her to the Christian money changer. He cashed Sandy's check for six hundred dollars and gave her thirty-one thousand naros in exchange.

David escorted her back to the car. "Today is dead man's market. All the sellers receive new shipments. We will go straight there." He drove her to the main city market and parked the car. After opening the back door for her he accompanied her into a giant building with open spaces instead of windows.

Vendors piled heaps of used clothes on large plastic tarps lining the passageways in every direction. The sellers held long batons and stood in front of each mound to lift clothes for buyers.

David pointed. "Each person shouts the cost of his goods. Everything in this pile is fifteen naros. The pile there is thirty. Over there are the sixty naros items, the most expensive."

"This is nothing like dead man's alley. Why is it called dead man's market?"

"No one but a dead person would give up his clothes. These dresses and skirts came from deceased people in your country. See this bag says, 'Good Will.' Some other bags say 'Salvation Army.' Good Christians send us the clothes of their dead relatives." David reached out. "Let me carry the baby so you can test the clothes."

How was she supposed to try the clothes on without a changing room? As Sandy handed Blessing to David she searched in every direction for someplace she could try on clothes, but there wasn't any.

She gave up and began looking through the clothes and spotted a blue and white striped, cotton dress. She lifted it up and thought it might fit her.

The trader beamed. "Test the dress."

"Right here?" Sandy's mouth fell wide open. "In front of all these shoppers?"

"Yes, my men and I will help you dress."

115

The dress fell from her shaking hands. She was already in enough trouble. There was no way she'd take off her clothes and let strange men dress her in others. The trader picked up the garment and unbuttoned the front. He stretched the neck wide open and faced Sandy, but she took a step back.

David shifted Blessing to the opposite arm. "Let these men dress you."

Sandy shook her head. "It doesn't seem appropriate."

"It is quite proper."

The dress seller lifted the spacious opening over Sandy's head. Two more men approached, and each held open a sleeve for her. In slow motion Sandy raised her arms and slid them through the armholes the men held open for her. She glanced at David who nodded. All three men tugged the dress down over Sandy's clothes without touching any part of her bust, waist, or hips. Sandy buttoned up the front while the trader held a tiny mirror before her. The garment was snug over her street clothes but should fit perfectly without them.

"Thank you. I'll buy this one." Sandy handed him the sixty naros. She unbuttoned the dress, bent down, and lifted the hem. The three men surrounded her and raised the dress up and over her head without touching any part of her anatomy.

She glanced around and noticed people had stopped to watch. "If this is normal, why is everyone looking at me?"

"White people do not come to dead man's market, so that's why they're watching you." With the baby in one arm, David rifled through the heap of clothes.

A full-skirted dress in her size fell to the edge of the pile. She picked it up and pointed to the label. "Look at this. It's Liz Claiborne."

"Is she a relative of yours?" David frowned. "Did someone take her clothes, and she's still alive?"

Sandy laughed so hard tears filled her eyes. She couldn't stop giggling to explain to David.

"Don't cry, Sister Sandy. If she is alive maybe you can send her dress back to her."

More tears ran down her face as she laughed harder and harder.

"Please don't cry, Sister Sandy. Buy her dress and you can take it to her."

The laughter kept coming, and she couldn't catch her breath.

David used his free hand to dig through the pile and handed her another dress. "Here is another one that belongs to that woman, Liz Claiborne."

The dress was in Sandy's size, so she took it. She found four more with full skirts for riding a motorcycle. She stopped laughing as she handed over the equivalent of a dollar for each dress.

"A woman called Liz Claiborne owns a big company and makes all these clothes. She puts her name in each dress to tell everyone she is the tailor who made it."

"In Africa, only if you own something are you allowed to write your name in it." David hesitated. "I cannot tell if you are laughing or crying. Sometimes I think you are laughing, but maybe you are crying."

"Sometimes I laugh so hard that I start crying. Other times I cry so hard I start laughing. Right now, I'm a happy lady."

A man covered with bras headed toward Sandy. Her mouth fell open as she stared at the garments hanging from the front of his neck. Numerous bras drooped from his extended arms. He wore a lacy, red Victoria Secret bra around his chest. Black bras stretched around his waist. She didn't mean to gawk but couldn't stop herself

A woman approached him and pointed to one of the bras. She tugged her blouse out of her skirt and pulled it up and over her head, exposing her breasts. The seller picked through the bras until he reached the one she had pointed to. He removed it and held it out to her by the shoulder straps. She walked up to it and put her arms through them. The woman turned around, and the bra seller fastened the hooks at her back.

David shook his head. "Christian ladies are not permitted to do that."

"Do what?"

"Ladies in our church are not allowed to remove their blouses and expose themselves in a public place. Here comes the wife of our church deacon. Watch how she buys a belt for the chest."

Did David call it a belt for the chest? No, that had to be a mistake.

The woman approached the bra seller and removed the bra she wanted from the man's arm. She stretched the bra out over her blouse and around her waist to fasten the hooks in front of her. She turned it and raised it to her chest while slipping her arms through the straps. With the bra outside her blouse, she adjusted the garment to determine if it would fit without her blouse.

"David, what did you call it?"

"He is selling belts for ladies' chests for thirty naros."

The idea of wearing a belt over her breasts threw Sandy into another fit of hilarity.

"David, this has been more entertaining than shopping in my country."

Sandy stuffed her new dresses and skirts into her backpack. She reached out for Blessing, but David carried the baby to the car. He drove her back to the guesthouse and helped Sandy and Blessing out of the vehicle.

Sandy was still laughing from the market adventures as she turned the corner to her room. Colonel Tsaou waited for her outside her door. She pointed to the wooden bench on the veranda. "Please sit down. How can I help you, sir?"

The officer didn't sit down, but towered over her, crossed his arms, and glared at her. "Your papers are not in order. I can make all the problems go away. Come with me to my village."

She staggered back a few steps. Her heart pounded harder and faster at his proposition. Holding Blessing, Sandy collapsed on the bench he had refused.

Lord, please help.

How could she send him away without being disrespectful?

Sandy stood. "Walk with me." She accompanied him to the main entrance of the guesthouse where numerous sellers congregated. She stopped in front of vendors who sold bread, bananas, matches, and charcoal.

She reached to shake his hand. "Thank you for coming to see me. I appreciate your kind visit."

"You will regret sending me away." Colonel Big stomped away.

Sandy walked back to her room and put her baby down. "Blessing, it's you and me fighting evil in the world. We have each other."

Then she remembered. "God is with us, and we'll make it."

Should she inform Mr. Jubilee of what Colonel Big wanted her to do? No. The medical director would see it as another problem she had caused. She'd keep quiet and pray for the best.

She closed her eyes and burst into tears. Colonel Big had already traveled to Koala to see her, and he might come back again. She bit her lip and rubbed her temple.

How could she stop him?

***

The days went by fast, and Sandy thanked God no other officers approached her. Perhaps all the immigration officials had forgotten about her.

On the morning of her departure someone knocked on her door. She opened it to see Helen standing on the other side. "Good morning. How are you?"

"I am well. I had to see you before you leave." Helen held out an exquisite pair of pink-knitted booties. "I made these for your baby."

Tears sprung to Sandy's eyes and slipped down her cheeks. "This makes me so happy." She threw her arms around the older woman. As Sandy hugged Helen, her stiff body yielded to the embrace, and she lifted her wrinkled arms to hug Sandy in return.

Sandy loved the ancient missionary. She sensed Helen cared for her and Blessing and accepted both of them. Turning the gorgeous booties over in her hands, Sandy beamed at the tiny, elaborate stitches. "These are beautiful." Too bad Sandy would leave Helen behind her. "You are the sweetest person I know. You've no idea how much this means to me."

"It's no big deal, just a pair of booties I knitted one afternoon."

119

"This is a huge act of kindness and I love you so much." Sandy sniffed and reached in her bag for a tissue.

"I intended to knit them much sooner, but I couldn't find any pink yarn in this whole country." Helen turned her head away, let out a deep sob, and sniffed. "I'm not used to so much emotion. I need to go."

"Thank you. I'll miss you and our chats."

Helen's eyes twinkled. "Sandy, try not to get into trouble."

"I'll try to be good, but sometimes it's not easy." Sandy giggled.

After the older woman left, two hefty African men arrived and pushed Sandy's motorcycle to her door at the guesthouse. David helped them lift the bike and slide it onto the roof of the Mercedes Benz.

David unlocked the trunk and pulled out a coil of plastic rope. He tied it around the handlebars and passed it through the open window of the front seat before tossing the rope to the opposite side. He wove the rope through the wheel spokes and passed it through the opposite window and then back to the other side. David fastened the cord ends with tight knots.

After carrying the luggage and sacks from Sandy's room, he loaded them into the trunk of the car and she climbed inside.

When they arrived at Koala, David took out Blessing's carton bed, the bags, and the three suitcases. He set them in front of the tiny mud house. He carried the ten cans of milk powder, a ten-pound bag of ground corn, a large jar of peanut butter, two loaves of bread, a box of one hundred tea bags, a bunch of bananas, and a papaya to the front door. He untied the motorcycle and called a couple of farmers, who were passing by, to help him get the bike down.

When they left, David said, "Those men think you bought the motorcycle for Pastor Paul and his wife. I hope that won't cause a problem."

Sandy shivered. Relations were already strained with Pastor Paul since she'd warned him about the dangerous practices his wife used to feed and bathe the children. If rumors spread that she had bought him a motorcycle, but the bike was for her to travel to the villages to vaccinate the children, would he be angry?

David handed Sandy a slip of paper. "Here is an emergency telephone number. There is only one phone cabin here. It is at the service station. You must pay fifteen naros to call us in Hose. The phones are still down since the problems, but keep this number for later in case you need to call." David left.

Sandy held Blessing and plopped down on the boulder by her front door. Her mud house, an isolated building, had no connection to the outside world. Tears raced down her face as loneliness took hold of her.

CHAPTER NINETEEN

Sandy chewed on her lip. If she left her baggage and groceries to hike to the chief's house for the key, someone might steal everything. Then she wouldn't have food for Blessing. Sandy glanced at the trail where the ladies voices grew louder and louder. Eve and Phoebe came toward her.

"I'm so glad to see you." Sandy stood.

"The chauffeur drove past our home and told us you'd arrived. We stopped at the chief's house and brought the key." Eve handed Sandy the tiny key and started to sweep the yard with the broom she brought.

Phoebe tapped another broom in the palm of her hand. "I will sweep inside the house. Wait out here until the dust settles."

Sandy sat back down on the huge stone. Footsteps stomped on the path as if the visitor wore boots, and he did. With a determined stride, Lieutenant Courteous marched toward her. Her heart plummeted. Were all the officers coming to Koala to intimidate her now? They must have their spies everywhere.

"Good afternoon, sir."

"How are you?" The lieutenant looked her up and down as if she wasn't quite respectable.

"I'm fine. The ladies are helping me clean my house. Would you like to sit on the tree root until they finish? I can bring a chair."

"No thank you, ma'am, Miss Calbrin. I'll come back when you are alone."

She would try her best never to be alone. Inhaling a deep breath, she closed her eyes to calm herself. If her new home weren't so small, she'd invite a young girl to stay with her, but there was scarcely enough room for the baby and her. The people didn't have many possessions, so maybe that's why they built small rooms.

After Phoebe and Eve swept, they lugged buckets of water from the well to fill the drum.

Sandy went inside and put some water on to boil. "Would you like bread and tea?"

"Yes, please." Eve put the brooms in the corner.

Phoebe sat on one of the wooden chairs. "Life is so dull without you and your bizarre ways."

"We missed you. I told everyone that nurses must hold the legs of men who are wounded to stop the blood flow." Eve set the mugs on the table.

"I appreciate your friendship. You make me feel welcome." Sandy reached for the kettle of boiling water. "Have you heard any more news about the strike? The post office is still closed and has been since the military coup last year. I want to receive packages and hear news from home."

Eve took a deep breath. "The last time there was a military coup, the banks and post office were closed for six months. It is best not to use them during these unsettling times."

"Would you like more bread?" Sandy offered.

Eve looked at her slice of bread. "No thank you. Why don't you put milk and sugar in your tea and eat butter on your bread like normal people do?"

Normal people? When had she ever been normal. She chuckled hearing that word again. If everyone put milk and sugar in their tea, she was noticeably different. She'd seen canned margarine, but it contained loads of chemical preservatives, so she preferred to eat her bread dry or with natural peanut butter.

"I haven't seen any butter since I arrived. Where can I buy it?"

"They sell it everywhere. It is in a small tin can and called margarine."

Choking on a giggle, Sandy set her cup down. She tried to stop from laughing. She took in a breath and held it but couldn't keep silent and burst into laughter. They most likely had never tasted real butter, only tinned lard.

"Sister Sandy, you are the happiest white lady I have ever known, and you laugh more than any other person." Eve smiled.

124

She wouldn't be laughing much longer if the officers visited her and found her alone.

***

With Blessing tied to her back, Sandy drove her motorcycle to a neighboring village. Every time Sandy changed the baby's diaper, the pastor's wife washed it and hung it to dry. Sandy prepared the baby's food and took a few minutes to feed her.

After Sandy had treated two hundred patients, the pastor's wife brought a tin tray and set it down. She served Sandy a big plate of beans and rice.

Driving home that evening, she couldn't stop smiling at the fulfilling day. All ten of her baby's diapers were clean and dry and so was the extra outfit Sandy had brought for Blessing. Both she and her baby were fed. She looked forward to a quiet evening playing with Blessing.

Thunder boomed as she drove along the road. A yellow sedan passed, pulled in front of her, and blocked her. Had the military officers brought a car to follow her around?

Her heart pounded faster and faster as she searched for a way to drive around the sedan and escape. She pressed her lips tightly together when three young African men, dressed in business suits, jumped out of the car and came toward her. One woman wearing traditional clothes trailed behind them.

The lady waved her arms. "Stop. Stop. Stop."

Maybe someone was sick and they needed help. Sandy turned off the engine and stepped off the motorbike. Sandy wasn't used to carrying her baby on her back while riding a motorcycle, so she untied Blessing to look her over. Maybe Blessing's head wasn't positioned correctly and they were warning her about it.

The oldest gentleman approached Sandy. "We are from the African International News Television called AINT. Where are you taking this African baby?"

"She was left at the hospital, and I am caring for her."

"Are you an American?" The gentleman stared at Sandy.

"Yes, but why do you want to know?"

125

The young woman in the blue and orange stroked the baby's chin. "This is a great human-interest story. We can do an interview right now."

Someone played a cruel joke on her. What kind of news people would want to interview her? They couldn't be genuine television employees. Besides, taking an abandoned baby wasn't newsworthy.

Even if they wanted an interview, she looked a mess. The wind had blown her ponytail in every direction. Grit stuck to her sweaty face, neck, and chest. Exhausted from giving vaccinations and weighing babies, she wanted to go home and relax. Her clothes reeked of urine from the children she had examined that morning.

"You can't do an interview now. It's getting dark. The rain is coming, and my baby is tired." Sandy put the baby on her back and remounted the motorcycle.

"Can we come to your house?"

To humor them, Sandy mumbled, "Yes, come."

They nodded and returned to their car. After the vehicle drove away, Sandy started the motorcycle.

Nothing would come of it for she hadn't told them where she lived.

***

Sandy wore a traditional purple and gold brocaded dress with a matching headscarf. She dressed Blessing in an identical garment to attend a local wedding three days later. After the ceremony, the news people walked into the church and headed toward her.

She was suddenly cold and her heart raced as she clutched Blessing tightly to her chest. How did the news people find her? Maybe it wasn't that difficult, since she was the only American in the region. She nodded at the television employees. Not wanting to create a scene, she stood and shook their hands.

"I am so happy we found you." The woman smiled. "Can we follow you home?"

No, you can't. She wouldn't let strangers come to her home. If they knew where she lived, they could show up any time and maybe make other demands on her. But it was useless to hide from them for they'd already found her in church, and could locate her anytime. It seemed best to do what they asked and get rid of them.

She should ask someone if there were any laws against her agreeing to the interview, but like before, there was no one she could ask. The chief, village elders, and pastor had already left the church.

Her voice wobbled. "Yes, follow me home."

Was being interviewed for national television against church regulations or worse, a local taboo? She should send them away, but it wasn't necessary for it would never amount to anything. Much of the furniture and equipment in most of the facilities had been destroyed during the government upheaval. Most likely the television cameras wouldn't work either. She had nothing to worry about.

The driver of the yellow car parked at her house. The logo 'AINT' on the side of the camera box suggested they were legitimate news people. A gray-haired newsman pulled the cameras out of the trunk. Two men unrolled a colossal wheel of electrical cords, but without electricity in the village there was no way to operate the camera or lights.

As they set up the equipment, Sandy announced, "Let me change my baby's diaper before we begin."

Five minutes later Sandy stepped out of her house. The roar of an engine startled her. It never crossed her mind they'd bring a generator. Her heart hammered louder than the motor. She carried Blessing toward the small group. Lights flashed. Cameras buzzed.

The young woman held the microphone in front of Sandy's mouth. "How did you get this baby?"

Sandy's throat constricted. She swallowed several times to work her mouth. There probably wasn't any film in the camera.

"The doctor at the hospital gave this baby to me to care for since her mother died in childbirth."

"What work do you do?"

"I work under the Evangelical Independent Church of Africa. I'm vaccinating children and establishing Under Fives clinics in the rural villages. The goal is to establish one hundred clinics where infants are weighed, receive malaria prophylaxis, and are treated for worms and other ailments."

"What prompted you to take this baby?"

"I wanted to care for her."

"Will you always be her mother?"

"That's in the Lord's hands. I'd like to teach mothers good child care."

"Could you put Blessing on your back and ride the motorcycle to conclude the film?"

Sandy tied Blessing to her back and mounted the bike.

"We will televise it from the state capital in three days." The young man rolled the electrical cord onto the black, wooden wheel and hoisted it into the trunk. "Thank you for the interview. May God bless you."

Sandy hoped she hadn't broken any taboos or laws by letting them film her, but something was bound to go wrong. No electricity. Equipment failures. Cable lines down. The interview would never be shown on television.

She held Blessing close to her. Surely, nothing could shake away her happiness or Blessing out of her hands.

CHAPTER TWENTY

Two days later Sandy rode her motorcycle toward home after vaccinating children. The bike bounced over rocks and ruts. After the road improved the motorbike still jerked, so she stopped to examine the tire, which was flat. She pushed the motorcycle off the road near the tall elephant grass and peered into the darkening landscape. Swarms of mosquitoes buzzed around her. She swatted them away from Blessing and slapped several insects that settled on her arm.

A gray-haired gentleman on a small scooter pulled off the road and parked. He headed toward her. "I recognize you from television last night. This must be Blessing."

Sandy asked, "What television?"

"You and Blessing were on the national news last night and the evening before last. I saw it twice."

"How could you? They told me they would not show it for three days."

"They announced your interview would be shown in every state on the local news over the next few weeks because many people asked to see it."

Sandy's heart pounded against her breastbone. Had it really been shown? Technical power failures occurred in every city. Mechanical breakdowns were common. Due to the lack of tools and replacement parts, lots of the equipment remained broken. Television programs in the national capital, Logatti, had been sporadic and unpredictable. She never imagined the film would be shown.

Icy fingers constricted her throat, and she shivered. If the stranger recognized her from a short, televised newscast, who else saw her? What would the church leaders do with her? Even worse, every military officer in the country would know where to find her. What had she done? Why had she ever agreed to that silly interview? Because if she hadn't, they would have kept coming back until she consented.

129

The gentleman smiled. "Blessing and you are more beautiful than you were on television."

"Thank you. By the way, I have a flat tire."

"I will go to the next village and call a mechanic for you." The gentleman remounted his scooter, revved the engine, and zoomed down the road.

It grew darker as Sandy slapped at more mosquitoes. A broken-down station wagon stopped. The middle-aged driver stepped out of the car. "I saw you on television in Logatti city last night. They telecast you and this baby across the nation."

Sandy closed her eyes and wanted to disappear. The situation was getting worse, but maybe the damage was done. She wished she could have seen the newscast. Without a television or electricity it was impossible.

"You can't stay here in the bush with a baby and these mosquitoes. I'll take you to the mechanic in the next village. You can wait inside his house while he repairs your tire." The gentleman opened the car door for her.

She had peace in her heart about going with a stranger, so she slid onto the seat. He drove her to the mechanic's house where she found the first elderly gentleman, and together they waited for the repairman.

An hour later, a local man covered in motor grease arrived. "I put your motorcycle in a safe location for the night. The melting machine is broken so I can't patch the tire until tomorrow. You'll have to spend the night here."

"Would you escort me to the pastor's house? I know him and his wife."

"Yes." He lifted Sandy's largest basket onto his head and picked up the other one.

Sandy found the pastor's wife at home. "My motorcycle cannot be repaired until tomorrow. There are no more taxis traveling tonight."

"Do not worry. You can stay in our guest room." Mrs. Pastor took Blessing. "How can I help you and your daughter?"

"Please soak a half cup of black-eyed peas and skin them before cooking. After they are soft, mash them with a fork. Since Blessing turned five months I've added them to her milk and corn porridge."

The pastor's wife tied Blessing to her back, handed Sandy a wrap-around skirt, and escorted her to the bathing stall.

Sandy bathed and washed Blessing. The pastor's wife handed Sandy a bowl. "Here are the cooked beans. I cannot mash them because I do not have a fork. We eat with our fingers. I have a spoon to stir gravies. Would that help?"

"I will try it." Sandy put Blessing on her lap and tried without success to mash the beans with the spoon. She mixed the lumpy concoction into the corn meal and milk which she fed to her baby.

That night, Blessing woke and vomited several times. Sandy gave the baby milk, but the child kept throwing up.

In the morning Sandy found the pastor's wife outside in the kitchen. "I need bottled water to prepare sugar and salt water for dehydration. Is there a shop nearby?"

"Market day will be in three days."

"I should go straight home to boil water to drink because my baby is getting dehydrated."

"What about your motorcycle?"

"I will take a taxi home. Would your husband ask the mechanic to bring my motorcycle to my house after he repairs the tire?"

"Yes, I will tell him. Please stay and let me make bean cakes for you."

"I need to be on my way with Blessing. She needs sugar and salt water for dehydration. Her clothes are filthy, and I need to change them."

"No one has ever seen your daughter dirty. Everyone speaks of how clean and neat she always appears. Besides, lots of children wear soiled, smelly clothes. It is okay." The pastor's wife hesitated for a moment. "But now that you are a celebrity it is important for you to always look your best."

"I'm not famous." Sandy shrugged.

But she was. Since the filming, everyone stared at her wherever she went. When she had managed the fitness center she'd been on display every day, but as a nationally-known mother she was a public figure day and night.

When she arrived home, the water drum was empty. Blessing kept vomiting, but Sandy wouldn't leave her baby alone in the house to fetch the water.

Someone knocked on the door, and Sandy opened it. The small farmer, dressed in neat clothes, gave her a letter. She opened it, read through the contents, and raised teary eyes to him. In a shaky voice, she whispered, "You're Blessing's father?"

"I came to see my daughter." He peered into the room.

Sandy handed Blessing, who screamed her lungs out, to the man. What would the father think of his vomit-covered daughter? The odor of the stinky diaper filled Sandy's nostrils. She blinked to halt her tears because she had failed as a mother. He would report her to Dr. Pelougu for not taking good care of his daughter.

He looked Blessing over as if he were a slave owner searching for blemishes or imperfections. The father handed the child back to Sandy and walked away.

Sandy sat down and bawled. Blessing's father had found his daughter in dirty clothes, crying, and in distress. Sandy couldn't take care of a baby in the middle of the African bush without running water and electricity, formulas, baby food, or diapers.

Phoebe came into the house and frowned at Sandy's tears. "Please stop crying. I will fill your water drum now. I had to take my sister to the hospital and couldn't do it yesterday."

Sandy gasped between deep sobs. "It's all over."

"What's over?"

"Blessing's father came to see her, and she looks like this." Sandy held the baby out to Phoebe.

"The man is used to dirty, crying babies. He had fourteen children. Do not worry about it. It will be fine."

But Sandy had a premonition it wouldn't be fine.

CHAPTER TWENTY-ONE

Sandy carried Blessing to the Under Fives clinic at the hospital where she was born.

The head nurse glared. "Is that baby sick?"

"She is perfectly fine. I came for her vaccinations. Here's her immunization record. She needs diphtheria, pertussis, tetanus, and measles."

"We do not give immunizations today. We only inoculate on Mondays and Wednesdays."

Sandy worked those days in the rural villages and couldn't return. The hospital was a four-hour taxi ride from her house making it more difficult to come back on another day.

The nurse snarled, "Come with me and take off the baby's clothes."

Something was wrong. Sandy's stomach fluttered. Nurses didn't remove clothes for an immunization.

The nurse snapped, "We have to weigh the child."

"I've checked her on my baby scale. She gained half of a pound, and I recorded it here." Sandy pointed it out on the card.

The nurse lifted Blessing and put her in the bucket scale. "She is losing weight. What are you doing to this baby?"

"Nothing." Tears filled Sandy's eyes. "She is not losing weight."

"Our scale is the official one for the government."

"Mine is the official one for the Health Organization for the World." Sandy sniffed. "She can't be losing weight for she eats every three hours."

Another nurse came into the room and pointed to a raised welt on Blessing's face. "You have let mosquitoes bite this baby."

Sandy opened and closed her eyes to suppress the rising flood of tears. She tried hard to be the perfect mother, but she was a terrible one. When she reached for Blessing's clothes to dress her, the baby sneezed.

The nurse yelled, "You are not keeping her warm. Go to the city and buy her a cardigan."

Sandy picked up Blessing and returned to the waiting room.

The head nurse screamed, "What kind of a mother are you? You should not be here."

Tears blurred Sandy's vision. Where else should a mother be to immunize her baby?

A nurse shouted at her in front of everyone. "You are not taking proper care of this child. You are a fool for coming on the wrong day. Come back at the right one."

But she'd never return not even on vaccination day. She would never walk through those doors again. Tears flowed down her cheeks. She wanted to scream in anger at the obnoxious nurses. She should have taken Blessing to Hose for immunizations, but she was afraid of running into the military officers there who had threatened her.

Sandy could have inoculated Blessing herself, but according to the law, the mother, guardian, or relative of an infant wasn't permitted to sign for the vaccination. If Sandy gave her the inoculation but didn't sign, then it wouldn't be recognized by other health workers.

She stumbled out of the hospital and stopped a taxi. After climbing in, a female passenger turned to Sandy. "Why are you crying? Please stop crying. You will make yourself sick."

Another passenger reached out and tickled Blessing. "You will hurt yourself, so stop weeping."

The female passenger behind Sandy said, "Tell me what is wrong, and maybe I can help."

"Everyone thinks I'm a bad mother, but I'm doing my best." Sandy looked down at her baby. "Blessing, I'm so sorry."

The woman gasped, "You're Mommy Blessing, the famous white lady who was on national television in all the cities in our nation."

"Why are you calling me Mommy Blessing?"

"Mothers are named after their firstborn child. If your first baby was named John, you would be called Mommy John. Blessing is your firstborn so you are Mommy Blessing. You are doing a great job. She is fat, healthy, and beautiful. Where did you get this lovely dress and matching bonnet?"

"I made them."

"Who told you that you are a bad mother?"

"The people at the hospital said I came on the wrong day to immunize Blessing."

"Don't mind them. Those workers are nasty to the women. Lots of mothers never return for immunizations because the nurses shout at them."

"That's terrible." Sandy sniffed back deeply to halt her tears. "I should do something about it. If the mothers do not vaccinate their babies, they can get terrible diseases."

The lady next to her shook her head. "You cannot turn a nasty medical worker into a sweet person. Lots of health personnel at the hospital are lazy and hateful. The doctor is a Nunaa man like the others but he was educated in Europe and learned how to be polite."

The taxi stopped at the station in Koala. Sandy stepped out of the vehicle. Eve came up to Sandy. "I am returning from the market and saw you get out of the taxi."

Sandy handed the baby to Eve, who tied Blessing to her back. Eve rocked back and forth and put the child to sleep. "I am worried about you. In your country, can a woman live alone without a man?"

"Yes, in America many women do."

"Is it because you have something special in your white body so you do not need a man?"

"God gives me strength to live alone. In the States we are taught to take care of ourselves."

"Do you drink a special medicine to stop your desires for a husband?"

"No." Sandy hiccupped then giggled. "No. Where did you hear that?"

"A pastor in the city told us that single, white ladies were not human. You don't have feelings like the rest of us and never need a man."

"Do you think I'm not human?"

"You are human. But among our people no woman is permitted to live by herself or stay single. We were put on earth to give birth. If a woman can't get a husband, she must marry anyone, even if it makes her the second or third wife."

Sandy raised her eyebrows. "Do Christian women do this?"

"Yes, many are pressured to marry and be part of a polygamous marriage. If we stay single we are not fulfilling our purpose on earth. It is a disgrace if we never have a child. Plus we need children to take care of us in our old age."

"I admire the way you care for your elderly parents."

"It is necessary because there are no old age pensions, retirements, or financial provisions."

"Here comes the taxi for Hose." Sandy reached out and took Blessing. "Will it cause problems if I live alone?"

But she didn't hear an answer as she climbed into the car and it drove off. Four hours later, she carried Blessing into the hospital and joined the other mothers in line.

Sandy approached the director of the immunization clinic, who sat behind a desk. "Are you immunizing babies?"

"Yes."

"I came for vaccinations. Here's my child's record." Sandy handed over the card.

The director scowled. "You call yourself a Christian. Why did you bring pants here?"

Sandy's heart raced. "My research indicated women in large developed African cities wore pants, and it was acceptable."

"You can see for yourself, this place is not as progressive as the literature suggests. There are many cultural taboos and different beliefs that have never been written."

"I understand that now."

"I hope you learned your lesson when you burned the pants. If the national church sends you away, what will you do with this baby?"

"If that time comes, the Lord will take care of her."

"Have you considered the consequences of your actions? If there's another military coup, and we are all evacuated, what will happen to this child? She cannot leave the country without legal papers. Or did you get them?"

"I'll trust God."

"You appear too spiritually minded to be any earthly good."

One minute Sandy was accused of being immoral and the next minute of being too religious.

"I can see why you're attached to this baby. She's a beautiful, healthy child. But what do you hope to accomplish by taking her?"

"Blessing is an example of good child care." She shifted Blessing's weight to the opposite hip.

"You are doing the impossible. Do you honestly believe these people will listen to you?"

"I pray and hope so."

"Here's your registration card. They are giving immunizations down the hall."

A nurse with a flat snub nose came up to Sandy and took Blessing for the immunization. She set the baby on the table. Blessing did not sit unassisted. "This baby is over four months and should be sitting alone. What is wrong with this child?"

"Nothing is wrong with her." Sandy lifted her baby and pressed her close to her chest.

The nurse raised her voice and took Blessing from Sandy again and put her on the table. "Sit. Sit, you lazy baby. Sit. Sit."

Tears sprang to Sandy's eyes. She covered her mouth not knowing whether to laugh at the absurdity of it or cry at the accusation that her baby was lazy. Wasn't six months the average age for sitting? All the women in the clinic stared at Sandy and her child. She wasn't a good mother, if her child couldn't do the skills other African children did. Sniffing several times, she wiped away a tear.

Another nurse with dilated nostrils glared at Blessing and snapped, "You are a lazy baby. Now sit."

A medical worker with thick protruding lips stopped in front of Blessing. "People believe this child is cursed. You must admit she is not normal."

Would Sandy ever convince the people Blessing wasn't cursed? Sandy's breath came out in ragged gasps. She was on the verge of tears. She turned her head away from the medical people, who had embarrassed her, and blinked several times to stop the tears.

Blessing cried when the nurse gave her the immunizations. Sandy lifted her baby and clutched her tightly to her chest as she walked out of the cubicle.

Helen came up to Sandy and put her hand on Sandy's shoulder. "Don't mind these medical workers. They are jealous of you."

"Why would they be envious of me?"

"Every time they've seen Blessing, she is always laughing and elegantly dressed. They feel threatened of the good job you are doing. They need to find something wrong to make themselves feel better, but African babies sit unassisted at four months." Helen stroked Blessing's cheek. "Their babies are tied upright to their mothers' backs from birth and spend many hours in a vertical position, which strengthens the back muscles. That prepares them to sit by themselves at an earlier age."

Sandy wiped away another tear. Had it not been for Helen's kind words, Sandy might have kept on bawling. "That makes sense."

Mr. Jubilee, the medical director, approached Sandy. "Hello. How are you? Did you bring the baby for immunization?"

"Yes." Sandy smiled.

"May I speak to you alone for a moment over there?" Mr. Jubilee pointed.

"Yes, of course." With Blessing in her arms, she followed him to the corner. Everyone in the clinic turned to watch them.

Mr. Jubilee stuffed his hands in his pockets and frowned. "A military officer came to me."

Sandy's heart beat faster. The officers were trying to frighten her again, but why?

"He plans to investigate you. I assured him you are here to help us and are working for us."

"Several military officers came to Koala to question me."

Mr. Jubilee shook his head. "Sister Sandy, I am sorry to tell you this, but you are the fish."

"What?"

"You Americans have a proverb, 'Everyone is watching the fish in the glass.' Be careful. Try not to offend anyone."

That wouldn't be easy. She'd try her best to please everyone. Maybe with God's grace she'd win the favor of the military officers.

Sandy found a taxi and squeezed inside with the other passengers. Wedged between two heavy women, she couldn't move.

When Blessing cried, Sandy patted her back. "It's all right. Let me make your food."

She always handed her baby to a lady in the taxi, so Sandy's hands were free to measure the black-eyed pea paste, corn, and milk powder, and put it in a metal cup. African women carried babies from the time they were youngsters and were always glad to help another mother.

Sandy held the flask and with her right hand unscrewed the lid. As she opened the thermos of boiled water, steam rose. She picked up the cup from between her legs and angled the flask close to the rim. Gripping the thermos, she tilted it as close to the cup of paste to pour the water without burning herself.

If the driver sped over a rough place, the motion would spill the boiling water onto her lap. She'd always taken a few risks, but only when she had no choice. Blessing was hungry and needed to eat. The woman to her left jiggled her arm, but at the same time the car slowed and there were no spills. Sandy stirred the hot water into the paste until it was like a thick milkshake. She handed the cup to one of the passengers while Sandy put the utensils away.

The vehicle bounced down the road at sixty miles an hour. Feeding a tiny baby from a cup would be more difficult. The woman who held Blessing took the cup and lifted the container to the baby's lips. "If I had not seen this with my own eyes, I would not have believed it. Isn't it amazing how this tiny infant drinks from a cup like an adult?"

"Feeding a child with a cup seems easy." Another woman smiled. "It is better than the choking method of force-feeding."

139

Another passenger said, "This is the Blessing baby. She is the famous child from television. She is a beautiful little girl. It is a pity the mother died for she would have enjoyed this laughing baby."

"Yes, she would have, because I enjoy her every day. She is my blessing."

The man behind Sandy tapped her shoulder. "I saw you and the baby on television last night in our state capital."

"Last night?" Sandy turned to the man.

"Yes. They have shown it several times from many different state capitals."

Every time someone told her about the program, Sandy wished she had seen the interview.

When the taxi stopped in Koala, Sandy stepped out of the vehicle and took a short-cut trail through the bush to her mud home. At the end of the path two military officers blocked her from going farther.

"Good evening, Miss Calbrin. You are under investigation."

CHAPTER TWENTY-TWO

Sandy wanted to run. Her stomach fluttered as the two officials blocked her way on the narrow trail. Her muscles tightened as she prepared to get away, but there was no escape. She couldn't sprint with Blessing on her back and carry a heavy backpack and basket of supplies.

She cleared her throat. "How can I help you?"

Lieutenant Courteous removed his cap and slapped it against his hand. "Excuse me, ma'am, Miss Calbrin. We came to see you and invite you to our village for the weekend."

Like a roadblock on the path the officers stood side by side impeding her way. she squared her shoulders, trying not to show fear. Planting her feet, she dug in her heels. Their cold glares like ice, chilled her.

Lord, please deliver me.

"We know you are a prostitute by night because of the pants in your room."

The air swooshed out of her lungs as if someone punched her in the chest. She had hoped the pants incident was behind her. Could she convince them of the truth? "I'm not a prostitute. I burned all the pants."

"Are you refusing our invitation for the weekend?"

"I must decline."

Lieutenant Scarface reached his arm out to touch Sandy's shoulder but dropped his hand. "Let's go to your house and talk about this in a reasonable manner."

She'd die before going into her house with two overbearing soldiers.

Blessing cried and Sandy said, "My baby is hungry."

On trembling limbs and heedless of possible snakes, Sandy turned to detour around them into the tall elephant grass.

They moved apart and let her pass between them.

141

Each step to her home brought her closer to ruin. Fear tightened her heart.

As they marched down the trail, Sandy talked to them. "Jesus loves you. He gave His life for you. He wants you to repent and believe so you can have eternal life in Heaven."

"Stop preaching at us. Be quiet," Lieutenant Scarface snarled. "We don't want anyone to hear us."

She spoke louder so someone would hear and come to her aid. "God loves you."

Their footsteps stampeded behind her like a herd of elephants about to trample her to death. The oversweet scent of Colonel Courteous's cologne filled the air and made her gag. She lowered her head to catch a whiff of her baby's soap.

How can I stop them, Lord?

An idea came to her. Maybe God gave her the tiny padlock and miniature key so they could be lost. If there was no key, no one could get into the house.

She would outwit them but also show them respect. If they killed her she would die. No, she wouldn't die. Her body would pass on, but her spirit would go to Heaven to be with Jesus. But who would take care of Blessing?

The men stopped with her in front of her house. Sandy glanced at the four trails leading to her home. No one appeared on the footpaths. She untied Blessing from her back and handed the baby to Lieutenant Scarface. "Hold Blessing while I look for the house key."

After he took the baby, she opened her backpack and rummaged around inside the sack. She pulled out a flask, a container of food, and change of clothes for Blessing. One by one and in slow motion she placed a coin purse, comb, sunglasses, sunscreen, and headscarf on the rocks in front of her house. When her fingers touched the key, she slipped it into the folds of her umbrella. She lifted her umbrella out of her bag and balanced it on a large rock closest to her house.

She resumed hunting through her bag but let her lower leg lean against the umbrella. It toppled to the ground behind the rock. The house key disappeared.

Lieutenant Courteous glanced at the crying baby. "What is taking you so long? Unlock this door right now. We cannot stay here. Someone might see us."

That was a good idea. Maybe someone would stop by and see them at her house. As she handed him the empty bag, her voice wobbled. "Look, the key is not in the backpack."

"Where is your house key?" The officer took her bag and looked in it. "What did you do with it?"

"It's gone." She lowered her head and plotted her next move. Her arms shook as she held them out for Blessing. Lifting her eyes, she glanced at their faces, not looking directly at them. She caught a glimpse of the trail, longing to see someone, but no one approached. Her thumping heart plummeted. What next?

Lieutenant Scarface raised his voice. "You tricked us! Where is that key? We want to take you inside."

Sandy kept her head turned away. "Would you like to go with me to the chief's house to collect the extra key?"

Lieutenant Courteous smoothed the collar of his uniform. "We'll be back."

They turned to the opposite trail, and Sandy walked behind them. Lieutenant Scarface looked back at her. "Are you following us?"

"I'm going to the chief's house to get the spare key."

The officers veered to the right down a narrower path, but Sandy kept walking toward the chief's home. The village leader was not there, but she met Phoebe.

Phoebe set her bucket of water on the ground. "I'm sorry to be late bringing your water. I had to cook for my sick sister."

"Two military officers threatened me. Do you think those officers would hurt me?"

"They would never risk harming you without knowing if your father was the ambassador, an American politician, or general."

"Those wicked men are waiting for an opportunity to be alone with me."

"Be careful."

143

"I'm trying, but they appeared out of nowhere." Sandy raised her hand. "He lifted his hand like this as if he would slap me."

"It is hard for me to believe they threatened you."

"They did."

"Sometimes they do things like that to scare people. There is no proof."

Sandy raised her eyebrows. "What do you mean no proof?"

"It was your word against theirs. No other person saw it." Phoebe picked the bucket up and followed Sandy. "Even if I arrived and saw it, no one would believe me, an African woman. No one would accept my word in favor of a military officer's."

***

A few days later Sandy tied Blessing to her back, mounted her motorcycle, and headed toward Odoo. It had rained the previous evening which made driving on the muddy trail more difficult. She halted in front of a dirty puddle before going around it and up the steep, massive hill. Putting the bike in the lowest gear, she navigated it at a snail's pace over the worst stretch of the climb.

The bike stalled in six inches of mud as she reached the top. She gripped the handlebars and slid off the seat. The kickstand sunk in the mud, and she shoved it back up in place. She glanced at her huge basket of drugs tied to the back of her bike. Blessing's bag of food and clothes dangled from the right handle. Her bag of water and necessities swung from the other side. If she turned the engine off and let it go, the bike would sink deep into the mud. When the sun came out it would dry up the mud with the bike stuck in it. She'd never get the motorcycle free.

Lord Jesus, please send some angels.

She tried to steady the bike with one hand, but couldn't. How could she save her basket of medications?

An African man chugged over the top of the crest on his motorcycle and Sandy called to him. "Help me, please."

He pulled his bike off the trail into the tall grasses on the side of the path and ran to her side. "Don't move. I saw you on television Monday night in the city."

"Thank you." Sandy smiled at him. "I'm grateful for your help."

He maneuvered her motorcycle out of the mud and pushed the bike alongside her. As she plodded up the steep knoll, Sandy pulled one foot up and placed it down in front of the other. A thick, dark mire coated her feet, ankles, and legs.

"We are halfway to the village." The stranger shoved her motorcycle the remaining five miles.

At the community, she hobbled to the church where a well-dressed woman reached out for Blessing. Another woman wearing torn clothes dropped her dirty hoe and picked up an empty bucket. A third woman lifted a straight-back chair and walked to Sandy. The woman set the chair on the ground, put her hands on Sandy's shoulders, and pushed her into the seat. She removed Sandy's flat shoes and ran away with them. The other woman who had taken the bucket returned with a full pail of water and set it down. She lifted Sandy's stinky, muddy feet, plunged them into the water, and used her hands to scrub them. The lady who had collected Sandy's shoes returned with a clean, wet pair.

After the women had ministered to Sandy, the villagers handed treatment cards to her. She pointed to the bench and called the first patient.

The wrinkled woman sat on the seat facing Sandy. "My heart is beating."

"Yes." Sandy put the stethoscope on the woman's chest. "Your heart is beating too fast. How long has it been doing this?" She wrote 110, possible tachycardia.

The patient scowled. "A long time. My head hurts, too."

Sandy examined the patient's swollen feet. "Do your feet hurt?"

"I said my head hurts, not my feet."

Sandy had no way of diagnosing heart disease. Even if she could, there were no cardiac drugs available there.

"You need to rest. Your feet are swollen because you have too much water in your body. All the fluid goes to the feet and makes them big. You must stop eating salt. It keeps this extra water in the body." Sandy wrote, "Consider congestive heart failure related to old age."

145

"How can anyone eat food without salt? It is not possible."

"Just try it. When you rest you must raise your legs higher than your head so the blood can flow freely." Sandy lifted the patient's legs.

By the end of the day, Sandy could barely put one foot in front of the other. She dreaded the ride home.

Several teenagers washed her motorcycle. It was sparkling clean by the time she was ready to leave. The hospitality of the local people in the villages touched her heart.

Too bad the military officers couldn't welcome her with the same kindness.

CHAPTER TWENTY-THREE

Early the following morning, Sandy carried Blessing to the taxi station and hired a vehicle traveling to Balitu.

When the driver reached the junction to the main north and south road, Sandy stepped out and opened her umbrella to shade Blessing in the carrier on her back from the hot sun. As she waited for the pastor of the Evangelical church, she breathed in the refreshing scent of mint and lifted her eyes to the bright blue that outlined the white puffy clouds. She had never enjoyed rural areas, but the African countryside was peaceful.

A motorcycle roared, and she twisted around. The pastor turned off his engine. "Good morning. I am glad to see you. There are two villages far in the bush, ten miles on a rough road. I told the people you would treat their sicknesses. They are waiting for you."

Sandy handed the basket of drugs, the supplies, and her bag of personal provisions to the pastor.

The pastor hoisted the loads to the rear of his motorcycle, pulled out a long, narrow strip of inner tube, and fastened the bags to the bike. She tucked her skirt around her legs and mounted the motorcycle behind the pastor.

He revved up the engine and maintained a fast speed, as she leaned forward and tilted to the side of the pastor's back. The bags behind Sandy slid into her lower back as he maneuvered the bike over the potholes.

"Please, slow down." She pleaded.

He zoomed into a deep hole at a reckless speed making her bounce up and down. Knifelike daggers shot through her backbone.

Sandy shouted, "Please, go slower."

"No, the rain is coming."

"The road is too rough. Slow down, pastor."

"We must keep moving for there is no shelter, and we cannot drive in the rain."

147

Reaching the village, Sandy slid off the bike.

Thank you, Lord.

She unpacked the medicines and set the bottles on the table. Then she handed Blessing to a woman to hold. Sandy sat down on a wooden chair under the baobab tree, collected the patient cards, and called the first patient.

The young African mother hung her head. "My son has scalp disease. It began with a white color and itching. All his hair fell out. Now he is bald."

After examining the little boy's head, Sandy said. "I'll scrub his scalp with soap and water to remove the germs. You must do this every day."

Sandy applied cream and handed a sack of pills and a bar of antibacterial soap to the mother.

After she had treated and vaccinated all the children in the Under Fives clinic, the pastor said. "I promised the people I would bring you to their village. It is ten miles farther in the bush. You must treat their sicknesses."

Sandy nodded, packed up the baskets, and handed the baggage to the pastor to secure to the bike. With Blessing in her arms, she mounted the motorcycle behind him. He revved up the engine, turned the bike around, and headed toward the second village.

As stabbing, knifelike pains seared her spine, she gasped to catch her breath. "Pastor, please stop."

The pastor halted. Her numb legs shook as she slid off the motorcycle, put the baby in the carrier, and fastened it on her back. To relieve the pain in her spine, she stretched her arms high over her head and lowered them a couple of times. She didn't want to get back on the bike but couldn't abandon the sick people who needed treatment. So she hobbled to the motorcycle and remounted.

At the end of the day, the pastor drove Sandy to the main junction to secure a taxi home. "I will wait with you until you get a vehicle to your village. You are a happy person, but isn't laughing too much a sin?"

"The Bible says a merry heart does good like medicine." She shifted Blessing to the opposite shoulder. "Before I came to Africa I wasn't as happy as I am today. After I started treating people and took Blessing, I realized what a selfish, greedy person I had been."

She wiped away a tear before it ran down her cheek. "I rededicated my life to the Lord. He filled me with an incredible peace and joy. Serving Jesus is fun and satisfying."

"The American Christians I knew were very serious." He straddled his motorcycle and leaned forward, letting his feet scrape the dust. "Many of them never talked to us person to person like you do, so they never understood us."

"I'm trying to understand you."

"We all see that quality in you." The pastor hesitated. "It is important to us that we support our children and parents."

"I am aware of your extended families."

"You Americans place more value in buildings and institutions than people."

Sandy stared down the road, saw an approaching taxi, and stepped forward. "What do you mean?"

Before he had time to answer, the taxi stopped. Through the open windows the chauffeur yelled, "Get in quickly. I'm in a hurry."

Sandy handed Blessing to the pastor and slid onto the seat of the station wagon. The pastor held the baby out to Sandy who took her child and closed the door. The driver roared down the bumpy, dirt road.

She wanted to understand the cultural differences and regretted she hadn't waited for the pastor's answer. But she had to take the taxi, for it might have been the last one traveling that night.

When she got home she prepared the medications for the next clinic and fed Blessing. She stepped outside to go to the pit latrine and bumped into Lieutenant Scarface. She froze and slapped a hand to her chest as she tried to catch her breath. Scarface had caught her alone at home.

"I have come about your visa problem."

149

"My visa problem?" She took a deep breath to slow her racing heart. "What do you mean?"

"Miss Calbrin, you have a four-month visa which must be submitted for the residence permit."

He pulled a file out from under his arm and flipped through some papers. "If you spend the weekend with me, I will take care of it for you. The only other way you can get a visa is to pay thirty thousand naros. You Christians working under the church are not permitted to give bribes."

It sounded like everyone else was permitted to bribe government officials. Military officers were not allowed to harass foreigners, and they were not permitted to threaten a lady with expulsion from the country if she didn't spend the weekend with one of them.

Clamping her jaws together, she gave him a chilly stare. Ice tightened like fingers around her throat. Her feet stayed frozen to the ground.

He moved closer. "Let's go into your house and talk about this. Do you still have your baby? Is she inside?"

Her limbs refused to move. She blinked and swallowed to suppress the rising flood of tears. His inquiry about Blessing was a threat. If she went in the house, he'd follow her. There was no one to help her, but God.

Lord, please help me.

Her mouth went dry. At last she whispered, "Blessing is asleep. I don't want to wake her."

"The baby will be fine for an hour."

She walked away from the house toward a tree root.

"Spend the weekend with me, and I will take care of you."

She sat down and looked up at him. "I will not commit such a sin."

"I am not a Christian, but in my religion it is not wrong to sleep with women."

"What is your religion?"

"I worship my ancestors."

"Have you thought about what will happen after you die?"

"I will join my ancestors across the big river of life. They have gone on ahead to prepare a place for me."

"Have you ever seen that place?"

"No one has seen it."

"How do you know it is a nice place, and that it even exists?"

"We never know if it is a good place, which is why we keep sacrificing animals to our ancestors. I am trying to make my great, great grandparents happy." He used his cap as a fan. "If you will not spend the weekend with me, give me money to buy more animals to sacrifice."

"I can't do that."

He put the papers in the file and closed it. "I know where you are, and I will be back. Do you understand?"

Her flesh crawled. She understood he would return again and again until he had what he wanted.

"I need to be going." The lieutenant marched down the trail.

Sandy went into her house, changed her baby's diaper, and fed her.

Distracted and upset over the officer's visit, she wasn't paying attention and didn't notice the deadly African snake until she caught a glimpse of it dangling from the curtain. The three-foot long mamba opened its inky, black mouth and spit out his hideous tongue.

She clutched Blessing closer and jumped away. "Help, Lord. Please send help."

Adam answered, "Sister Sandy."

With a shaky voice, she stuttered over and over. "Come in. Come in. Come in."

He entered the small room. "I was passing by on my way home from the farm when I heard your scream." Adam took one glance at the snake and raced away.

Sandy backed away from the serpent, holding her daughter tighter. Why did Adam abandon her? He should have stayed to help her kill the lethal snake. He had helped clean up dirty dressings, scrubbed urine and putrid stools from the floor, but he now deserted her and her baby at the first sign of danger.

She never took her eyes off the serpent and followed its movements behind the bed. It slithered into the corner. Staring at the creature took her mind off its danger. Sweat ran down her face and into her eyes. The serpent stopped moving. Sandy didn't budge.

Adam returned with a long, thick pole. He stepped closer to the serpent and shrieked a wail, which startled Sandy and made Blessing cry. The snake lashed out. Adam whacked it several times with the rod. He smashed the serpent against the screen and it ripped. The snake slithered outside through the tear.

With Blessing in her arms, she followed Adam outside. His initial blows stunned the creature. It curled and shook, so Adam beat it again with the rod.

"We should whack off its head to make sure it's dead," Sandy ordered. "Get my machete in the kitchen."

After severing the head from the body, Adam glared at Blessing. "Your baby appears to be cursed, Sister Sandy. Look at what happened. Is this the only time a snake attacked you since you came to Africa?"

"Yes, but if Blessing were cursed, wouldn't I already be dead of a snake bite?"

"Maybe. This snake's bite is fatal. Without refrigeration, we cannot keep anti-venom. The villagers call it the ten-step snake because a victim can only walk ten steps before dropping dead."

Sandy shivered.

Adam scooped the snake's body up onto the end of the long, heavy baton. The snake's body dangled from the rod as Adam lifted it. He carried it several yards away and tossed it into the tall grasses next to the house. Surely nothing else could happen to Sandy that day.

Adam returned with Sandy's machete. "Your baby has brought danger to the village."

"The snake is dead. There's nothing to worry about now."

"These snakes travel by twos, so that means more trouble. I searched through the bushes but didn't see its mate. Now it can hurt or kill someone. Your baby is responsible."

"My baby is innocent."

"When I tell the chief about this, he and the elders will call a meeting to decide what to do."

Would they demand she give up Blessing?

CHAPTER TWENTY-FOUR

In three months Sandy had established fifty Under Fives clinics and treated patients in as many villages. Three evenings a week, she cared for the sick in Koala.

Lieutenant Courteous marched into the clinic. "Good morning."

Adam stopped sweeping the floor and brought a chair for the officer. "Sit down."

The lieutenant opened his briefcase. "The government passed a new law. Every alien must carry a personal identification card. This way we know precisely where you are at all times or where you are going. You must come and present your papers at the police station."

Sandy pursed her lips and exhaled through her nose. Nodding, she said, "I will come."

"Tomorrow morning."

"Yes."

The lieutenant smirked. "You cannot travel to any village unless you bring the new alien's book to the police station and secure our permission."

"Permission?"

"Yes. You must ask us any time you want to travel to a village."

The military officers wanted to terrorize her, but surely they hadn't made the law just for her. Could she keep standing up to the officials? She had to, if she were going to vaccinate all the children, but how? Military officers watched, followed, and hounded her.

It would be easier and less dangerous to return to the fitness center. But if she left, what would happen to her baby and all the others she didn't vaccinate? She couldn't leave, yet.

After the officer departed, an older female handed Sandy a health card. A huge mass hung from the patient's neck.

Sandy palpated the goiter. "Does this hurt?"

"No."

"How long have you had this?"

"Since I was a young girl, and nothing can help it. I came today because snakes are moving around inside my stomach. They bite my abdomen and come out in my stool."

Sandy wrote 'round worms' on the health card and scribbled, Mebendazole.

After she collected the fee, the woman departed. "Adam, I've seen many large goiter tumors here."

Adam wrote notes on the next card. "That last woman had an evil spirit that got stuck in her throat and didn't leave."

"That's not the cause of this sickness. Eating iodized salt and fish prevent goiters and stop the little growths from becoming larger. When I was in the capital city, I didn't see any of these tumors, but people eat fish which prevents it."

Adam shrugged. "We have no ocean to catch fish, so you may be right, Sister Sandy."

"It's too bad they can't bring all that fish inland to these villages or at least bring the salt from the sea."

"Our people will always believe an evil spirit lives in those tumors."

After treating all the patients, Sandy packed her bag to leave. Adam carried the sack and escorted her home.

Sandy unlocked her door and Adam carried her bags into the small house. He set them on the table. "I would like to see what the carpenters did?"

"Go look at the new, secure screened windows."

Adam ran his hand up and down a frame. "You bought the highest quality of wire netting. No one or nothing can get inside now."

"I want to keep my baby safe."

"And you, too." Adam turned to leave. "Goodbye."

After supper each evening the game started. Sandy covered her face with the cloth. "Peek-a-boo game, Blessing." Their play lasted until bedtime.

Sandy loved the special hours with her sweet baby but didn't have time that evening. She opened her exercise book and jotted notes for a

156

health lecture. When it was time for bed, she put Blessing in her cardboard box, blew out her two bush lanterns, and slid into bed.

A blood-curdling scream pierced the peaceful night. Sandy leaped up and reached for Blessing in the dark. She lit the lantern and examined her baby, but there weren't any wounds or scratches on Blessing. There were no snakes in the room, either.

Blessing laughed and laughed and laughed.

Sandy put her baby back in the cardboard box. Blessing pumped her legs and arms up and down. Sandy covered the baby again.

The child giggled. "Ha, ha, ha, ha, ha, ha, ha."

"Blessing, what are you doing?"

The baby cackled and kicked as she moved her little arms and legs.

Sandy picked her up again. She carried the child to bed and lay down beside her baby. "Blessing, it's time to go to sleep. It's late, and we are not playing games tonight. Please go to sleep."

When Blessing closed her eyes, Sandy carried the baby to her makeshift crib. Blessing blinked, but Sandy assumed it was a reflex and blew out the lantern before returning to bed. Howling screams jolted Sandy upright. Rushing to her baby, Sandy lit the lantern and stared down at Blessing, a little giggling runner who raised and lowered her arms and legs.

"Blessing, we are not playing games tonight. Go to sleep." Sandy picked up her daughter and walked the floor with her. Blessing smiled and giggled. After two hours and a third time going through the routine, the baby slept. Could a six-month infant have missed peek-a-boo time? Or had Blessing invented her own game of scaring Mommy in the dark? Was Blessing smart enough to do that?

The next morning Sandy tied Blessing to her back and walked two miles into the village center to the police station. Lieutenant Courteous and Lieutenant Scarface sat on a wooden bench outside the building and smoked cigarettes. Had they been transferred from Hose to Koala?

"Good morning." Sandy halted before the officers. "I've come to apply for an alien's book."

Lieutenant Scarface tossed his cigarette to the ground. "Good morning." He stood and walked with Sandy inside the building where another officer sat behind a desk. "Miss Calbrin is here for her alien's book."

"Please have a seat." Colonel Renita was printed on his nametag.

He opened a desk drawer, pulled out a tin box, and searched through it. Taking an alien's book from the stack held together with a rubber band, he lifted his head toward Sandy. "May I see your passport, please?"

Sandy reached in her backpack and retrieved the document. "Here it is."

The colonel picked up an ink pen and printed her name in capital letters in her new identification card. On the next line he wrote out, UNITED STATES of AMERICA. He flipped to page three and jotted her visa number. Then he turned to page four and wrote Koala on the line marked village. He dated it, stamped it, and signed his name in the book.

"Miss Calbrin, the new law requires that you report here anytime you want to leave Koala. We must stamp this book indicating the time of your departure and where you are going. You must check in again the moment you return."

"Sir, I have fifty Under Fives Clinics in the surrounding villages. Does that mean I need to check in and out all these times?" Sandy grimaced and shook her head.

"The government is tightening reigns on all foreigners. I am sorry you will have to suffer so many trips here to the police station, but it is the law." Colonel Renita heaved a sigh. "I know you have come to help our people. I have heard good things about you."

She reached out for the document. Had government officials established these regulations to trap her? Or did they want all foreigners to get discouraged and leave the country? Would the military and police officers make life miserable for her until she complied with their demands? But Colonel Renita seemed almost kind, and she nicknamed him, 'Colonel Helpful.'

Maybe God sent the colonel to assist her, but maybe not.

CHAPTER TWENTY-FIVE

Sandy stopped at the base of the muddy mountain and surveyed the slippery trail to Odoo. Her motorcycle would stall in the mud, and she'd never be able to drive to the village on top of the hill. So she parked her bike at the bottom of the peak and collected her bags and basket. After putting Blessing in the carrier on her back, she began the ten-mile hike up the steep mount.

"Blessing, I'm glad I kept in shape all these years. I shouldn't be out of breath by the time we reach the top."

After trekking two miles, Blessing cried for food. Sandy stopped and sat on a giant tree root to prepare the corn cereal for her baby. Sandy slapped flies away from her child and dodged several swarms of buzzing mosquitoes.

She protected Blessing. "I love you dearly. Right now I wish I had someone to take care of me in the middle of the jungle."

The sweet scent of orange blossoms revived her and she forgot about the insects. Surveying the lush hills, she let the clean, crisp air strengthen her. She turned her face into the breeze and caught its coolness.

Lord, thank you for taking care of us.

She loved and adored her baby and couldn't imagine life without Blessing. Unless God solved the visa problem and stopped the military officers from stalking her, Sandy might not be able to stay in the country much longer.

After Blessing ate, Sandy started hiking again. The sun rose halfway overhead indicating ten in the morning. She stumbled into the village and collapsed on the nearest bench.

The villagers gawked at her, but the pastor asked, "Where is your motorcycle?"

"It is at the bottom of the hill."

"Did you walk all the way to our village on foot, carrying that baby and all these loads?"

"Yes."

"My deacon and I will bring your motorcycle after you have finished."

Later in the afternoon, the men rode double on the pastor's motorcycle to her bike. They brought her motorbike back to the village. Their kindness warmed her heart.

By the end of the day, the hot sun dried up the road, so she wouldn't sink in the thick mud. Sandy, with Blessing on her back, hopped on her rescued motorcycle and headed home.

She stopped at the police station in Koala.

Lieutenant Courteous greeted her. "Good evening. Colonel Renita has traveled. So I will take care of your problem."

"I've came to report back from Odoo. I need permission to travel to Jaretti to teach at a health conference for a week."

"Sit in that chair."

She sat for an hour. "Excuse me, sir, but I need to go home. My baby is hungry."

"Be patient. I will take care of your card."

An hour later, Lieutenant Scarface entered the office and scowled at Sandy. "You are under investigation. Come with me."

She had no idea where he wanted her to go and didn't want to leave with him, but refusing him might make the situation worse. She picked up Blessing and put the baby on her shoulder.

Lord, go with me.

As she followed Lieutenant Scarface outside to the back of the building, she searched the yard, but no one was there. Her flesh crawled and knees weakened.

Lieutenant Scarface turned and faced her. "I do not want to make life difficult for you. Give me three thousand naros, and I will never bother you again."

What a relief. He only wanted money. She had thought he might beat her or rape her. Still her chest constricted and throat froze. Today it would be three thousand. Next week it would be another three thousand, and the following week it would be more. When would it all end? "I'm a Christian and cannot sin before my God."

160

"Do you want trouble?"

"No sir, I don't want trouble."

He raised his hand as if to strike her, but a loud voice stopped him.

"What are you doing?" Colonel Helpful walked up to them.

Lieutenant Scarface dropped his hand and stepped away from Sandy. "There was a biting ant on this lady's face. So I removed it."

Colonel Helpful glared. "Lieutenant Coutene claims you called this lady outside. What do you want with her?"

"I wanted to speak a word alone with her."

Colonel Helpful glared at Sandy. "Miss Calbrin, what did this officer say?"

Was Colonel Helpful a good guy or a bad guy? It didn't matter. Either way, it would be dangerous speaking against a government official.

Lord please help.

She clamped her jaws shut and followed Colonel Helpful into the police station.

He frowned. "Why are you here, Miss Calbrin?"

Sandy's heart beat faster. Did the colonel think she seduced his officers out back behind the building? Surely, he wouldn't think that about her, but if he did, she was in more trouble.

She grimaced. "I need my alien's identification card stamped with permission to travel. I gave it to the other officer."

"What have you been doing since you arrived?"

"I was sitting here in this chair until the officer called me out back."

"Why?"

Her throat tightened. Tears blurred her vision. She choked up and was unable to speak. Colonel Helpful shrugged and sat down behind the desk. "Where are you traveling tomorrow?"

She lifted her head. "Jaretti for a health seminar."

He stamped her alien's book and handed it to her. "I wish you a safe and pleasant journey, Miss Calbrin."

Her limbs shook so much, she wasn't sure she'd get home.

161

Lord God, please stop these immigration officers from hounding me.

***

At the conclusion of the health seminar in Jaretti, Sandy put Blessing in her cloth carrier. Lifting her right arm, she slid the baby with Blessing's face toward Sandy's back. She tied the infant to her before hiking down the dirt trail to the major taxi station. No one appeared on the road in the early morning hours, and no one was in the station except one teenager.

"Excuse me, are there any taxis traveling to Koala today?"

The young boy who appeared about fifteen and wore dirty farm clothes looked Sandy over from head to toe. "A taxi will not leave for two days from this station, but I can help you."

He snatched Sandy's bag from her hand.

"Wait. Stop. How can you help me?"

He set the bag on his head. "I will take you to a good taxi station. Follow me."

They made a right turn and trekked down the main road. Sandy pinched her nose and opened her mouth. Urine and excreta stench watered her eyes. Garbage heaps and burning piles of refuge covered the fields and lined the street. Slimy, black liquid dribbled down the mounds of trash onto Sandy's feet and legs as she hiked past the dumps. Cars splashed putrid slime on her.

The teenager turned and smiled at her. "Do you know American girl I can marry? Would you marry me?"

Was it a genuine proposal? She put her hand to her forehead and furrowed her brows. Turning to the boy, she studied his somber expression. He was too young and couldn't be serious. As cars drove by, horns honked, and traders screamed their wares, but she kept silent.

"Will you marry me?"

Sandy found her voice. "Why do you want to marry an American girl?"

"So I can live in America and be rich like all of you."

She froze. Did they think all Americans were wealthy or just her? Shame pressed hard in her chest. She'd worked hard since college and saved her money. Maybe it was time to do something about the sick, suffering, and impoverished people, but where could she begin when it seemed everyone needed help.

Sandy shrugged. "Not everyone in America is rich."

"That is what you say, but we believe all of you are wealthy."

Several men, dressed in flowing robes, skullcaps, and flip-flops walked past them. A barefoot man, wearing blue and white striped, flannel pajamas, darted between them and shoved her toward a heap of garbage. She stepped in it. Sewage and refuse tainted the air. She coughed and gagged but stepped back from the pile of trash.

Sandy pasted a sober expression on her face. "Right now, I'd like to be married to God."

"You took this poor cursed African baby. Are you like one of the Catholic nuns?" The young boy scowled. "I can understand and accept if you are married to God now, but what about later? Would you leave God to marry me?"

"Aren't young people required to marry someone from their own tribe?"

He nodded. "Many of our parents want us to marry someone from our own village."

"My parents want me to marry someone from my home town."

"I understand. That is the cultural way. We must respect our parents."

After a mile-long walk they reached an obscure taxi station. She marched to the gate guard. "Where are the taxis?"

"There are no transports this morning. If you wait, some of the privately owned vehicles will arrive this afternoon."

"Will any of them be traveling to Koala?"

"Yes, one will come in the afternoon."

She didn't look forward to the long wait in a deserted taxi station, but there were no other options. She set her backpack on the ground and untied Blessing.

163

The young teenager maintained a grip on her sack. "You are a rich, white lady. Pay me for carrying your bag."

She dug into her backpack and retrieved an African naro bill worth seven dollars, but she kept searching for a smaller one. The teenager snatched the money out of her fingers and ran down the road.

Scowling at his back, she shook her head. She found a large, flat rock under a tree, adjusted the baby in the crook of her arm, and tucked her skirt in tight all around her before sitting down.

A little girl, carrying a tray of bananas on her head, approached Sandy. The child sold five bananas for fifteen naros. Sandy handed the fruit seller some coins and invited the small girl to sit down and chat with her. The child pointed to the bananas, shrugged her shoulders, and walked away.

Passengers began to arrive at the station. A young woman, dressed in an expensive satin brocade skirt and blouse with matching head tie, joined Sandy on her rock.

"You are Mommy Blessing, aren't you?"

Everyone who had a television in his home in Norgia must know her. She smiled. "Yes."

"I saw the program four times and loved you for taking this baby. Have any bad things happened to you since you took this child into your home?"

Pants were discovered in her closet. She was accused of prostitution and having an illegitimate baby. The mamba attacked. There was a new immigration law forcing her to report to the police station. Officials stalked and harassed her, and apparently she was under investigation.

"No, nothing bad has happened that's related to my baby."

"I am talking about disease." The woman shook her head. "Have you had any sicknesses since you took this baby?"

"No."

"That's strange, don't you think?"

"It's not strange. I'm a Christian and believe Jesus protects me."

"I'm a Christian too, but evil spirits trouble me at night."

"Have you prayed to Jesus and asked for His protection?"

164

"No, I asked the Virgin Mary to protect me."

"Next time after you ask the Virgin Mary, ask Jesus to protect you."

"I will try it."

The sun had moved directly overhead indicating it was noon. She turned to the young lady. "Are you traveling to Koala?"

"I'm taking the taxi to Koala, but I am getting out before Koala. My name is Beatrice. Can I hold the baby for a while?"

"Yes, you may, but aren't you afraid of her?"

"No." Beatrice reached out for the baby. "You, an important and smart white lady, took this baby into your home and nothing bad happened to you. It proves you have a greater power to neutralize the curse of the baby."

Sandy handed Blessing to the young lady. "Jesus Christ, the Son of God, is the power in me."

"Yes, I believe that." Beatrice put Blessing on her lap and played with her.

"Do you know a good place to urinate?" Sandy looked around the taxi station. "I don't see any pit latrines or bushes."

"Go down that alley past the Heinz tomato sign and turn right." Beatrice pointed. "Lots of people urinate there."

Should she leave Blessing with the young woman or take the baby with her? She had never left her baby with a total stranger. In the villages she only allowed the women recommended by the pastor's wife to carry Blessing. If Sandy left the baby with Beatrice, perhaps the girl might try to harm Blessing. Did Beatrice believe the child was cursed? Sandy shivered.

Two well-dressed women approached. One of them stared at Sandy. "You're Mommy Blessing."

"Yes."

"Can I hold baby Blessing?"

Sandy nodded at Beatrice who handed Blessing to the newcomer. The woman examined the baby's dress, pink booties, matching bonnet, and plastic bag pants. "Blessing, you are a beautiful baby. You have a clever mother, too."

"I need to urinate and do not want to trouble you with my baby." Sandy stretched her arms out to take Blessing from the woman.

The lady kept holding the baby. "The child is no trouble. We are taking a taxi to Koala where we will get a connecting vehicle to the border. We will watch your daughter for you."

Sandy didn't know them and shouldn't leave her baby with them, but she glanced at their baggage and spotted a Bible. In Africa, born-again believers always carried their Bibles. Sandy sensed she could trust the women. More passengers arrived in the taxi station and several pointed toward Sandy and Blessing. Sandy had peace about leaving her baby with the ladies.

She headed in the direction of the place that many people used as a latrine. No one was there. Walking gingerly around heaps of human wastes, she tiptoed through the rancid puddles of urine, and soiled papers. Holding her breath, she tried not to gag from the disgusting odor. The fumes brought tears to her eyes. She searched but there were no pit latrines, only isolated garbage heaps.

After Sandy finished, she walked carefully through the field of sewage back to the station. A chauffeur in a sedan with bald tires pulled up in front of the women. The driver leaned his head out the window. "I am traveling to Koala. Would you like to go now?"

Beatrice stood, "Yes, there are four of us."

The ladies and Blessing climbed into the taxi. During the trip, the women took turns feeding and holding Blessing.

When Sandy arrived home, she found Colonel Big sitting on a log near her front door.

He stood. "Good afternoon. I hope you and the baby are well."

"We are returning from Jaretti."

"I hope you had a pleasant journey." He wore an impassive expression. "You are being investigated and must report to the immigration headquarters in the national capital, Logatti to see Colonel Jio this week."

Sandy took a deep breath. It had to be another ruse to make her go to the headquarters. The officers in Hose had been terrifying enough. She didn't want to face more of them in Logatti. "Is it necessary?"

166

"Yes, it is." He smirked.

"I will make arrangements to travel there to see him."

He leered. "Maybe you would prefer to give me money, so I could take care of this problem for you."

"I don't have anything for you. I just returned from a long trip where I taught health lectures."

Colonel Big glared. "When will you pay me money for my trips to your house to carry out this government business on your behalf?"

His insolence shocked her. Sandy suppressed a gasp. How much bolder would he get? If the officers left her alone, they wouldn't need any money for transportation to come and trouble her.

"Let's walk together to the pastor's house. We can discuss this problem of your need for money."

"You are not taking me seriously. You will get yourself in grave trouble without my help. We military are in charge and have the power to send you out of this country or do whatever we want with you."

It felt like someone punched her, knocking the air out of her. "The only influence you have is the power that God Almighty allows you to have. I'm going to the pastor's house. Would you like to come?"

Colonel Big stomped off.

"Blessing, we won another round, but how much longer will I be able to hold off the military officers?"

And when will it all end?

CHAPTER TWENTY-SIX

A few days later, Sandy stuffed food, diapers, and clothes in a small cloth sack. She filled her backpack and hiked to the station, where she rented a seat in a taxi traveling to the national immigration headquarters in Logatti.

After six hours, the vehicle stopped at the main office. Sandy went to the receptionist's desk. "Good afternoon. I was told to report to Colonel Jio."

The woman stood. "Come with me." She accompanied Sandy down the hall and to an officer wearing a badge that read "Colonel Jio."

The tall, middle-aged official reached for her hand. "Miss Sandra Calbrin, you are as beautiful as your photos."

She tilted her head. What pictures had he seen of her?

"My subordinates informed me you were coming. As you know, you are being investigated. My men suspect you of carrying out illegal activities in our country. May I see your passport?"

Sandy pulled it out of her bag. "Here it is."

"Give the baby to my secretary and come into this office."

"I will not leave my daughter."

"As you wish." Colonel Jio pointed to a chair. "Sit here."

Sandy sat in the wooden chair and held Blessing on her lap.

When the baby cried, Sandy prepared porridge and held the cup to the child's lips. The ten military officers in the busy office stopped shuffling papers and stared at the tiny infant drinking from a cup.

A sergeant approached Sandy. "I have never seen a baby drinking from a cup. Your daughter giggles and sips as if she likes it."

"We are impressed by your devotion to one of our children." Colonel Jio moved closer to Sandy. "Your church president has been trying to get a working visa for you. After the political difficulties, your papers were sent to the wrong offices. We now have the documents but cannot renew your visa. Your papers are not in order, which is why you are under investigation."

Sandy drew her brows together. "I don't understand."

"Someone applied on 10/11/75. It means the form was submitted on November 10, 1975. However, look at the next line." Colonel Jio lowered the passport to her. "Do you see the 11/10/75? On October 11, 1975, it expired before it was issued which invalidates it."

Her gaze clouded as she studied the dates in the passport. "To me the dates indicate the original application was stamped October 11, 1975 and expired on November 10, 1975."

"I'd heard you Americans write the month before the day. In our country the day is always before the month."

"How did this happen?" Sandy bit her lip. "It must be a human error. It was issued to me by your embassy in Washington D.C."

"It is a mistake, but we never make mistakes. Someone, who may work in the embassy and prepared the initial transient visas, wrote the date in an inappropriate manner."

"Since it is in the past, and I now have a four-month preliminary visa for a permanent visa, doesn't that cancel the first one?"

"No, it does not." Colonel Jio stood and motioned for Sandy to step into the corridor.

Sandy set the baby's cup down, held Blessing in her arms, and left her bags to follow him into the hall.

Colonel Jio closed the door behind him and lowered his voice. "If you, Miss Calbrin will come home with me and spend time with me, I will straighten this problem out for you."

The blood pulsed in her ears. She lifted a clammy hand to rub her temple. Why couldn't the officers leave her alone? She took a deep breath to calm her shakes. She had traveled all the way to the capital city to ward off more threatening officers. Her trip had been for nothing. She wasted valuable time and resources to be harassed all over again. Her throat constricted, and she blinked away the tears.

Lord Jesus, please help me.

"Sir, I follow my Savior, Jesus Christ. I will not go to your home and spend time with you."

"I will impound your passport until you agree to satisfy me."

He couldn't do that, could he? Yes, the officers were in charge and could do whatever they wanted. Blessing had started crying because Sandy had stopped feeding her. Sandy's vision blurred with unshed tears.

"You cannot stay in Norgia with an impounded passport. If you do not cooperate, we will send you away."

Give up.

Sandy was tired of everything. Worn out from the long, uncomfortable trip and exhausted from the constant harassment, she admitted defeat. Fatigue and the stress of avoiding officers drained her. Staying strong and doing the right thing was too hard.

Her voice cracked. "Do what you will. My God will not leave me."

"We will escort you to the next plane leaving the country. You will be officially deported and never allowed to come back. We will not give you papers to take this baby with you."

She tried to serve God, but the government and its officers were against her. She only wanted to help. Sandy hung her head and fought the urge to scream.

Colonel Jio opened the door to the main office where the officers worked. He glared at Sandy. "Go back in my office."

She went inside and finished feeding Blessing. Sandy reached in her bag for a diaper to change her baby. After putting a clean one on Blessing, Sandy tickled her daughter. Blessing kicked her legs and pumped her arms.

The sergeant watched. "You act as if you love that black baby of yours."

"I do." Sandy smiled, but wiped a runaway tear off her cheek.

Sandy had the joy of the Lord in her, and Blessing fulfilled her. Vaccinating the children, treating the sick, and helping people to get well gave Sandy a deep satisfaction.

Picking up Blessing, she kissed her and then lifted her eyes, glancing around the room at the silent men. The officers had stopped what they were doing and were staring at her.

171

A military man with the rank of general on his shoulder stepped into the office. His eyes stopped at Sandy and lit up. "You're Mommy Blessing. I saw you on television. It's wonderful what you have done with this baby. How is she?"

"She's great." Sandy kissed Blessing again, and the child giggled.

The general looked around at the room full of officers. "What's going on here?"

Colonel Jio and a junior officer jabbered in a local language before handing Sandy's passport to the general. He flipped through the pages and examined the document. "This temporary visa application is not in order. Have you seen the dates?"

Sandy's voice wobbled. "Yes, sir."

"I am sorry to make your time here end sour."

"This is not sour. I am a child of God and do not believe my Heavenly Father would give me something bitter." She hadn't spoken the words, but a voice not quite hers had declared them.

"Here's your passport." The general nodded. "As the officer in charge, I have the authority not to impound your passport and to return it to you, but please have your church president correct the problem right away."

Through wet eyes Sandy beamed. "Thank you, sir."

As she exited the national immigration office, she turned right to walk to the road and hail a taxi. A weight had been lifted from her shoulders. *Thank you, Lord.* She reached into her bag for a tissue to dry her eyes. Her problems weren't over, yet. She had to get her visa dates straightened out. Was it even possible? Thank God she hadn't been carried off to spend the weekend with that awful man.

The government had a valid reason for the investigation. She would travel straight to Hose to speak with Mr. Jubilee.

She walked past a woman frying fish bodies. Sandy stopped and turned around. "Where are the fish heads and tails?"

"We send them to the interior where there is no refrigeration. Here in the city there is electricity and refrigerators for us to store the fish bodies."

It made no sense. All parts of a fish could be dried and sent inland. She glared at the overweight woman with a glowing complexion, wearing gold jewelry and expensive tailor-made clothes. Wealthy, city people must hoard the fish bodies.

A taxi stopped, and Sandy slid inside of it. She closed her eyes and saw images of machine guns and military interrogations. Officers' threats raced through her tormented mind. She couldn't stay in the country with an invalid visa in her passport. If Mr. Jubilee couldn't straighten out the problem she'd have to leave.

What would happen to Blessing?

CHAPTER TWENTY-SEVEN

Sandy climbed into a van traveling to Hose. It was after office hours when the vehicle arrived in front of the church headquarters.

With Blessing in her arms, she climbed out of the vehicle. Seeing a light in Mr. Jubilee's window, she knocked.

He opened the door. "Come in. How are you and Blessing?"

"We're fine. Thank you." Sandy pulled her passport out of her backpack.

"Please sit down." Mr. Jubilee sat in the chair facing Sandy.

"Several military officers threatened to impound my passport and deport me because of the wrong dates stamped in it." Sandy flipped through the small book and opened the page to them. "Right here."

Mr. Jubilee stared at the figures and shook his head. "Did you know in our country the day is written before the month?"

"I didn't know it until I went to the capital this morning. The military officers pointed it out to me."

"This is not serious. Anyone could see it is a human error."

"The military officers scared me."

"It sounds as if they are always frightening you, but they like to intimidate people."

"These are more than just shock tactics. They want me to spend the weekend with them, which I keep refusing."

"They would never suggest something so evil to you. Perhaps you misunderstood them. They could get in lots of trouble if they implied you should do something like that."

"I'm telling the truth." Sandy stared at his doubtful expression, willing him to believe her.

Sighing loudly, he let the air out of his lungs. "We must be careful. Talking against military officers, police, and government policies can cause lots of problems. You must never say anything unfavorable about them, even if it is the truth. You could be thrown in prison for speaking negatively about the government or tossed out of the country and never allowed to work in Africa."

"Sir, I'm trying to be careful, but they sneak up and appear without warning."

"It is their job to creep up behind people to catch the evildoers. I am sure you are being as cautious as you can." Mr. Jubilee took a deep breath before speaking. "Between us, I overheard talk of another military coup. Perhaps that is the reason the military seem to be tightening control. You must never repeat this."

"No, I will not speak of it to anyone."

"Would you like me to transfer you back to Hose for a few weeks? If we watch over you here at the church headquarters, perhaps, that would discourage the officers from pursuing you."

"No, thank you. I've not finished vaccinating all the children yet. Besides, there are many sick people in Koala and the surrounding villages. God wants me to stay there. How can we reach our goal of a hundred Under Fives Clinics in that region if I move back to Hose?"

"Can you get a young lady to stay with you as a live-in chaperone?"

"The young ladies who would be suitable have returned to school. The girls remaining in the village are too young. I'd be worried a military officer would threaten them. Besides, none of the little girls in Koala speak English, and I haven't learned enough of the language to communicate directly."

"How can I help? The military officers are powerful. It is their word against anyone else's word, including mine or that of the church president."

"The Lord is on my side, and He keeps sending guardian angels. Can you take care of this passport problem?"

"Leave it with me. I'll get it straightened out, but it will take some time."

Sandy found a taxi returning to Koala that evening before dark. She stopped at the military police headquarters to have her alien's book stamped. The station stayed open twenty-four hours a day, which must be why the extra soldiers from Hose had been transferred there. Maybe it had nothing to do with her, or everything to do with her.

Lieutenant Scarface sat in the office. "Come in and have a seat."

"Thank you." Sandy handed him the alien's book.

The officer shoved the book to the corner of his desk. "Give me money for stamping your book."

Sandy shook her head.

"Sit there and think about it."

No one entered the office during the entire time she sat in the chair. He opened the door to let the fading light in. When it became dark, he lit several bush lanterns.

Please Lord, let him stamp my book.

She should get up and walk out of the office. But his hard, cold eyes riveted her to the chair. He would harm her if she moved.

A few minutes later Colonel Helpful came into the office. He cocked an eyebrow at her. "What are you doing here?"

"I need a stamp in my alien's book."

Colonel Helpful took her book, flipped through the pages, studied the last entry, stamped the page, signed it, and handed it back to her.

"Miss Calbrin, I apologize for your inconvenience of having to report here for this legal process."

"Sir, I appreciate your kindness and help."

"You are not doing anything illegal." The colonel turned and glared at Lieutenant Scarface. "I will talk to my superiors about getting you exempt from this procedure. I know it is a hardship for you."

But poor Colonel Helpful was outnumbered by Lieutenant Courteous, Lieutenant Scarface, and Colonel Big. Did Colonel Helpful have any power to assist her?

***

Early the following morning, Sandy packed her bags. She picked up Blessing for the trip to Jouw and hired a taxi.

A hundred miles later, Sandy with Blessing in her arms climbed out of the vehicle at the designated junction. She waited at the fork in the road for the pastor.

177

When he arrived, she slipped the baby into the cloth carrier and fastened it onto her back. Her skirt lifted six inches.

The pastor turned his head away from her. "Madam, your tie is showing."

Eve had warned Sandy there was no '*th*' sound in the local languages. Exposing the tongue was a taboo. Pulling the tongue back from the bottom of the upper teeth to pronounce the sound was repulsive in the culture. So tie meant thigh.

The pastor stepped away as Sandy lowered her skirt to cover her legs before mounting the motorcycle. He drove at high-speed over the rough, dirt road as if she were a piece of steel welded to the bike. Holding onto the male driver was banned, so she had learned over the months to use her thighs to grip the seat.

"Today I will drive slowly because of the baby."

His slow equaled Sandy's high-speed. Sandy bounced up and down on the end of the motorcycle with Blessing tied to her back. She almost tumbled off the bike three times. As it zoomed down the road, daggers stabbed her back and shoulders over and over. When the pastor stopped, she stepped off the motorcycle and untied Blessing from her back.

The pastor glanced at Sandy. "Madam, your tie is showing again."

She tugged her skirt lower. "Thank you for telling me, so I can keep myself presentable."

In the Under Fives Clinic she vaccinated ninety-five babies. After Blessing had fallen asleep the pastor's wife put the baby on a bed in her house.

Sandy checked on Blessing at one o'clock in the afternoon, since it was the baby's time to eat. Knowing everyone would want to play with Blessing, Sandy let her baby sleep. Later when Sandy entered the room her heart banged and dropped in her chest. Blessing lay in the middle of the bed. Four chickens hopped up and down around her. Three goats chewed on Blessing's feet or near her feet. Sandy couldn't tell which.

She rushed to her baby and picked her up. Her precious child didn't move. *Please let her not be hurt, Lord.* With shaking hands she crushed her baby to her chest. The child's thumping heart comforted Sandy. Tears ran down Sandy's cheeks, and she wiped them away. She looked at Blessing who opened her eyes and smiled.

Thank you, Lord.

Babies were safer from wild animals and falls if they were tied to their mothers' backs. Local people called Sandy the perfect mother, but mothers could make mistakes like everyone else.

CHAPTER TWENTY-EIGHT

Sandy carried Blessing to the hospital for another set of immunizations. The long line of waiting mothers went up and down the hall several times. There were four times more women than the previous month.

The woman behind Sandy tapped her on the shoulder. "You're Mommy Blessing. Is this Baby Blessing?"

"Yes."

"I saw you on television five different times. Your baby isn't sucking her finger like other children. Did you give her a medicine to make her stop?"

"She has never sucked her finger."

"My baby sucks her thumb all the time. I can't get her to stop."

"Have you tried a speck of red pepper? Taste it first to make sure it's not too hot for the baby."

A second woman approached Sandy. "Explain how to prepare the porridge that Blessing drinks? It must be special to keep her healthy and fat."

"Soak beans overnight, skin them, cook them, and mash them. Add one large spoon of powdered milk and hot water until it is a thick drink and then add a spoon of peanut butter or red palm oil."

A third woman headed toward Sandy. "You know how to take care of a black baby. We are following your advice and have come to vaccinate our children. My child is eight months. How can I get her to sleep through the night?"

"Mix a large spoon of oil in her night feeding. It will keep the food in her stomach longer and help her stay satisfied to sleep."

Another lady turned to Sandy. "What about the personal sicknesses?"

"I understand, like diseases in private parts."

"Not that. A personal sickness is one that belongs to the person. It is a sickness the person is supposed to have, for him personally."

181

"I don't believe anyone is supposed to have a sickness. Do you believe that?"

"Yes, I do." The lady shrugged. "My baby has been lean ever since he was born. It is his personal sickness."

"Do you breastfeed?"

"Yes."

"Do you give anything else to the baby?"

"I give river water."

"Why?"

"It is our culture. Everyone drinks river water in our village."

"If you want the baby to gain weight, you must not give river water. Give only breast milk. Your baby appears to be only two months old. All he needs is breast milk."

"I will try it." The mother nodded. "My other children have fevers all the time. What causes them?"

"Mosquitoes do. You can prevent malarial fevers."

"Wouldn't we have to kill every mosquito to stop it, which would be impossible?"

"Couldn't you reduce the number of mosquitoes by getting rid of the stagnant water, tall grasses, and high crops where they breed? Sleep under a net and put screens on the windows."

"We could cut our grass. We don't have mosquito nets and screens because they cost money."

Sandy whispered in Blessing's ear. "You did it. You persuaded mothers to take better care of their children. You're the most effective health teacher these people have ever seen. You are a special blessing."

What would she do if Blessing's father took her away? She had a premonition the man would return to cause trouble. Sandy shuddered.

***

A week later, Sandy found Blessing's father waiting for her when she arrived home. Taking a deep breath, she invited him inside her house.

He sat down. "Mommy Blessing, I have come for my daughter."

182

Sandy's heart pounded like beating drums calling the people to war. She put her hand on her chest hoping the man wouldn't hear the loud thumps.

Please help me, Lord.

The man snapped, "You have taken my daughter. Either give her to me or give me money for her."

"Sir, are you suggesting I buy your daughter?" Her voice sounded weak. "Selling children is illegal."

"Just give me money, and you can keep her longer."

Her heart landed with a thud in her lower stomach. She would hand Blessing over to him if she thought he loved her. If he wanted his baby, he should take her without demands for money.

The Lord's quiet voice whispered. **Give him Blessing.**

No, Lord, I can't.

Surrender your baby.

She squeezed her eyes closed for several seconds. *Give me strength, Lord.* Submitting to God's will was best. With trembling hands she held Blessing out to her father.

The man took his daughter, but he shook his head. "I don't want this baby. I want money."

Sandy's mouth went dry as she managed to whisper, "She is your daughter. You should take her."

"Give me money, and you can keep her."

"It's illegal to give money for children. I won't do it."

He handed Blessing back to Sandy. "I will come back with my uncle. Goodbye." He went outside and stormed down the trail.

Sandy collapsed in a chair. Tears raced down her cheeks. The father had the legal right to take his daughter but seemed only interested in money.

After she had composed herself, Sandy hiked to the military police station to stamp her alien's book. She seemed to spend half her life there, waiting. She entered the small, official building. The cracked cement-plastered walls indicated the building had been there for a long time. Even the ancient tin roof showed age.

"I came for you to stamp my alien's book."

Lieutenant Courteous glared. "Come back next week."

"I can't. I need to travel to Hose to collect more vaccinations for the Under Fives Clinics."

"I'll stamp the book later." He pointed. "Sit there while I think about it."

Sandy was tired of delays and excuses. She blinked to ward off the threatening tears. Like a little child being punished, she sat in the corner the rest of the day. She couldn't think of one positive thing about the long wait. What good could come from being forced to sit from morning to evening?

Love your enemies. Pray for those who persecute you.

She started praying for the salvation of those who mistreated her.

When Colonel Helpful arrived, he spoke sharply to Lieutenant Courteous. "What is she doing here?"

"She is waiting for me to stamp her book."

Colonel Renita snapped, "Stamp it for her. Don't you realize she is Mommy Blessing? Maybe she will go on television again. We want her to speak well of us. Don't make her wait all day."

Lieutenant Courteous opened the drawer and pulled out the inkpad. After he stamped the book, he signed it. With a slight bow, he handed it to Sandy.

Round two for Sandy. *Thank you, Lord, that Colonel Helpful came to my aid.*

She visualized more days of waiting in the police station, or worse. Scarface would catch her one day and haul her off. She'd seen the evil in his cold, black eyes.

***

Sandy traveled on her motorcycle to Ogsohogo, a village located on the main road. After setting up the Under Fives Clinic, she called the first patient.

A mother came forward and pushed her two-year-old toward Sandy, who twisted her head away and held her breath from the stench. The child smelled like rancid garbage and a sewer.

For several minutes Sandy breathed in and out through her mouth. Looking the child over from head to toe, she noticed globs of what appeared to be excreta dangled from clumps of his hair. Dirt, sticks, and straw stuck out from his head. Sandy extended her hand toward the child's head.

"Stop!" The pastor had raised his hand and his voice. "Don't touch the baby's head."

"What is wrong? I wanted to feel his skin to check for a fever."

"You can touch the baby's face but not the top of his head. He is a *Faafo* child."

"What does it mean?"

"He was born in a certain position, in a special manner, and at a unique time. From the moment of his birth no one is allowed to touch his head."

"Are you saying no one has washed this child's head since he was born?"

The pastor shrugged. "No one is allowed to do that."

"That is unhygienic, and he can get many sicknesses."

The mother pulled the child closer to her. "He is strong and special."

"Yes, I agree that he is a beautiful little boy. Why did you bring him?"

The mother lifted her little boy's shirt and placed the back of her right hand on his chest. "He has a hot body."

Sandy stroked the child's chest. Exquisite huge eyes, the whites of which were pure and clear stared at her. A well-shaped nose, straight-white baby teeth, and a big grin met her as she assessed the child.

"Pastor, what does *Faafo* mean?"

"True Christians do not believe it. In spirit worship, the family thinks an evil being controls this child. If anyone lays a hand on the boy's head he is defying the spirit. The wicked demons will get angry."

"What do they think will happen?"

"A long time ago when a child was born in the same manner as this one, the parents washed his head. Wicked demons called the child back to the spirit world because the parents did not respect the leader of the dark world. That was the end of the child."

"Thank you for telling me." Sandy counted out pills for malarial fever, which she handed to the mother.

A police car stopped in front of the patients. Lieutenant Scarface climbed out. He motioned with his hand for Sandy to leave the people and approach him. She didn't want to cause a scene, so she went to him. He wouldn't harm or threaten her in front of all the patients.

He lowered his voice. "Good morning, Miss Calbrin. Have you decided to give me money so I can help you?"

"Sir, I can't do that."

"I can make life difficult for you."

"But my God can make life good for me."

The words must have come from the Lord for she could never have formulated a snappy comeback like that.

"You will regret your decision." Lieutenant Scarface glowered and lifted his hand as if he would slap her but dropped it. He stepped back into the car and drove away.

Sandy returned to her patients.

Her translator handed her the patient treatment cards. "That immigration officer appears to be quite interested in you. Have you noticed?"

"Yes, I have." Sandy clenched her jaw. "I try to avoid him."

"It is wise to stay away from the police and military. Sometimes we do not know what side they are on until trouble erupts."

The pastor of a neighboring village arrived. "When you are finished treating these people, we need you to come to our community and treat the sick. It is eight miles on a rough road."

Sandy rolled her eyes. When an African referred to a road as rough, it was not passable by any vehicle. She nodded.

She drove slowly on the treacherous path for over an hour. She maneuvered her bike over rocks and potholes, but it wasn't a proper road.

After treating fifty patients, she packed her supplies. "I don't know if I can come back. Driving the motorbike on this rough road was nearly impossible. The loose rocks and potholes almost threw me several times from the bike."

"Could you please try? We need your help."

"With God's help, I'll try."

As she pulled away from the village, it was dark. The first part of the trail was flat and smooth. When she reached the long section of ruts, she veered around to the right where the furrows weren't as deep.

She hesitated at the fork in the trail before turning to the left. Deeper holes and sharper bends emerged at every twist and turn. She should have stayed in the village and slept in one of the mud houses the people offered her, but she wanted a cup of tea and to sleep in her own bed. She had purchased a new foam cushion and looked forward to it.

The farthest village that day had been only twenty miles from her home. According to the odometer, she'd already traveled thirty miles since leaving and had no idea where she was. The lights of her motorcycle dimmed which meant weak bulbs or a low battery. It was harder to see, but the trail couldn't get any worse.

Her heart pounded. It looked like she had driven into a jungle. Her hands tightened on the handlebars. She was lost, miles from civilization, and in the pitch-dark. Without landmarks or signs she had no way of finding her way.

Something moved in the tall grasses on the right side of the road. She shivered. A mountain lion could eat her and her baby. Or she and Blessing would be gored to death by a wild boar. Maybe they'd be torn apart by a leopard who stalked sub-Saharan Africa.

The battery light grew weaker making it even harder to see. Up ahead a massive army of soldier ants marched across the trail. If she stopped to catch her breath or find another direction, the ants would eat her alive. Up and down, on and over the hills she rode. If she ran out of gas she'd be forced to halt. Without fuel, she'd never get away from the dangers in the African bush.

Lord, please help.

Her eyes stared straight ahead into the darkness as she willed herself to find the path home. She gripped the handlebars tighter. Blisters erupted on her sweaty palms. As she drove on and on, her limbs grew stiffer and tenser. Her motorcycle might soar off the rocky precipice. Blessing and she would fall to their deaths.

Dying wouldn't be bad. Her spirit would go on living with the Lord in Heaven. Maybe God would deliver her because sick people still needed treatment.

Lord, please help me get home.

She slowed the bike, peered ahead into the darkness, and recognized a bend in the road. She'd been driving in circles on a little trail around and around the mountain peak.

Her gas tank was on empty.

CHAPTER TWENTY-NINE

Sandy stopped the bike for a moment to study the trail on the left. It led to the main road. She was thirty miles from home.

She arrived at midnight, and her gas tank was below the empty mark. With Blessing in her arms she stumbled into her home.

Exhaustion kept her in bed the next morning a little longer than usual, but she forced herself to get up. Her movements slowed as she dressed. Muscles she didn't know she had throbbed. The blisters on her hands had ripped open.

Before she could check in at the police station, she had to buy gasoline. A hundred yards before the gas pump, her motorcycle died, so she started pushing it.

Colonel Helpful was getting his own gas tank filled. He waved to Sandy, left his motorbike, and ran to her. "Let me help."

"Thank you. I'm out of fuel."

He grabbed the handlebars and shoved her motorcycle up to the pump. "I didn't think you Americans ever ran out of gas. A white man told me that when his tank was half-full, he always filled it up."

"That's smart to do." She wiped the sweat from her forehead. "There's only one station in Koala. Whenever my gas tank is at the halfway point, the station is always closed."

"Yes, it closes when they have no fuel."

"I'm on my way to the police station to check in. I was too exhausted last night to stop, and I'm sorry. I should have, but sometimes I must wait a long time before the officers stamp my book."

She clamped her jaws together, regretting that she'd spoken before thinking. Had she insulted the military officer? If she had, she was in big trouble. She should never have mentioned the officers taking a long time, but it was too late. Her heart pounded as she glanced at Colonel Helpful's troubled expression.

"Do you have your alien's book with you?" He asked. "Give it to me."

With a shaking hand, she reached for the book in her backpack. She could scarcely breathe as she handed it to him. He would probably tear it into a million pieces and send an armed guard to escort her out of the country.

He opened the book, scribbled his initials and the date on the bottom of the page, and handed it back to her. "We will keep this just between us."

Keep what between them? He couldn't be talking about the identification card. She shouldn't keep a secret with a colonel. What if he was doing something illegal and had implicated her?

She whispered, "I don't understand."

"You are exhausted, and your hands are bandaged. I wrote my signature, which is the same as if I'd stamped it. The next time you see me in the station, I will stamp over it. It will be fine."

Sandy didn't think it would be fine. Were they making up the rules as they went along? Maybe if she mentioned it, she would get him in trouble. So she remained silent. She pasted a smile on her face and took her book. "Thank you, I appreciate your kindness."

"Don't mention this to anyone."

Her blood pulsed in her temples. Colonel Helpful was always kind and stamped her book immediately. If he were on duty all the time, she wouldn't have any problems.

Would his signature in her book now without the stamp cause more problems?

***

The following morning, she met Colonel Helpful, Scarface, and Courteous inside the police station. She smiled and greeted them before handing her book to Colonel Helpful. He took it, opened the desk drawer, and stamped the book on top of his notation of the previous day. He stamped it again giving her permission to travel that day.

"Thank you." She slid the book in her backpack. That was easy. Colonel Helpful seemed to be one of the good guys.

She drove to the village. After unpacking her basket of medicines, she set up her clinic and began vaccinating all the children.

The first woman brought her baby. "My child's urine is yellow."

Sandy bit her tongue and choked on a giggle. "What color is it normally?"

"It is like water. It has been yellow for a week, and my child has a hot body."

"It's possible she has an infection. I'll give you antibiotics."

"Thank you. Why does Blessing wear a napkin?"

"I don't like her to urinate on people."

"Why can't you teach your baby to urinate properly?"

Cocking an eye, Sandy dropped her pen. Was there an improper and proper way for a baby to urinate? For a third world country, there seemed to be a lot of normal and abnormal behaviors, improper and proper ways, and rules for good and evil.

The woman lifted her hand. "When a baby makes a certain movement on the mother's back she takes him off. She props him between her spread ankles and legs on the ground, and holds him in a sitting position so he can urinate. Even a two-month-old baby can do this. Your baby is intelligent, but she is not smart enough to urinate properly."

Sandy suppressed a giggle. "I've seen local mothers train babies like this, but I'm not an African woman, and I don't know how to do it."

"You have an African baby, so you should be an African mother."

"I'll never be an African mother."

After the clinic, the church deacon accompanied Sandy to the junction. Sandy held Blessing as she stood by the side of the road to wait for a taxi. When a vehicle stopped the deacon opened the door. Two men jumped out, shoved Sandy into the sedan, and jumped in after her. She swiveled her head to the right and stared into the bloodshot eyes of the passenger. When the one next to her opened his mouth, she jerked her head away from the alcohol stench.

She had no sense of direction until the taxi turned toward her village, and then she relaxed a bit. Several miles later, the driver picked up more drunk men. She balanced on the front edge of the back seat between the intoxicated fellows. Two men had squeezed into each of the bucket seats in front.

The passenger to her right stared at her. "I'm coming home with you tonight. You are a nice woman. You are beautiful, and I love white ladies."

She breathed through her mouth to avoid his putrid breath and sour body odor. The road ahead of her lifted and fell. With her free hand she steadied herself on the edge of the seat. The taxi bounced down the bumpy road at eighty miles an hour. Holding onto the baby and keeping herself on the seat was a challenge.

When Blessing cried for food, Sandy pulled out the flask to pour hot water into the pureed corn cereal, milk powder, and bean paste. Sandy always handed Blessing to a female passenger to hold while she mixed the drink, but she didn't want to give Blessing to any of the drunken men.

The fellow on the left mumbled with slurred speech. "May I help you?"

Sandy handed him the container. "Hold the jar still, please. I don't want to burn you. I need to pour the hot water."

She held her breath as his fingers tightened around the cup. It would serve him right if she burned him, but she didn't want to cause pain. After adding the boiled water, she searched through the bag and found the spoon to stir the baby food. She poured it without spills into Blessing's cup. She held the goblet steady for her baby to drink. The infant sipped five ounces without spills.

Bam! An explosion jarred the vehicle. It swerved left and right down the road. Wham! Bump a bump a bump! She dropped Blessing's cup on the floor. A tire must have come off the rim. She grabbed the edge of the seat with one hand and gripped her baby tighter with the other one. The driver lost control of the vehicle, and it turned into some thick bushes in a field.

The taxi was only a mile from home. So she slid out of the car to walk the rest of the way. Then thunder crashed. She jumped, and Blessing cried. The rain fell and lightning flashed across the dark sky.

Shivers raced up and down Sandy's spine. She climbed back inside the car.

The man who had held the baby's cup left the taxi, weaving on unsteady legs back and forth down the middle of the road. Two men left and walked across the field and into a bar.

Sandy could stand outside in the storm or sit inside with the drunken men. She put her sleeping baby on the seat between her and the two remaining men.

One of them stammered, "I'm coming home with you tonight to get on with you."

She kept her mouth closed. Lightning bolts illuminated the black night. She slumped back in the seat.

Thirty minutes later, the rain stopped. The driver changed the tire. The only passengers left were Sandy and the man who wanted to come home with her. The chauffeur drove her to her house. The drunken fellow jumped out and grabbed her baskets.

Sandy reached out and snatched her belongings out of his hands. "Thank you."

The man slid back into the car with the grinning driver who shouted, "Good night, Mommy Blessing."

The driver must have known her and been watching out for her, but some days she wished she were invisible. Sandy smiled and waved. She had won another battle, but how many more were ahead of her?

***

Early the next morning, Sandy climbed into a taxi. The chauffeur turned to her. "Good morning, Mommy Blessing."

"Good morning."

He drove past the middle school that headed out of the village. Hundreds of children ran out of the classrooms and yelled, "Mommy Blessing. Mommy Blessing. Mommy Blessing." The youngsters lifted both arms to wave.

Sandy waved to the school children, feeling like a princess in a parade. Villagers, patients, chauffeurs, and other passengers addressed her as Mommy Blessing everywhere she went. Being called Mommy

193

Blessing reminded her of Mommy Santa Claus as if she were expected to shower gifts on everyone around her. The national fame she'd received as Mommy Blessing overwhelmed her for she was always on display.

The driver stopped the vehicle to collect another passenger and turned his head to Sandy. "Last night after I left you at your home, I took that last fellow to his house. I deposited the taxi at the station and went home. One of the local drivers and two men drove the vehicle after me. They were in a bad accident, and all three of them were killed."

Her heart dropped like a rock to the pit of her stomach.

"This is the accident." The chauffeur stopped next to the demolished vehicle.

She inhaled slowly to fill her lungs and clasped Blessing closer to her. She and Blessing might have been killed, too.

Lord thank you for saving us.

After vaccinating the children that day, Sandy returned home. When she was nearly to her house, she almost turned away.

A chief, wearing a red and gold hat, held a staff with strips of goat skin wound around it, which signaled he had come for official business. He was sitting beside Blessing's father and another older gentleman on a log near Sandy's front door.

"Good afternoon." The blood pounded in Sandy's ears. "Please come in."

"I've come to see my daughter." Blessing's father stood and went inside with the two men. "This is the chief of my village and the other man is my uncle."

She pointed to the chairs. "Please sit down." Then she handed the baby to her father.

"My daughter is beautiful. She looks so smart." The father gave the baby back to Sandy. "Mommy, I want you to keep my daughter, but give me money for her."

Her voice cracked. "Sir, it is illegal to sell a child."

"I am not selling my child. I want you to give me money so you can keep her."

194

Her breathing came out in ragged gasps. It sounded like selling a child to her, and she was already in enough trouble. She pressed her fingers over her mouth. Little by little she tried to catch her breath.

The chief scowled at her. "Mommy Blessing, everyone knows you are a good mother. You must keep this baby and raise her as your own daughter. It is only reasonable that you give the father money for his daughter. If you raise her, she will grow up and take care of you when you are old."

She rubbed her head as if to ward off a headache. "I understand your culture of caring for aged parents, but I could never deny a father his own daughter."

Sandy blinked again to suppress the rising flood of tears. A drop slid down her cheek, and she wiped it away. He could take Blessing home, proving he had the authority to do it.

The father said, "You can take better care of her than I can. Please keep her. I do not want this baby. We will go, but we will return after discussing this problem with all the village elders. Goodbye."

She collapsed on the chair and clutched her baby to her chest. Sandy wiped away the tears that slipped down her cheeks. The chiefs discussed serious problems with community elders and persuaded the village men to their thinking. The chief would be back with more men.

If only the father loved Blessing, but it seemed he only wanted money.

The Lord would never shake Blessing out of her hands.

CHAPTER THIRTY

The next morning when Phoebe arrived, Sandy was surprised to see her carrying a baby seat.

Sandy chuckled. "Where did you get that?"

"I found it in the trash a long time ago and saved it. We don't use things like this, but I thought you might."

"Thank you." Sandy went into her bedroom and returned with two lengths of rope, three plastic cords, and two belts from her dress. She wound the lines around the little chair to the back of her motorcycle behind the wooden box of medicines and tied them.

After fastening her bags, the basket, and her baby to the baby chair, she drove to Odoo. At the bottom of the massive hill, she parked the motorcycle. Should she attempt the slippery ride up the mountain? Yes, she could do it with God's help. Without Blessing's weight on her back, she had more control of the bike and also wasn't afraid of injuring her child.

She put the motorbike in low gear and took a deep breath as she slowly began the treacherous ascent. Halfway up the peak, the motorcycle slid into a deep, long groove. The bike headed toward the edge of a steep cliff. She lost control of the motorcycle, and it slid closer and closer to the precipitous crest. Sandy turned off the engine and braked. The jolt threw her off the seat. She landed on her back on the rocky hillside. Her head hit a rock. For several moments, she couldn't move. Then she slowly rolled onto her stomach and lifted to her hands and knees.

Her baby screamed over and over again. Where was Blessing? Sandy came to her senses and shrieked, "Blessing, Blessing!"

Every limb in Sandy's body shook, and her breathing grew ragged. The baby wasn't on Sandy's back. In her painful, disoriented state she couldn't remember where she'd put her precious child that morning. Her head pounded as if it might explode and she couldn't think clearly.

The trees and bushes moved around in circles. Her heart beat faster as she became dizzier.

With teary eyes she searched left and right. "Blessing, where are you?" If the baby had been tied to Sandy, the baby would have been dead when Sandy had landed on her back.

Her motorcycle was gone. Had the bike zoomed off the cliff with Blessing tied to it? Sandy's heart dropped to the pit of her stomach. She crawled to the ridge several yards in front of her. Spotting her motorcycle on the crest, she gasped. It was about to tip off the ledge and into the ravine.

Blessing shrieked. She was secured in the little chair which hung in midair on top of the precipitous edge.

Still on her knees, Sandy crawled closer. Blessing yelled louder and cried. Covering her face, Sandy sobbed. She hadn't the strength to pull the large motorcycle back onto solid ground as it kept shifting in midair. Her trembling limbs might knock the bike off the precipice. Tears raced down her cheeks.

Lord, please save Blessing.

On quivering legs she struggled to get up, but collapsed again in the stones and mud. Shooting pains held her to the ground.

Lord, please help.

She stared up the mountain but couldn't believe what she saw.

It was him, but why would her Lord send the devil to help her? She wept so hard, she couldn't breathe. Her limbs shook. Why was one of her tormenters there, when she'd prayed to God for help?

Colonel Big rode a motorcycle over the hill from the opposite direction and was coming closer to her. She was certain it was Colonel Tsaou.

He yelled, "Stay right there. I'm coming to help you."

She didn't want his help, but she had to save her daughter. What would he demand in exchange for his aid? She'd do anything if he'd only rescue her baby from plunging to her death. He parked his motorcycle in the tall grasses off the path and marched toward her. His size alone terrified her, but then he knelt down in the mud next to her. He reached for the teetering bike and gently pulled it little by little toward him onto solid ground. He raised the bike upright as if it weighed less than the baby. Blessing in her little seat kept screaming.

Sandy sniffed. "My baby is frightened."

Colonel Big asked in a tender voice, "Can you move?"

"I'm not sure." Her foot and arm felt like they were broken.

He reached out, took her hands, and pulled her to her feet. She took a few tentative steps toward the bike. "Let me untie my baby and hold her."

Colonel Big held the bike steady as Sandy unfastened Blessing and clutched the baby in her arms. Sandy sobbed with tears of relief streaming down her cheeks.

He pushed the motorcycle out of the deep mud and into a cluster of thick shrubs. After parking the bike, he turned to her. He extended his right hand, but she jumped away and shivered from his intense scrutiny.

His look changed to compassion. "Why back away from me? I wanted to see where the blood on your face is coming from. It looks like you hit your head. There's blood everywhere. Can you tell me where you are injured?"

Sandy stood still and took a deep breath with her baby still clutched to her chest. "Thank you for helping me, Colonel Tsaou."

He would expect payment. She was alone in a tropical forest with Colonel Big. What would he demand from her? She reached up with her free hand to wipe away sweat before it dripped into her eyes, but her fingers and palm were covered with blood. He pulled a handkerchief from his pocket. More blood dripped from her arms. He dabbed at the flow from her forearm. Her limbs stung as if a million knives stabbed her.

Colonel Big pointed to her blood-coated legs. "You are seriously injured." He looked her over from head to toe, but not lustfully as he had done on other occasions. "Where were you going?"

"I have patients in Odoo to treat. The people are waiting for me."

He handed her the handkerchief, but she shook her head. So he wiped down his dirty uniform. "I will push your motorcycle over the worst stretch of the road and come back to collect mine."

His kindness caused her to cry even harder. Sandy, still wearing her flip-flops, trudged next to him on the muddy trail. She couldn't suppress her tears as Blessing clung to her like a monkey sticking to its momma.

Sweat dripped from the colonel's face, and his military boots were filthy as he pushed the bike uphill over the rugged terrain. "I find myself quite fond of you. You are a special woman, not just beautiful on the outside but the inside, too. I could love you."

Her mouth fell open. *Love me?* No, he couldn't. All he wanted was to sleep with her or spend the weekend with her. The colonel didn't care for her.

She limped up the trail. Every limb and muscle in her body throbbed.

Twenty minutes later, Colonel Big and Sandy halted at a flat place on the path. He held the bike steady for Sandy as she tied Blessing into her little seat. Sandy remounted the motorcycle and looked in Colonel Big's eyes and saw compassion.

It so startled her that her voice wobbled. "Thank you. I'm grateful for your help."

By the time she'd reached the village, her hands, arms, and legs were completely covered in blood. A lady brought a chair for Sandy. Another village woman took Blessing. The third woman brought a bucket of water, washed Sandy's feet and handed her muddy shoes to another lady.

Daggers shot through Sandy's back as she washed and wrapped bandages around her arms and legs. She swallowed two aspirins, but wanted to take a hot bath, lie down, and rest.

Praying for strength, she collected the patient treatment cards to care for the sick.

A woman with a baby sat in the chair across from Sandy. "My daughter is seven months old, but she is weak."

With a deep sigh of pain, Sandy bent to examine the child. "She only weighs eleven pounds and is malnourished and anemic. What are you feeding her?"

"Corn gruel in a feeding bottle."

200

"Stop giving the bottle. Make the porridge thick and add a spoon of oil. Feed your child in a sitting position with a cup and spoon."

"I will try it. I would love to see my baby become fat and beautiful like Blessing."

After the sun set, the pastor brought a bush lantern. Sandy finished treating the patients and packed the supplies. Her shoulders slumped as she tied the basket and bags to the motorcycle. She stared down the dim path, shook her head, and let the tears flow. She didn't want to get on the motorcycle ever again. But the bike was her only means to go home. Grabbing the handlebars, she mounted the motorcycle.

Knives sliced her back again and again as she bounced up and down rolling down the hill over the rocks. With each jolt, switchblades pierced her arms, legs, and back. Her throbbing bones screamed with every sharp intake of breath. Tremors of pain ran up and down her spine as the motorcycle wavered on the mountainous trail.

Outside of Koala she turned onto the path leading to her home. She parked the bike at the front door. Her chest pounded as she unfastened the belts to Blessing's car seat. Sandy slid one foot in front of the other and carried her baby inside. She wanted to fall into bed but needed to prepare food, feed Blessing, and get her ready for bed. And she had to unpack the bags and baskets from the motorcycle and restock her supplies.

Give me strength, Lord.

After putting Blessing to bed, Sandy propelled one foot ahead of the other one and shuffled to the outside latrine. She went inside her home and washed away the blood. With shaking hands she replaced the dressings on her wounds.

As she stumbled into bed, the lingering one-hundred-and-twenty-degrees heated up the aluminum roof. Her tiny home felt like an oven.

Colonel Big would demand a big favor for his help. She shivered as she drifted off to sleep.

CHAPTER THIRTY-ONE

Sandy moaned in agony as she pushed herself to sit and shoved away from the bed. Her painful legs shook, but she took a tentative step. Knives shot through her back, arms, and legs.

After dressing and getting the baby fed and dressed, Sandy picked up Blessing and walked to the police station.

She stepped into the building. "Good morning, sir."

"Good morning, Miss Calbrin." Colonel Helpful drew his brows together. "Colonel Tsaou visited me last night. We are trying to seek special permission for you."

Why would Colonel Tsaou work with Colonel Renita to help her? Her gaze clouded. Either Colonel Renita was evil like Colonel Tsaou, or Colonel Tsaou had changed. Maybe the colonel was building up a pile of good deeds on her behalf so he could secure a giant favor from her one day.

With softened eyes Colonel Helpful peered straight into Sandy's face. "If you had sanction you would no longer need to report to us every time you go and come from a village." A shadow covered part of his mouth as it drew back a little at the corners. He raised his hand and pulled his military cap lower over his face as if to conceal his pleasure.

What did his hidden smile mean? Were they plotting something?

She flashed a beam of appreciation. "Thank you. I'm grateful and could visit more villages to treat many patients."

"You are helping our people. We do not want you to suffer. Colonel *Tsaou* said you had an accident yesterday. How are you feeling?"

Sandy lifted her bandaged forearms and looked down at her dressed knees. "I landed on a pile of sharp rocks and have cuts and bruises."

"You should take it easy for a few days."

"I would like to rest, but I have many more babies to vaccinate before another epidemic hits."

He handed her the stamped book. She left and walked to the taxi station to hire a vehicle. Thirty minutes later the driver let her out at the junction where she met the pastor of Dooma on his bike.

"The village is hard to find so I will carry you there on my motorcycle." He tied Sandy's basket and two large bags to his bike.

With Blessing in her arms she mounted behind him. He headed down the rocky path. Several miles later, the motorcycle bounced with a loud thud and stopped.

He turned the engine off. "I have a flat tire and will have to push the motorcycle to the village."

Sandy tied Blessing to her back. "How far is it?"

"Seven more miles."

Her foot throbbed, but she squared her shoulders and limped down the trail. After hiking a mile, they met a stranger coming toward them on a motorcycle.

The pastor shook hands with the young man. "This is the chief's son. He will carry you on his motorbike into the village."

There was no seat behind the driver, so Sandy did her best to balance on a three-inch wide metal bar. She had learned to use her thighs to hold on since custom forbid touching the driver. Searing pains shot through her aching back and legs as she used her muscles to grip the bar on which she sat.

As they reached the first cluster of mud homes, she yelled, "Please stop, I need to rest a minute." Numb from the bouncing motorcycle going over the rocks, she tumbled off the bike, lost her balance, and landed on the ground.

Several women bent toward her and grabbed her upper arms to lift her. They swatted the dirt off her dress and legs with their hands.

Sandy turned to the chief's son. "How much farther is the village?"

"Not far."

In Africa, "not far" was relevant and always farther than implied. She stretched her back to reduce the pain and nodded at the chief's son before sliding onto the metal bar behind him.

Jolts of electricity radiated down her back, buttocks, and legs as she maintained her balance on the steel bar. An iron rod, no matter how one sat on it, would never be comfortable. Heavy rains fell. Sandy was surprised the driver didn't stop. Every bone in her body throbbed. She wrapped Blessing in a blanket to protect her from the wind and cold and asked the driver, "Can you keep going in this storm?"

"We have to keep moving to reach shelter."

The rain soaked through the top blanket, but Blessing slept soundly inside, snug and dry. Rain drenched Sandy's hair and clothes. When the driver stopped, Sandy slid off the back of the motorcycle and handed Blessing to a woman.

The rain had stopped, so Sandy lifted her skirt and wrung the water out of it. She felt comfortable exposing her half-slip because the Africans told her a lady's underclothes were just a spare set of clothes. The local women often wore slips alone as skirts. Sandy pressed her wet dress flat down over her body and reached under it to pull her sodden half-slip down. She hung the garment over a tree branch.

The village chief walked up to Sandy, and his son translated for her. "Thank you for coming to our town. My father says you must hold the clinic inside his palace. It is over there." He pointed.

Sandy surveyed the mud structure, which held no resemblance to a palace. She shrugged and turned to the chief's son. "I can treat the sick in your father's home. Will you be translating for me?"

"I need to leave, but the students from the high school will soon arrive." The chief's son carried her basket. "One of them will translate."

Ten minutes later a young teenager approached Sandy. "I took first place in English at school and will interpret for you." So he translated for the sixty patients who came.

She pushed through her pain to finish vaccinating all the children. When she was through, she packed her medications. "I need to leave before dark."

The interpreter nodded. "No worry. I made preparations for you to reach home." He pointed. "Here they come."

She turned to three young girls. "How are these children going to get me home?"

"They will carry your bags to the junction." Her translator set one of Sandy's baskets on top of each of the girls' heads.

She grinned at the children who came almost to her shoulder and looked about ten years old. Sandy tied Blessing to her back and held the umbrella over her baby to protect her from the light drizzle that had started. The carriers untied their outer skirts and shook them open. They reached up and spread them on top of the loads covering their heads. The cloth swayed around them, keeping them dry. Wearing blouses and panties, the girls led the way.

Sandy couldn't hike ten miles with her injured foot, so she stopped the girls outside the village. She lifted the loads off the heads of the children and set her bags on the ground. Turning to the girls, she pointed to the village, and thanked the girls in their language. They shook their heads and reached down for the bags and basket and set them back on their heads. Sandy pasted a fierce expression on her face and lifted the baskets off the girls' heads again. Sandy crossed her arms and glared at the children.

She pointed back to the village. "Go home. I can't let you walk ten miles to the junction and home again in the dark."

The girls shook their heads and put Sandy's loads on top of their heads again. Her heart melted at their determination to carry her supplies. She took the bags off their heads and pointed to her bandaged foot. "Oh. Ouch."

She sat down on a boulder which she should have done earlier, clutched her foot, and moaned. Shaking her head, she pointed at the girls and motioned them to go back home. They sat down with her on the boulder and shook their heads.

Lord, please send help.

A minute later, a man driving a Mercedes Benz stopped on the cow path. Sandy had never seen any cars on that trail.

The driver, wearing a business suit, turned in his seat to Sandy. "If you give me one thousand naros I will take you to the junction."

Motorcycles charged fifteen naros, but she was stranded with a baby and an injured foot. Nightfall was coming.

"Can you please send these girls home?"

206

The man spoke to the little girls in another language. They grinned, lifted their hands to wave at Sandy, and turned toward the village.

She paid the man the equivalent of twenty dollars and stepped into the car. She sat next to the woman in the backseat. It was dark when they reached the paved junction.

Sandy joined the thirty people trying to flag down the few cars on the road. A long line of brilliant lights wavered in the distance. What was it? Two lights screeched to a halt in front of her.

A man from her village yelled, "Hurry up, Mommy Blessing! Get inside the vehicle."

Sandy clutched Blessing closer as rough hands shoved her onto the back seat. Someone tossed her loads to the car floor and slammed the door. It locked. She settled back on the seat with Blessing in her arms.

As the driver increased his speed, she glanced at the speedometer. The racing car traveled ninety miles an hour and tossed her from side to side. She sniffed in the odor of new upholstery. The clean leathery scent reminded her of the classy convertible she'd left behind in the States. She rubbed her hand on the leather seat under the torn plastic protection. The driver braked, and Sandy pitched to the floor.

Lord Jesus, please help.

Blessing's eyes darted left and right.

Sandy whispered. "Blessing, have we been kidnapped?"

The baby giggled. Sandy grinned at her child before getting back on the seat and looking in the driver's mirror to get his attention. "Excuse me, sir, where are you going?"

"We are traveling to the farthest city in the north, one thousand miles away. This vehicle is part of a ten-car convoy going to the major city."

"Why are you going so fast?"

"Our contract says we must arrive by tomorrow morning at seven. We are not allowed to stop for any reason but did for you because you are Mommy Blessing."

She wished once again she wasn't so famous.

"We cannot take you to your village, but we can drop you on the road leading to your home. We will slow down, and you can hop out of the car."

They expected her to leap out of a traveling car with a baby in her arms and an injured foot. If she slipped, she might break her other foot or Blessing could be hurt. How would she get her three containers of supplies out of the speeding vehicle? Maybe if she placed her basket and bags to her right and the car slowed, she could fling open the door, toss the luggage out, and leap. It would take her twenty seconds, but would she land with Blessing without another injury?

All vehicles slowed to twenty miles an hour on a stretch of rough, road close to the village. As predicted, the driver reduced speed to thirty miles an hour.

She called, "Stop for a moment, and I will jump out."

The vehicle braked before a huge pothole. She flung open the door and hurled the containers out on the ground. With Blessing in her arms, Sandy leaped and landed on her feet. Pains shot through her injured foot.

Sandy checked her baskets and bags which had landed upside down in different places. Carefully she stepped over the rocks in the pitch-dark and oriented herself to her exact location.

A young man on a motorcycle stopped. "Can I give you a lift to your house?"

In that moment, she was grateful everyone knew her. She tied Blessing to her back while the man fastened her loads to his bike. After she mounted the motorcycle, the man maneuvered the bike over the holes on the dirt path to her home.

As she put Blessing to bed, she sighed in exhaustion. Her days were so much more fulfilling than they had ever been in the States. But with the threats of Blessing's father, visa problems, and harassing officers, would she survive?

CHAPTER THIRTY-TWO

Sandy was preparing for the clinic when men's voices startled her. She glanced out the window. Her heart beat faster.

Colonel Jio had come all the way from the national immigration office.

Her knuckles turned white as she gripped the handle of the front door and stepped outside. "Good morning." She pointed to a mango tree. "Let's sit down under the shade. My house gets so warm."

He remained standing. "Has the church officer straightened out the date problem in your visa?"

"No, but he is working on it."

Colonel Jio leered. "You must come with me."

"Where? Why?"

"You are being investigated. We learned you are carrying on an illegal business of prostitution here in Koala."

"No, I'm not."

"Is it true that you had twenty pairs of trousers in your house to supply all the prostitutes with their outfits?"

Sandy's breathing grew ragged. Her voice wobbled. "I had trousers in my house, but I burned all of them."

"What happened to the females you were training to be prostitutes?"

"There were no women. I don't know any prostitutes."

"How can you deny this, when you are alone here in the bush and your home is isolated from all others? This is the ideal location for a house of prostitution."

"I didn't choose this house. The village chief told me to stay here."

"Do you have a witness to vouch for your whereabouts each night?" Colonel Jio removed his hat and waved it in front of his face like a fan. "Since you are alone at night, you can carry out any illegal activities you want."

The scent of his strong cologne gagged Sandy. Sweat soaked through his polyester uniform. Its stench made her mouth go dry. She searched the trail and wished someone would come to her aid. Eve warned her that living alone could be a problem. Too bad she hadn't found a village girl to stay with her.

"Find someone to take that baby and come with me."

She dug her heels in. "Where?"

"To the headquarters."

"In the capital city?"

"Yes. You will come into our private custody. Then the church officers will see how serious it is. The dates on your passport must be changed, or you will need to leave the country."

An icy tremor ran up and down her backbone. She shuddered. "I'll get my Father to help." Her Father God would never leave her or forsake her.

"Is he important?"

"Yes, he is very worthy."

"If you have a high-ranking father looking after you, I will give you two weeks to get this straightened out, or we will incarcerate you. Good day." He stomped off down the trail.

Sandy collapsed on the boulder behind her. How could a closet full of jeans cause so many problems? She had rededicated her life to the Lord after burning them. She had been reading her Bible every day. The Lord would not abandon her.

Maybe she was reaping the consequences of her past actions.

***

After preparing for the village clinic in Butou, Sandy picked up Blessing and her loads to hike to the junction for a taxi.

A vehicle stopped and drove her to the village.

When she arrived, she set the treatments on the table and began caring for the sick.

A young woman glared at her. "It is bizarre that your baby laughs all the time and is happy."

"Why is it strange?" Sandy held Blessing on her lap.

210

"We think she is happy that she killed her mother, which makes her cursed."

"Blessing did not kill her mother. She giggles because she hears me laugh and copies me. I feed her every three hours, which keeps her happy. She stays with me all the time and feels secure so she doesn't cry."

The village chief approached Sandy. "One of the women in our village has the brain sickness."

Sandy had treated people with epilepsy, which the local people referred to as brain sickness. "Is she taking medicine for it?"

"No. Her eyes roll inside her head, her tongue hangs, and water comes out of her mouth. She shakes and falls into the fire."

"I have pills that may help her."

"She is a young woman married to an old man. They had a baby." The chief looked around as if searching for an answer. "We want you to take the child away from her."

"What?" Sandy gasped. "I can't take a baby away from a mother."

"You took Blessing."

"I didn't take my baby away from her mother. She died. The doctor at the hospital gave the child to me, and I have the father's permission to care for her."

"Please take this woman's child."

"I can't take care of another baby. I must finish the vaccinations and treat patients." She smiled. "How could I possibly carry two babies on my back and ride a motorcycle?"

"I understand, but we are tired of helping this couple and their small baby. We give them food, clothes, and firewood."

"May I see the mother with the brain sickness?"

The chief pointed. "Here she comes, and she is carrying her child."

Sandy walked up to the woman. "Good morning. Please sit down here. How are you feeling, today?"

"I'm fine, thank you."

"What is your name, and how old are you?"

"I am Ayato, and I am about twenty years old."

"Where do you live, and what do you do?"

"I live here in the village with my husband, and I am the mother of this baby."

The chief interrupted. "She has the low I.Q. disease, too."

Sandy lowered her voice so only the chief would hear. "But, sir, she does not appear to be mentally challenged."

Sandy placed Blessing in the woman's free arm and took the woman's baby from her. Sandy examined the clean, attractive child who was about four months old. "This child is cared for, well-nourished, and healthy."

She handed the baby back to the mother and picked up Blessing. "Go and call your husband."

The woman put her infant on her shoulder and departed. An hour later the wife brought a gray-haired man. They sat on a wooden bench nearby. The wrinkled old father tickled his baby and made her giggle.

Sandy couldn't break up the delightful family. At the end of the day after all the patients departed, the village elders arrived. Sandy had no idea what she would tell them.

Lord Jesus, please give me your words.

The chief sat next to Sandy on a bench and looked at her. "What is your decision?"

"I'd like to question the parents." With Blessing on her lap, Sandy smiled at the elderly gentleman. "How are you feeling today, sir?"

"Well, thank you."

"Are you the husband of this woman? Is she your wife?" She wanted to make it clear because there were different words for a wife, a concubine, and a woman.

The old man turned to his homely wife. "Yes."

"Are you the father of this baby?"

He puffed out his chest and took a deep breath. "Yes."

"Do you like your wife?"

He looked at his wife again and grinned. "Yes."

"Do you like your baby?"

"Oh, yes." He kept smiling.

"There are people who feel your wife cannot take good care of the baby. Your wife has seizures, which cause her to fall into the fire. How do you feel about this?"

"She has not had any attacks since she delivered this baby."

"Can your wife care for this child?"

"She needs help."

"What kind of help does she need?"

The man hung his head and remained silent.

Sandy took a deep breath and looked at the father. "If you gave me your baby, and I found a good home for her, she would have new parents and not grow up with you as her father. Is this what you want?"

He shook his head with such force his whole body jiggled. "No. No. No." His violent protest almost made him drop the baby. When he stopped shaking, he wiped his watery eyes.

"I can give you, your wife, and baby free treatments each month. I have medicine for your wife to help stop the fits. Would this help you?"

The ancient man lifted his head and responded with a huge toothless grin. "Thank you."

After Sandy agreed to sanction their union by giving them free medicine, the villagers consented to feed and clothe them. It wasn't a major decision like King Solomon dividing the living child, but Sandy's heart swelled in pride.

With his wooden cane dangling from his arm, the husband favored one leg over the other as he hobbled away. He joggled the baby in his arms. The wife swung the plastic sack of pills by her side and strolled in a sedate fashion next to her husband.

Sandy brushed away a few tears of joy. Nothing could destroy the family's happiness.

What if something happened to Sandy and the family no longer received the medical treatment? The feeble man might drop dead, or the wife could forget to take her medicine. If the mother was holding her baby and fell into the fire, they might both die.

She had no other choice but to trust God.

213

CHAPTER THIRTY-THREE

Sandy's gas tank was almost empty. The solitary service station appeared to be open, so she stopped to fill up her tank. Best to get gasoline when it was available.

Maybe she'd meet Colonel Helpful again, and he'd take care of her identification book so she wouldn't have to go back to the police station. With fewer trips to the police station, she'd have more time to finish the vaccinations. She wasn't comfortable having secrets with military officers that might get her into trouble. Still Colonel Renita had been helpful. With a smile on her face, she scanned the area hoping to see Colonel Helpful.

A van filled with mothers and babies drove up to the pump. The driver jumped out of the taxi to purchase gasoline. The passengers climbed out of the vehicle and marched toward Sandy who had her baby tied to her back.

"Mommy Blessing. Mommy Blessing. Mommy Blessing," they shouted.

She turned to them.

"Your daughter is so beautiful." A woman tugged Blessing's bonnet lower. "Mommy Blessing, I am happy to meet you."

A well-dressed young lady patted Blessing's back. "You know so much about our children. I stopped giving a baby bottle, but my child refuses to drink from a cup. What can I do?"

"Add a little sugar to the porridge. When your child opens her mouth, put a small spoonful on her tongue. After she tastes how delicious the food is, she will want to eat it."

Another lady stroked Blessing's cheek. "Where did you buy this exquisite bonnet?"

"I sew all her dresses with matching hats."

"Can we see the rest of her outfit?"

Sandy untied Blessing from her back and pulled the child out of the cloth carrier so the people could see her.

"You dress her so beautifully. Everything matches. She is a gorgeous child."

The women returned to the van, and the driver left. After the attendant filled Sandy's fuel tank, she paid him with a large bill.

The employee searched through his coin purse. "I need to look for change." He turned away to leave.

"I'll wait."

Lieutenant Courteous and Lieutenant Scarface drove up riding double on a motorcycle. They pulled into the gas station and stepped off the bike.

"Good evening, Miss Calbrin."

Sandy turned to them. "Good evening."

They moved in front of her. Scarface put his arms out touching the pump on each side of her, forcing her up against the metal dispenser. With the baby in her arms and the nozzle of the gas hose pressed into her backside, and with Scarface keeping his arms in place, she couldn't escape.

He leaned closer and whispered, "We have you now."

Lieutenant Courteous crossed his arms. "What did you give to Colonel Tsaou and Colonel Renita?"

"Excuse me?" She cocked an eyebrow and shook her head. "I don't understand what you are talking about. I didn't give them anything."

Lieutenant Scarface bared his teeth. "What favor did you promise them in exchange for seeking sanction for you?"

She turned her head to escape his sweaty, unwashed body. The gagging stench of stinky cigarette breath nauseated her.

They wouldn't dare hurt her out in the open, or would they? Her heart thumped faster and harder. She pressed Blessing closer to her chest.

Sweat ran down Sandy's forehead and dripped off her chin. "I didn't promise anyone anything."

"You gave them money or guaranteed them a special favor. You no longer have to report to the police to get permission to enter and leave this village." Lieutenant Courteous scowled.

216

Lieutenant Scarface glowered. "We want a little of what you gave them."

"I didn't give them anything."

Lieutenant Courteous snapped, "Those men would never assist you unless you gave them a reason to help you. If you won't give us some physical pleasure, at least give us money."

Her chest constricted with a sharp intake of breath. Still sandwiched between Scarface and the pump, she glanced down the road, hoping for deliverance.

Lord, send the pastor, Mr. Jubilee, the village chief. Someone.

A moment later, she sighed in relief when three cars pulled into the isolated gas station.

Scarface lowered his arms and glared. "You haven't seen the last of us."

When Colonel Big and Colonel Helpful agreed to get sanction for her, it had created more problems. She'd promised nothing, nor had she given anything to the officers, but if the rest of the immigration officials thought she'd given favors or money to the men, they'd keep stalking her.

Another vehicle drove up to the pump. It forced the officers and Sandy to move away from the metal dispenser. The attendant returned and handed her the change from her payment. She tied Blessing to her back and stepped to her motorcycle. After mounting it, she gripped the handlebars tightly to stop her shakes. She lifted her foot and kicked the pedal to start the engine. Her trembling foot slipped off of it. She tried again to start the motorcycle, but failed. On the third attempt, the engine roared. Her legs wouldn't move. She wanted to sit there and bawl, but she wouldn't do it in front of the officers. She grasped the handlebars tighter and took a deep breath.

Adrenalin soared through her body as she drove the bike forward. She dared not look back at the officers. She went to the police station and parked her bike. She carried Blessing with her inside the building.

Colonel Helpful stood and extended his hand. "Colonel Tsaou and I secured sanction for you. It is no longer necessary to report here when you travel to villages within the state, but if you leave the state you will need to come to the station."

"Thank you for your help. I am very grateful."

"It is the least we can do. You have treated so many people in the villages and vaccinated our children."

"I will be traveling out of state for a week." Sandy handed the alien's book to him.

After stamping it, Colonel Helpful handed it back to her. "Have a safe and pleasant trip."

When she returned home, Phoebe was waiting for her. The woman reached for Blessing. "Good evening, Sister Sandy." Phoebe carried the baby into the house. "She is the happiest baby I've ever seen. You spend lots of time amusing yourself with her."

Without pacifiers, toys, or swings to occupy Blessing, Sandy played with her baby. "I love Blessing and enjoy my time with her."

"Everyone sees how much you love this baby."

Sandy took Blessing. "I'm glad you stopped by and appreciate everything you do for me. Tomorrow I will be traveling by taxi to a village six hundred miles north to vaccinate all the children and teach health classes. I will be gone a week. It will not be necessary for you to wash clothes or fetch water for me during that time."

Phoebe sat down. "Would you like me to go to the market to buy supplies for your trip?"

"That would be helpful. Thank you." Sandy handed her the money. "I need bread, peanut butter, and powdered milk."

Phoebe departed, and Sandy packed Blessing's clothes.

Thirty minutes later Adam, Eve, and Phoebe came to the house.

Sandy took the bag of supplies. "Thank you so much. Would you join me for tea?"

Eve put the water on to boil. "Sister Sandy, I am now again on break from the university. May I help you in the Koala clinic while I am on vacation?"

"Of course, you can, but I only need one person. The clinic is small and the pastor sent Adam to help."

218

He tossed six sugar cubes in his tea and stirred it. "No worry. We will speak to the pastor and make the arrangements."

A small child cried. Sandy jumped up and looked toward the door as a man called. "Excuse. Excuse. Excuse."

Sandy went outside. Phoebe, Eve, and Adam followed her.

"My daughter is in terrible pain. Can you pull her tooth?"

"Sir, I cannot do that. She needs to see a dentist."

"There is only one in the national capital, which is too far away."

The child, about nine years old, appeared healthy, so Sandy said, "Open your mouth." She put her hand on the girl's shoulder.

The girl put the fingers of her right hand in her mouth, pinched the lower, back tooth, and jiggled it.

Sandy peered into the mouth. "Adam, could you bring a bucket of water and bar of soap, please?"

He brought the pail and put it next to Sandy. Using a plastic cup, he poured cup after cup of water over Sandy's hands as she rubbed soap on them and scrubbed. Adam poured more cups of water over her hands to rinse away the soap.

She shook her hands free of water and put her right hand inside the girl's mouth and gently wiggled the tooth. A small amount of thick, yellow pus oozed out from the gum around the tooth. She had never pulled a tooth, but it didn't appear too difficult. She'd read the basic steps in an old medical handbook for the tropics. The tooth had to come out to release the pus, or the infection could spread through the child's body.

Adam brought the medicine basket and set it next to Sandy.

"Is there a mechanic here in the village?"

"Yes."

"Can you go and ask if I can borrow one of those tools that can squeeze a bolt?"

"It is called a pincher." Adam left.

Sandy looked at Eve. "Go to the church and bring a small wooden bench." Sandy turned to Phoebe. "Please put a large pot of water on to boil. Cut up a strip of cotton bandage into small squares and drop the pieces into the boiling water."

Within ten minutes Adam returned with a small pair of pliers. Sandy scrubbed them for five minutes with soap, water, and bleach. "Phoebe, please put these in the boiling water for me."

Eve returned with a wooden bench balanced upside down on her head. She came into the yard and set the bench down.

A car engine grew louder. The vehicle stopped and parked in front of them. David and Helen climbed out of the Mercedes Benz.

The older missionary walked to Sandy and smiled. "I wanted to stop and see your home."

"It is good to see you. Can you stay for a visit? I need to take out a rotten tooth."

"David brought me, and we are on our way to Hose. I can only stay a few minutes. I need to check on a rumor. Are you teaching health in churches on Sundays?"

"Yes, I am. I teach health classes on Sundays in the surrounding churches."

"Why are you training the people in church?"

"Christians are the most likely group of folks to change. They have already left their pagan forms of ancestor worship and idols to follow Christ. If they have changed to worship Christ, they may likely listen to new ideas, turn from unsafe traditions, and practice healthy principles."

"That's not what I meant. Why are you using God's day to worship Him for health teaching?"

"The Lord wants us to be in good health. If we have healthy bodies, souls, and minds, we can serve God better."

"I see your point, but it has never been done."

Sandy couldn't suppress her giggle. "So I heard."

Helen looked around Sandy's mud house. She dropped her hands at her sides and tilted her head. "Why are you living like an African?"

"From the moment I arrived, people told me they wanted to go to America to get rich. I couldn't live as a well-to-do woman for it would be flaunting my wealth and might convince Africans that all Americans were well-off."

Helen shook her head. "Why are you living in a mud house when you could have a proper cement house with running water?"

"If I show the people I'm willing to live as they live, I can earn their respect."

"That's a noble gesture, but aren't you suffering for it?"

"No, I'm not. The relationships I've built with the local people in Koala are worth more than my comfort."

"We could rent you one of our houses in Hose, and you could live like us."

"I like it here in Koala."

Eve brought a chair for Helen, but the older woman remained standing.

"Please have a seat." Sandy turned to the little girl and put her hands lightly on her shoulder. "It should only take a few minutes to pull the tooth."

Phoebe brought the pot of boiling water and set it next to Sandy by the bench. With a shaking hand, Sandy used her long wooden spoon to lift the pliers from the steaming liquid. She dropped them on a clean cloth. Then she washed her hands again. She touched the pliers with her fingertip, but they were still too hot to use. She waited longer for them to cool. After several minutes, she picked up the tool and gripped the handles.

Helen's eyes grew large. "You must not use a mechanic's pliers to pull a tooth."

"It's all that is available." Sandy smiled at the child. "Lie down on this bench and close your eyes. I will take out that awful tooth." She spoke with confidence, but her insides turned to mush.

The root could break off in the gum, or the tooth could shatter into pieces. She wouldn't be able to fix that.

Lord Jesus, guide my hands.

Sandy knelt down in the dirt facing the child's head. "Open your mouth."

Sandy touched the girl's trembling shoulders and positioned the nose of the pliers at the base of the tooth and squeezed the handles closed. With a gentle wrist motion she rocked the tooth back and forth about twenty times. Sandy tugged it free. It came out intact with its complete root. Thick, putrid pus oozed from the gum.

With her wooden spoon Sandy lifted out the hot sterile bandages. She swung each one slightly midair allowing it to cool. Several slipped off and back into the pot. She used the boiled ones to soak up the escaping pus from the gum and tossed the contaminated squares to the ground. She continued soaking up pus with more sterile squares. After all the drainage seeped out of the opening, a slow trickle of blood dripped out of the gum, a good sign. She pinched the two edges of the gum together and held it tight until the bleeding stopped. She wadded up a small sterile dressing and stuffed it in the hole between the teeth and pressed on it.

Sandy pulled the girl to a sitting position. "Bite down and close your mouth."

Helen's eyes widened. "You are amazing. I know of no other person who would attempt to pull a tooth using a mechanic's pliers."

"I had to manage with what I had."

"Great to see you again. I must be on my way. Goodbye."

Sandy raised her hand and waved to Helen as she got into the car.

The little girl smiled, looked up at her father, and spoke in her language.

"My daughter said all the pain is gone. Can you pull the other one?"

Sandy couldn't believe what she heard.

The little girl opened her mouth and pointed to another tooth. Sandy peered into the girl's mouth. The bleeding had stopped. Several other teeth were seriously decayed.

Now what?

CHAPTER THIRTY-FOUR

Sandy welcomed Eve into her home early the next morning. "Thank you for coming to carry my baggage to the taxi station."

Eve lifted the heaviest bag and set it on her head before picking up the two baskets. She led the way down the twisting trail.

At the station, Sandy hailed a taxi traveling north and climbed into it. Throughout the day, she prepared food for Blessing, which she drank from her metal cup. The temperature rose. It became so hot that Sandy and Blessing were covered in sweat.

Later in the afternoon Sandy's drinking water had finished. Then the taxi broke down in the bush and the passengers sat on rocks under a shady baobab tree. Sandy removed Blessing's clothes and used the little bonnet to fan the baby.

A young woman, hawking bottled Coca Cola, marched to the stranded passengers. "Buy one." She yelled.

Sandy bought a warm soft drink and poured the liquid into Blessing's cup. When the baby tasted it, she puckered her lips and stopped drinking. Then Blessing smiled at her mother and sipped a little at a time, until she finished a half a cup. Sandy would never recommend Coca Cola for an eight-month-old baby, but if the choice was between drinking a sweet soft drink or dehydrating in the African bush, the drink was preferable.

The driver repaired the rusted-out taxi and called the passengers to return to the vehicle. A little while later, he stopped at a small European store. Sandy bought a liter of filtered water. She and her daughter drank it before they reached the village.

It was dark when the station wagon stopped. "This is the end of the trip, last stop. Get out." He removed Sandy's bags from the vehicle and all the passengers left the taxi.

"You can't stop here." Sandy slid out of the taxi. "We are in the middle of nowhere. I thought we were going to Hetai."

223

"There are no passengers who want to travel there this evening, and I cannot go with only one person." The driver climbed into the taxi and drove away.

She stood with the eight male passengers who had been in the vehicle with her. They surrounded her, but she sensed no danger from them.

One of the men pointed down the road. "We live here in the village of Steggai and will wait with you, Mommy Blessing. We cannot leave you alone by the side of the road. It is dangerous. This is the headquarters for armed robbers."

Shivers ran up and down her spine. The men maintained a circle of protection around her and Blessing. She shifted her baby to the opposite hip.

Lord, please protect us.

Not one of the men touched her or her belongings. Sandy breathed easier as she waited in the dark with them.

When another taxi arrived, the men loaded Sandy, Blessing, and the bags into the sedan. Her protectors scattered into the darkness before she had a chance to even thank them.

At midnight the taxi reached Hetai. The villagers came forward one by one and said, "We have waited all day for you."

"I apologize. I had problems on the journey." She sat on the wooden bench someone brought to her.

A woman set a bucket of steaming, boiled water near her. "This is for your bath."

Sandy cringed. Her clothes were soaked in sweat. African hospitality always amazed her as she watched another woman put a bucket of tepid well water next to the steaming one. Tired visitors were always given water to bathe after a journey. The people would be offended if she refused the bath water.

She picked up a large, clean washtub and poured the lukewarm water into the basin. Then she took off Blessing's clothes and put her baby in the bath. The crowd moved closer.

A woman dipped her hand in the water. "Madam, you should bathe your baby the proper way with boiling water."

224

"It's over one hundred degrees tonight. My baby and I would prefer a nice, cool bath."

Blessing giggled and splashed water. It splattered on the villagers who jumped away.

"This baby is strange." A woman glared at Sandy. "She laughs when you bathe her. Our babies always cry. Have you always washed your daughter without boiling water?"

"Yes, and she has never been sick a single day."

After Blessing was bathed, a woman handed Sandy a bowl of mashed soybeans and a thermos filled with boiled water. Sandy mixed the beans with milk powder and poured some hot water into it to warm it. She filled Blessing's little cup and fed her baby. With milk-covered lips the baby stopped between sips and turned to grin at everyone in the crowd.

"This is an amazing child. She is happy and laughs when you bathe and feed her." The pastor's wife reached out for Blessing. "You should take your bath now."

Sandy didn't want to leave Blessing with one of the women. Anyone might think it her duty to bathe Blessing in boiling water after Sandy had left. She couldn't shake her uneasy feelings. Each of the mothers Sandy met had been bathing her baby in hot water, except the ones that Sandy had convinced not to do it. Blessing wouldn't be safe.

She carried Blessing to the pastor and put her daughter in his arms. "Sir, Blessing had a pleasant bath. She doesn't need any more baths, and she is happy. Promise me that you will not allow anyone to bathe my baby in hot water."

The pastor grimaced. "I promise."

Securing the pastor's vow in front of all the village leaders guaranteed Blessing's safety.

Sandy glanced at the three buckets of boiling water for her bath. How could she avoid taking a hot bath without offending the poor villagers?

She went to the pastor's wife. "Thank you for boiling this water for my bath. In my family we do not bathe in hot water. Maybe someone else can use it."

"Are you normal?"

She'd heard that question so many times since she arrived in Africa from so many people. Sandy wasn't normal. No woman in her right mind would ever be in some of the places and situations Sandy had been in over the last few months.

Maybe she was different. If she wasn't in her right mind, maybe she'd been transformed to have the mind of Christ.

She drank black tea, took cold baths, slept without a light, and ate natural peanut butter without red peppers.

A young man arrived with a bucket of water. He tossed a plastic cup in it, turned on a flashlight, and accompanied Sandy to a three-foot-by-three-foot stall constructed of palm leaves. As she went into the stall, she gagged from the overpowering stench of urine. She stepped on the soggy earth, held her breath, and washed as fast as possible. She left the stall quickly.

She returned to the yard where the villagers had gathered. The pastor's wife handed Blessing to Sandy. "Did your daughter ever use a baby bottle?"

"No. She always drank from a cup. You can see her increased growth on this card." Sandy held Blessing's growth chart under several lighted bush lanterns. Her baby's monthly weight had been recorded like a perfect mountain.

"We heard you took an orphan child. We did not think you would bring her all this distance. You should have left her at home with a small girl."

"Blessing comes with me every day to all my clinics and health classes. I love my child and like having her with me."

Sandy visited with the women and answered their questions about their babies. A giant man with scars across his face approached her. "You must report to the police station tomorrow morning."

Not again. Did all the military officers follow her to that remote village?

***

After breakfast the next morning, Sandy asked the pastor's wife, "Would you or someone else in the church accompany me to the

226

police headquarters to stamp my alien's book? I don't know where the station is."

"You are a stranger. We are happy to help you." The pastor's wife stepped outside and shouted. Two young girls arrived. "Escort Mommy Blessing to the police station."

The tallest girl took Blessing and tied her to her back. The other one lifted the backpack and set it on her head. Sandy followed the girls down a narrow trail and stopped in front of a broken-down building.

The gentleman of the previous evening stood up from the desk. "I must check your identification card." He wore a grungy uniform with sergeant stripes on the sleeves.

Sandy took her backpack and reached in the bag. She pulled out her alien's book and handed it to the soldier.

He flipped through the pages and pressed the book open to an empty one. He stamped and signed it. "You will need to come back on the day you want to leave for Koala."

"Yes, I know. Thank you."

"I hope our military officers are agreeable."

"Two officers secured sanction for me so I no longer need to check in and out if I am traveling within the state."

"Why would they obtain special favor for you? What did you give them or do for them?"

Sandy's heart plummeted. She had spoken impulsively and should not have mentioned sanction. Her words, which had been meant to be kind, had backfired. Her chest tightened. She wished she'd have kept her mouth closed. How could such a nice act get so misunderstood? Now she needed to convince him she didn't do or give anything.

"They were kind to me. I didn't do anything."

"No one would help you unless you gave something. Tell me what you did for them to make them help you."

"I'm a Christian and would not lie to you. The officers were helpful. I didn't give them anything." Without wavering, Sandy squared her shoulders.

"Maybe someone would help you because you are very beautiful."

She glanced down at her old used clothes from dead man's market that hung on her. She no longer wore makeup or styled her hair and held no resemblance to the sophisticated manager of a fitness center. She was far from beautiful.

"Will you stay here in the village this entire week?"

"Yes. I will vaccinate all the children and teach a complete series of health lectures."

"I will keep your alien's identity card with me."

He couldn't do that. It was illegal. The reason a foreigner carried a national identification card was to prove his identity. She needed the book to show other officials. She was told to never argue with a military officer. Government officers were always right, even though the vile man in front of her hadn't brushed his blackened-yellow teeth, taken a bath, or washed his uniform.

"If I meet another military authority, and he wants to see my alien's book, what should I do?"

"Do not worry. I'm in charge and am the only military figure in the village."

She rubbed her temple to ward off an oncoming headache. She would have no witnesses. Her word against his. Every nerve screamed. She blinked over and over to hide the threatening tears. Nodding, she stepped out of the office.

The oldest girl stared at Sandy's teary eyes. "Why are you crying? What did he do to you? We didn't see anything."

But that was the point. No one ever saw anything.

CHAPTER THIRTY-FIVE

After a week of vaccinating babies and treating the sick, Sandy packed to return home to Koala.

The pastor's children accompanied her to the police station. She was surprised the sergeant handed her the alien's book and wished her a safe trip. She hated the control the military officers and soldiers wielded over her. The nation bordered on dictatorship, so she had little choice.

She reached Koala late that night and decided to go to the police station to get her book stamped the next morning.

Colonel Helpful was on duty. After checking Sandy into the state he handed the book to her.

After that, she went on to her village clinic at Odoo. She parked her motorcycle at the base of the hill to wait for transportation. She stood a long time on the side of the road, but finally a noisy pick-up truck stopped beside her. She walked to the back to climb inside with the other passengers.

The driver pulled Sandy's bags out of her hands. "You must sit up front with me."

She didn't want special treatment, nor did she want to sit with the driver.

He set her bags on the floorboard of the passenger seat. "If one of the military officers saw you in the back end of my truck, he would yell at me for mistreating you."

She laughed and couldn't imagine the military officers mistreating the driver for that, because they had been mistreating, harassing, and threatening her. They'd praise the driver.

"The other women are in the back end." Sandy smiled.

"They sit there every week going to the market and are used to it. You are an important white lady, Mommy Blessing, and not used to trucks. You are a stranger in our country, and we must treat you with respect."

The local people treated her with dignity. Church leaders respected her, but the military and police officers didn't. But what if she'd brought the problem on herself by bringing her jeans? Maybe if she'd never agreed to the national television program, she would never have been singled out as Mommy Blessing.

With her baby in her arms, she climbed into the truck cab. It bounced along the rocky road for about half an hour. And then bang! Crash! The truck smashed down. What happened?

She got out of the truck and stared at another catastrophe. The rear axle had broken off, and the vehicle tilted into the dirt road.

Ten mothers with children climbed down from the back end of the truck and hiked to the shade of a colossal mango tree. They hunted through the grass for large flat rocks which they layered on top of each other to use as little stools. The women loosened the knots at their waists and untied the babies from their backs. They sat down on the rocks and held their children on their laps. Half of them lowered the front of their blouses to nurse their little ones.

Sandy waved away the flies and slapped at the gnats that buzzed beneath the shade. Blessing wailed and Sandy hiked back to the broken vehicle and lifted out her bag of supplies. She returned to the shade and sat on a pile of flat rocks. After mixing the milk and mashed black-eyed peas, she held the cup to Blessing's mouth.

Everyone watched Sandy, but one of the mothers spoke. "She is drinking from a cup. Why don't you give her the feeding bottle?"

"Baby bottles are made of plastic and rubber. Dangerous sicknesses can live inside the plastic container and nipple. God made breast milk. It is better and more nutritious."

After Blessing had eaten and gone to sleep, one mother held her child out to Sandy. "My baby has a cough. Can you look at her?"

Sandy examined the little girl and wrote a prescription. "She has bronchitis and needs antibiotics."

Another woman complained, "My baby has a fever."

Sandy examined that child. "She has malaria. Here is the medicine for it."

"My child's skin is coming loose."

"Do you bathe her in boiling water?"

"Yes, but I add a little river water and black, local soap."

"Her skin is burned." Sandy looked over the mothers. "Here's ointment for her skin and antibiotics. Stop bathing your children in boiling water."

"My child is losing weight."

"He is malnourished and anemic. Here are vitamins, but you must feed him an egg each day or add peanut butter to the corn porridge."

Two hours later, after diagnosing and prescribing treatments for the children, Sandy treated the mothers. She was taking a woman's blood pressure when an elderly gentleman drove up on a motorcycle.

The driver parked the bike and walked over to Sandy. "The people have waited for you in Odoo since morning." He peered around at the mothers and children. "Why did you stop to treat these women instead of coming to our village to help us?"

"The truck broke down." Sandy pointed. "Look at that axle."

He went to the broken-down vehicle. "This was not your fault, but you should get on the back of my motorcycle and come with me."

Sandy handed her basket and bags to him, and he tied them to the motorcycle. With Blessing in her arms she mounted the bike behind the man. "Thank you for coming to get me."

Over the months Sandy had slowly changed. She was no longer stressed out if her plan wasn't followed or her schedule was interrupted. She had learned to take life in stride and flow with the events. When the vehicle broke down, she didn't worry about getting to Odoo. If it was the will of God, the Lord would get her there. Maybe God allowed the truck to break there, so she could treat those children and teach the stranded mothers better health care.

Sandy had become more adaptable and was turning into a calmer woman, willing to accept the new paths the Lord took her down. Praying and reading the Bible each morning had given her peace, contentment, and direction in her life.

The driver slowed the bike. "Every month you have a problem driving to our village. When you did not arrive we decided to look for you."

"Thank you. I appreciate it."

When she reached the village, she wasn't tired. Over the last few months, she had hiked the ten miles in the sun, got stuck in the mud, or had an accident.

Late that night when she arrived home, she fed and bathed Blessing and played with her before putting her to bed. An hour later, she went into the bedroom to check on her baby.

As she was getting ready for bed, the stench of vomit irritated her nostrils. She hurried to Blessing who lay without moving. White curdles covered the infant's face, hair, and clothes. Splatters coated the walls, the floor, and inside the cardboard box. Sandy's heart beat faster as she picked up her baby. When Blessing opened her eyes, Sandy's heart rate slowed, but it didn't return to normal.

Blessing's eyelids lowered and raised like it was a great effort. Sandy pressed her child against her own heart, and carried Blessing to the kitchen.

Sandy examined the remainder of food that she'd given Blessing earlier and tears filled Sandy's eyes. She'd forgotten to dilute the porridge with water and had fed Blessing a doubly-concentrated amount of soybean paste which had made her child sick. As Blessing vomited again with a wretched expression on her face, it tore Sandy's heart. She'd been exhausted that night as she made the food and now her baby suffered. When Blessing's stomach was empty, she had dry heaves. With Blessing in her arms, she mixed a hydration drink of sugar, salt, and water. She held the cup for the child to sip the fluids, but the baby kept vomiting as she continued giving the fluid.

An hour later, Blessing stopped heaving and kept the fluids in her stomach. The rest of the night Sandy kept a vigilant eye on Blessing.

When Blessing woke, Sandy fed her sips of half milk and half sugar/salt solution. The child smiled at her mother.

"Blessing, I love you more than anyone on earth. I am so sorry."

Her baby grinned as if saying, "It's okay, Mommy, I'm going to be fine."

Tears filled Sandy's eyes and ran down her cheeks as she clasped her precious child to her. She'd never forgive herself if anything ever happened to her baby.

They traveled to the main north and south junction by taxi.

A pastor on a motorcycle met Sandy. "I've come to carry you and your daughter to the clinic." After she was settled on the back of the bike, he revved up the engine and drove twice as fast as she normally did.

Sandy was about to open her mouth to suggest slowing down when the front tire dropped in a deep pothole. Her heart hit the pit of her stomach like a rock. She gripped Blessing closer to her chest as she flew from the bike. Her back twisted as she landed.

"Ouch." Sharp blades sliced her spine again and again. She sat up and checked out Blessing, still in her arms. The baby didn't have a scratch on her body. The child smiled up at her.

Sandy squeezed her eyes shut and groaned. Knives stabbed her back. Daggers sliced her leg. Every bone in her left foot throbbed. Thank God her right foot had healed from the last injury. Tears blurred her vision as she examined the gashes on her arms and cuts on her legs. Blood flowed out of a long laceration running down her left leg. She gasped, unable to catch her breath.

The pastor gave her a dirty, smelly cloth. "I am so sorry."

She handed Blessing to the pastor and struggled to stand. She couldn't put any weight on her injured leg. The pastor extended his hand and pulled her up.

"Thank you for this cloth, but I need soap and clean water to wash my legs and feet."

"We are in the middle of the bush. There are no people and no buckets of water."

They remounted the motorcycle. The pastor stopped at the first mud house, parked the bike, and went to the door. He returned with a bucket. "Here is water to wash."

"Thank you. Can you untie that basket from your motorcycle so I can get a roll of dressings?"

He handed Sandy the drug basket. "Give me the baby."

She did, and then she poured cups of water over her legs. With the bar of soap, she scrubbed her calves and feet. After rinsing them, she dressed the wounds before climbing back on the motorcycle.

The pastor drove slowly to the village.

She hobbled around the Under Fives Clinic. When she sat down, she tried to wiggle her toes but couldn't. It might be a sign she had broken a bone or two in her foot. She treated patients, counted pills, and prayed for strength as beating mallets hammered every bone in her body.

Not again. How could she finish the vaccinations if she kept having accidents and getting injured?

***

By morning it felt like switchblades were slicing through her back, hips, and legs. With Blessing in her arms, Sandy shuffled to the stove to fry some eggs. Her left foot was swollen three times its size, and she couldn't move her toes. Tears filled her eyes and ran down her cheeks. What was she going to do? How could she go to work? She had taken a couple weeks off when she had sprained her right foot. It looked like she would need to take more time off.

A vehicle stopped and the doctor of the hospital climbed out of his sedan and came to the house.

She opened the door. "Come in."

"I wanted to see how you and Blessing were doing."

"Sit down." Through tears of pain, Sandy limped to a chair. "We are doing well, but I had an accident yesterday. I'm so glad you stopped by."

He glanced down at Sandy's swollen foot, and his jaw dropped.

She sat down. "Please have a seat." Lifting her foot with care, she put it on a third chair.

The doctor examined the injury. "It looks like you have several broken bones. You need to go to the hospital for an x-ray and possibly a cast."

"I don't have time for x-rays. There are two villages far into the bush, on the path of the measles epidemic. Children could die if I don't

234

vaccinate them soon. I've only established seventy Under Fives Clinics. The program goal is one hundred."

"I could send a taxi driver to inform the villages of your accident. We could delay the program until you get a cast on your foot or are back on your feet. How many patients are you treating each month?"

"About two thousand."

"It is obvious you love the people." He let out a deep sigh. "I wanted to come sooner, but I traveled to England for a three-month seminar. This is the first chance I've had to visit."

"I appreciate your concern. If I need to hire a driver to go to the village to tell them, then I should go in the taxi myself and treat the sick while I am there."

"You need to take care of yourself so you can care for Blessing and the patients."

"I will."

The doctor stood and glanced over at Blessing, who slept in the cardboard box. "How is the baby doing?"

"She is fine, but her father came and asked for money in exchange for her."

The doctor shook his head. "He signed a paper saying you could keep her, unless he wants to take her back. Don't give him money. If you do, he will ask for more each time he comes."

"I would never give him money, and I didn't. Will he cause a problem?"

"People who ask for money all the time and never receive it, will stop asking. He'll probably bring his brothers to ask for money."

Sandy giggled. "He already brought two uncles."

"Be smart. Don't antagonize him or his relatives. Pray that God will give you wisdom when you speak to him."

"Thank you. With God's grace, I'll do my best."

"Stay seated. I'm going to my car for a minute."

He returned with an ace bandage in his hand and a sterile dressing. After sitting, he removed the cloth dressing and placed gauze dressing on the top of her foot where the skin had been ripped off of it.

Unrolling the ace bandage, he wrapped her foot. Knives of fire shot through her leg, and her eyes blurred with tears.

The throbbing persisted no matter how her foot was wrapped. She tried to keep off of it and elevate her leg when she sat down, but it was difficult.

***

A few days later as she hobbled around to cook, tend her baby, and prepare medications, she heard men's voices. She limped to the window and breathed faster at the sight of Blessing's father and his two uncles.

She opened the door to the visitors. "Good morning. I am happy to see you. Did you come for your daughter? It has been difficult caring for her with my broken foot. Please take her if you would like her."

Blessing's father and his uncles barked a quick laugh.

The old chief snarled, "We do not want the baby. Can't you keep her any longer?"

"I can keep her, but you see for yourselves that I cannot get around easily. Can you give me money to hire another lady to do the extra chores?"

The father snapped, "Are you asking us for money?"

"Why yes, of course. You're her father."

The chief's mouth dropped open and he glared. "If you are going to keep this child, you must pay the father money for her."

"How can I pay the father when I need money to hire a girl to help me? I cannot get around with this broken foot." Sandy groaned as she hopped about in the small room on her good leg. The men gaped at her injury. Her foot, covered in dressings, was four times larger than the other one.

"We cannot give you money."

"I was hoping you could give me funds." She lowered her head so they wouldn't see the amusement in her eyes. She held her breath to halt the giggles.

"Help you!" The uncle shouted, "You are a rich white lady. You should be helping us."

"I can't assist you when I'm suffering like this." Sandy pointed to her injured foot. Once again she took a deep breath, lowered her head, and put her hand to her chest to stop herself from laughing.

The father raised his voice. "I am getting tired of coming here and not getting anything from you."

It's about time you got tired of asking for money.

Sandy whispered, "Take your daughter, sir. Then you will at least have her. You could raise her, and she can care for you in your old age."

The father growled. "I do not want another daughter. Give me something?"

"Take Blessing." Sandy handed him the baby.

"I don't want my daughter. It's best if you keep her. Will you keep her for me?"

Sandy pasted an expression of extreme anguish on her face and nodded slowly. "I will keep her, but it will be difficult caring for her with this injury. You should try to help and give me some money."

The father turned to his uncle. "I see no reason to come back. Mommy Blessing is too powerful for us. She will not give me anything, and I do not want another mouth to feed. I do not want this baby."

The men stormed out of the house and down the trail.

Sandy sat down and bawled. She wept tears of happiness. Maybe the men were gone forever. She thought of nearly losing Blessing, and she kept crying.

The military police were the only ones who could take Blessing away now, but would they?

She shuddered.

CHAPTER THIRTY-SIX

After three weeks the swelling and pain in Sandy's foot had diminished so she was able to move all her toes, except her little toe, which remained twice its size and unbendable. She would never be able to wear closed shoes or heels again. Still, it had been months since she'd worn designer stilettos, but she no longer missed her elegant wardrobe.

She rode her motorcycle to Tagbari and set up the clinic. She handed Blessing to one of the women who tied the baby to her back and disappeared.

After vaccinating, weighing, and treating all the babies, she cared for the sick adults. She treated all the patients and packed the medicines and supplies.

Sandy turned to the pastor's wife. "Please call the woman who took Blessing. It's time to go home."

The lady brought the baby. Sandy gasped and snatched Blessing out of the older woman's arms. "What happened to my baby?"

"Nothing," The woman stuttered.

Blessing clung to Sandy as if the baby had been rescued from the jaws of a lion. "Blessing has bites all over her body, scratches on her nose, her hair ribbons are untied, and her beautiful dress is filthy and torn."

Several persons raised their fists at the woman and spoke harshly to her in another language.

Sandy lifted her hand as if to halt traffic. "Leave the woman alone."

The pastor's wife held her little boy as she said, "Blessing is so smart and beautiful. She always wears an adorable bonnet to match her dress." She paused. "We are sorry this woman did not take proper care of your daughter."

"I forgive her." Sandy washed the dirt off Blessing's face and arms.

"At first no one wanted to hold your baby because of the curse on her. When we saw that no sickness came to you and you didn't die, we believed that Jesus living in you is greater than the curse on the child."

"Do you think Blessing is no longer cursed?"

"We are not sure. Some of the women are undecided, which is why they wanted to hold your baby and study her. It was this woman's turn to take your daughter. The woman is not reliable. Please come back to our village."

"Of course, I will return to your village."

"Some people believe that the good in you went into the baby. They hope some of the good will rub off on them. There is only a limited supply of good. We need to get it while the supply lasts."

This made no sense to Sandy. "Do you think one day the good in the world will end?"

"We Christians believe there will always be good in people who know Jesus, but there are many old beliefs that still imprison our people."

Sandy applied antibiotic cream to the wounds, dressed Blessing in clean clothes, and straightened her hair ribbons.

The pastor's wife carried one of Sandy's bags to the motorcycle. "You are smart because you know how to care for our children better than we can take care of them. I have never seen Blessing sick."

Sandy wondered why she and Blessing were never ill. They were surrounded by unhealthy people, filth, and germs. It made no sense, unless it was another one of those miracles.

***

Several nights later after work as Sandy was bathing Blessing, she felt a lump on the baby's neck. Sandy's mouth tightened. She put her hand again on Blessing's face and neck to confirm the enlarged cervical lymph nodes. Sandy's stomach fluttered. She couldn't breathe. With shaking limbs she lifted the baby out of the water and pressed her close to her own heart. "Did that strange woman in the village the other day hurt you and give you an infection?"

Please, God, keep Blessing healthy.

She put her child down, went to her medical basket, and lifted out a bottle of powdered antibiotics. With a trembling hand she poured boiled water into the tiny bottle and shook it. After mixing it, she put a spoon of the medicine to Blessing's lips.

After two weeks of antibiotics for the infection, Blessing's lymph nodes were still swollen. Sandy shuddered at the possible sicknesses that ran through her tormented mind. Blessing had no fever, no diarrhea, no vomiting, and only a slight cough at night. The child did not appear in distress and even laughed more than normal. Sandy's eyes blinked faster to halt the tears as she considered the most logical disease. Her heart plummeted to the pit of her stomach.

No, it can't be that. But if it was, her daughter needed treatment immediately. She tossed food and clothes into a bag. With Blessing in her arms, she ran to the taxi station where she hired a vehicle to take her to the hospital.

There the doctor examined Blessing. "She needs a tuberculosis test."

Sandy's fears had come to pass. Her heart beat faster. She hoped and prayed her diagnosis would be wrong. Sandy cried with her daughter as the child was restrained for the chest x-ray. When the lab technician drew two milliliters of blood from Blessing, she screamed. Her little face was wet with tears. Through Sandy's blurry vision, she wiped Blessing's face. *Please Lord, not tuberculosis.* But the remaining alternative was even worse.

Sandy spent most of the night praying. When the sun lit her little house she stood and dressed. If Blessing had tuberculosis, or a more fatal disease, and died, Sandy wouldn't want to live. With her baby in her arms, she walked to the church and sat in the last pew so she could rest her back against the wall and pray uninterrupted.

She stared straight ahead as every sickness from a list in a medical textbook ran through her tortured mind.

The elders flipped open the lopsided wooden shutters that lined the sides of the primitive mud church. A gentle cross-breeze flowed through the cool building. A cockroach landed Sandy's head, and she knocked it off with the back of her hand. Dust, insects, and straw

241

fluttered down from the thatch roof as an elder slammed open the remaining doors. Several chickens and a rooster flew through the openings and landed on the podium. Two black and white goats headed to the communion table. They slid underneath it and lowered themselves to the packed mud floor. A stray, mangy dog covered in flies limped to a front pew and scrunched under it. The animal folded its legs and closed its eyes.

It looked like it prayed, so Sandy closed her eyes and returned to her prayers.

The pastor's wife touched Sandy's arms. "Is something wrong?"

"I'm not sure." Sandy sobbed. "I took Blessing to the hospital for tests."

"What kind of exam did she need? I can see she is becoming blacker and blacker. Does that mean she is sick? I thought she would turn white when she lived with you."

Through her tears Sandy managed a smile. "Blessing's birth parents were black, so she is, too. Surely you did not think the color of Blessing's skin would change, did you?"

"I thought something would happen. You are her accepted mother, and you are white."

"Blessing's skin color will never change."

Sandy glanced at the door. The doctor from the hospital marched into the church and headed toward her. She struggled to take in air. A doctor coming in person always meant bad news. Her eyes blurred and burned. The blood pulsed in her temples.

Her voice wobbled. "Good morning, doctor."

"Good morning." He sat next to her on the wooden bench, set his briefcase on his lap, and opened it. "I know you are anxious about your daughter's test results. So I wanted to drop them on my way to Hose this morning."

"Thank you." She squeezed her lips together until they hurt as her heart pounded faster and faster.

The doctor took Blessing's health card from his briefcase and grinned at Sandy. "All the tuberculosis tests came back negative and also the other tests."

With trembling hands, she reached for the card and flipped it open to read. "Child recovers from viral infection. Baby is okay." She brushed away a few tears.

Then gunfire erupted. Sandy swiveled her head toward it while church members ran to the windows. There were no machine guns or other weapons in the peaceful community of Koala. Popping sounds shook the quiet Sunday morning. Sandy joined everyone else at the row of windows.

"What's happening?" Sandy whispered. "What does this mean?"

Brisk clomping steps grew louder and louder. They approached the church. A squad of military men marched past the sanctuary and down the dusty cow path.

Pastor Paul turned to Sandy and shook his head. "It means nothing. The troops are headed north, not south toward Logatti. If there were political problems they would march toward the national capital."

"I disagree." The doctor grimaced. "No soldiers ever organize unless they are planning something. We are not permitted to speak about political or government problems, but you and Blessing should be prepared."

"For what?"

"I can't say." The doctor hesitated. "I suggest you pack your bags in case of an emergency."

Sandy glanced over at the pastor and his wife, who both nodded.

"I hope the roads will not be blocked because I need to reach Hose to collect medicines." The doctor turned to go.

"I wish you a safe journey." Sandy shook his hand.

She should go home and pack, but why? What would she do, or where would she go? If political problems were coming, she'd be watched. There was no place she could hide with her baby. Everyone knew she was Mommy Blessing.

The pastor raised his voice and faced the villagers. "Please sit down and let us start the service." He stood before the congregation and folded his hands. "We must pray for Mr. Dugumou's wife. She was released from the hospital and is at home resting. Pray that God will bless them with a child."

After the service, Sandy approached one of the elder's wives. "How serious is Mrs. Dugumou's condition?"

"She has had many miscarriages. The doctor at the hospital said only through a miracle of God would the couple ever be able to have a child. They have been married fifteen years."

An earsplitting blast, like a bomb, shook the ground and pierced the air. Another explosion rattled the church beams. Dust and grasses fluttered to the floor. Members of the congregation dropped to the ground and covered their heads.

Sandy wrapped her arms more tightly around her baby and turned to the row of windows. She stared straight ahead at more soldiers, who carried weapons, marched past the church, and headed east.

Sandy glanced over at Mr. Dugumou who nodded at her. Blessing giggled.

Give Blessing to Mr. and Mrs. Dugumou.

No, Lord. I won't give Blessing to anyone.

CHAPTER THIRTY-SEVEN

She couldn't give Blessing up and would not surrender her to anyone. The Lord could never ask that of her. God had given her the child and wouldn't want her to give Blessing to another person. Sandy sniffed back the tears, but some slipped down her face. The baby was hers, her precious Blessing.

When another explosion shook the bush timbers, Sandy shivered, gripping her baby tighter. A third military company marched past the church. Several soldiers raised their voices and pointed at Sandy. "Look, there's Mommy Blessing from television."

Tears ran down her cheeks. Everyone in the country knew her and Blessing, which meant there were no places she could hide. She wiped away her tears. Why had she ever agreed to that television interview?

People believed she was a rich, white lady. The soldiers could kidnap Blessing and demand money from Sandy or threaten to inflict horrible pain on her baby. Or worse.

If you love Blessing, you must surrender her.

I can't.

You can with my help.

Sandy glanced to the left. Mr. Dugumou grinned at her as if he could almost read what was going through her mind.

She needed a moment alone with God. Wiping her tears away with the back of her hand, she approached Mr. Dugumou. "Sir, would you hold Blessing so I can use the pit latrine? Thank you."

He took the baby. Blessing grinned and giggled at Mr. Dugumou, who laughed along with the child.

Sandy walked toward the toilet. Giving up her child was too much to ask of any mother. What woman could do such a thing?

Mary gave up her son Jesus so the world could be saved. Hannah gave up Samuel to serve God in the temple. With God it was possible. Sandy's breathing grew ragged.

Did God want her to do it? And if so, could she?

She took a deep breath and stepped out of the pit latrine and walked back to the church.

Lord, I can't do this.

You can with my help.

Mr. Dugumou handed Blessing to Sandy. "She is a beautiful, special child. My wife and I could love a baby like this."

And Sandy loved the baby. Her heart dropped like a rock in the pit of her abdomen at the thought of losing her.

Mr. and Mrs. Dugumou would love and take care of Blessing.

Surrender Blessing?

Did she have the strength to give up Blessing?

"Mr. Dugumou, could you and your wife come to my house this afternoon?"

He nodded and then Phoebe, Adam, and Eve approached Sandy. Adam reached out for Sandy's backpack. "We will escort you to your home, since there are soldiers passing through our community."

"There are many problems in the country. Anyone speaking against the government will disappear or be thrown in prison." Eve took Blessing and slid the baby onto her back.

Adam led the way. "The soldiers of the opposing party headed north on the main road right in front of the church. One of my uncles followed and saw them turn onto a back trail, outside of Koala, which leads south to the capital city."

"What does it mean?" Sandy walked behind him.

Adam sighed. "If the soldiers are hiking and have no form of transportation it may take them a couple of weeks to reach the capital, where the government offices are located."

"You and Blessing may be in grave danger," Eve said. "We will do our best to help you, but you must be reasonable."

Sandy tilted her head. "What are you talking about?"

Phoebe whispered, "Do you have a passport and legal papers for Blessing?"

"No. The father only gave me custody but said he never wanted the child."

"You must give Blessing back to her father so you can get safely out of the country. You can't hide because you are famous."

Blessing's father didn't want his daughter, and he admitted he couldn't take care of her.

Adam shrugged. "Those soldiers were from all parts of the country, and they recognized you. The only way to save you and Blessing is for each of you to go your separate ways."

Fine, but it would be her last resort, and only if necessary to save her daughter.

Reaching home, Sandy dug out the contract Blessing's father signed. She spread open the single sheet and pressed it flat on the table. She read the words out loud. "If Miss Sandra Calbrin is unable to care for my child, and I do not come to claim her, it is her decision and task to secure another person or persons to care for my daughter."

With her index finger, Sandy stroked the father's thumbprint at the bottom of the sheet. And then she wept again. The solution was in front of her, but she didn't like it. Would she have the strength to give up her precious child, whom she loved more than anyone on earth?

A few moments later, Mr. and Mrs. Dugumou arrived.

She pasted a smile on her face, opened the door, and invited them inside. After they were seated she sat down facing them. Mrs. Dugumou took Blessing, put her on her lap, and played with her. "She is such a beautiful, perfect child, and she is so happy."

Sandy's vision blurred. "How much do you know about the military problems?"

"All the white people, the foreigners, must leave the country, but Blessing isn't an alien. She is one of us."

Sandy sniffed back her tears. "Almost everyone in Norgia has seen us on television. Everywhere I travel people know us."

"It's true, Mommy Blessing. You are a national celebrity. You and Blessing could never hide. If you need to leave the country, you must let Blessing stay behind with people who love her. It would be the only way to save both of you."

"I would never put my baby's life in danger." Sandy turned to the couple. "Someone could take her and threaten to harm her, if I didn't agree to their demands."

Mr. and Mrs. Dugumou both gasped loudly and covered their mouths.

Over the last few months, Sandy had been learning to surrender and she finally whispered, "Would you and your wife like to keep Blessing and care for her?"

"You are Mommy Blessing. You are her real mother and the only mother she knows. Everyone has seen how much you love this child. Can you give her up?" Mrs. Dugumou shook her head.

Sandy blinked as tears ran down her face. "Sometimes a mother must surrender her baby to save her life. Remember the two prostitutes who stood before King Solomon, both claiming the one living baby. To save the life of her baby from being sliced into two, the birth mother was willing to give her child to the other woman."

Mr. and Mrs. Dugumou lowered their heads as Sandy wept.

"We would be happy to take her," Mr. Dugumou murmured. "There are many evil people in our country who would try to hurt you and Blessing."

Mrs. Dugumou pointed to the scars on her face. "You can see for yourself how different our tribal tattoos are from the people in Koala, so Blessing would be completely safe with us. We will move back to my hometown where we will fit in with everyone else. We've been away a long time and no one will question us having a child now."

Sandy had noticed the three-one-inch-long horizontal lines under their eyes. "Blessing's skin is flawless without tribal scars and tattoos."

"That would be no problem." Mr. Dugumou tickled Blessing's stomach. "We are older than the young married people today and have been Christians longer. People know that we would never cut our children because the Bible tells us not to cut or tattoo our bodies. They are the temples of God."

"My wife's family lives close to the border. It is on the opposite side of the country. They are illiterate people and do not have electricity or televisions. They never heard of you or Blessing. We can take the baby with us, and she will be safe. We will love her as our own daughter and raise her as a Christian."

Sandy furrowed her brow. She could keep Blessing and go to Mrs. Dugumou's village with her child, but if the military forced all foreigners to leave, she would need to evacuate with the others. After the political conflicts were resolved, maybe she could come back to visit.

Mrs. Dugumou hugged Blessing. "She is such a sweet, agreeable child. We will love her always and take good care of her."

Sandy's eyes glassed over with tears.

Give them your baby.

She would give her cherished baby to them, but would she regret it one day? God's peace filled her heart, but could she hand her baby over to them?

"It's best if you left right away for your new home. I will give you the money to hire a taxi and leave."

Sandy stroked Blessing's cheek. The baby giggled as she always did. "I will miss you so much."

Another explosion shook her tin roof. If Mr. and Mrs. Dugumou left immediately with Blessing, Sandy would have no time to change her mind. It was the right decision. Could she do it? She closed her eyes for a brief moment.

Lord, please give me strength.

Mr. Dugumou stood. "I will help you pack her things. No one ever comes to my wife's village. It is too isolated and far away from civilization, but you will always be welcome there, if it is ever possible for you to return."

She put all of Blessing's little dresses with matching bonnets, and the pink booties, which were too small, in the large sack. She set the cups, spoons, jars, and containers of food in another bag and added the cloth carrier. It wasn't necessary because Mrs. Dugumou stood, leaned forward and unfastened her long wrap-around skirt to tie Blessing to her back. All traces a baby had ever been in Sandy's house were slowly disappearing. She kept nothing for herself, not even Blessing's bath soap. She wanted no sign of Blessing in case the military officers visited and harassed her. Her hands shook and heart pounded as she jammed the little blankets she had made into the bag.

With troops marching through the village, military officers like Lieutenant Scarface and Lieutenant Courteous could be on their way to her house at that moment to threaten her daughter's life.

With tears running down her face, Sandy kissed her baby and then looked at Mr. and Mrs. Dugumou. "Blessing will be safe with you. Go with God."

Mrs. Dugumou's eyes moistened. "We will raise Blessing to know God's love and to serve Him. We will teach her the language and our culture."

If she took Blessing and held her in her arms one last time, she'd never be able to give her up. So she stood rigidly, squared her shoulders, and tried to smile in spite of her sobs. Blessing's new parents carried her off down the bush trail toward their new home.

God's peace filled Sandy's empty heart, but what would fill her empty arms?

CHAPTER THIRTY-EIGHT

Sandy sobbed. Her heart exploded into a million pieces. Daggers pierced deep into her spirit. Emptiness filled her soul. Profound loneliness swept over her.

Blessing was gone. Solitude crept into every corner. Aloneness pervaded the two rooms of her house.

She needed to hold her daughter again and sniff in Blessing's soap scent one more time. She longed to see that cute little smile once more.

The quiet of the room suffocated her. Sandy lay on the bed and wept. She must have dozed, for Lieutenant Scarface's voice jolted her awake.

"Miss Sandra Calbrin."

Sandy went to the window and peered into the yard. Lieutenant Courteous and Lieutenant Scarface stood there. She dressed, grabbed her bag, and walked outside.

"Good morning." Sandy attempted a smile.

"We came to ask you questions."

"What are they?"

"Let's go inside your house."

"I'm already late for the prayer meeting at church."

On trembling legs, Sandy walked away from them and headed toward the trail. She gave the officers no choice but to follow her. Reaching the church, Sandy went inside and selected a wooden bench in the back, so members could continue praying in a quiet manner in front.

She pointed to the cracked seat, put a finger to her lips, and whispered, "Please sit down."

"Miss Calbrin, where is your baby? You never go anywhere without your Blessing."

Sandy put her shaking hands in her lap and interwove her fingers. "She has gone with her father."

"When did she leave?"

"She left last night."

"When she returns, bring her to the military police. We are doing an investigation on your child."

Sandy willed the threatening tears to stop and swallowed, staring ahead. "When she returns, I will bring her."

Blessing was safe. She tried to breathe easier, but her heart rose to her throat.

After the officers departed, she stayed behind with the church members to pray for peace and safety in the country. When the meeting ended, she walked home. For the first time in her life, loneliness consumed her.

She wept throughout the following day and kept glancing at the clock. She put the kettle of water on to boil when it was time to feed Blessing.

In the middle of the night Blessing giggled. Sandy leaped out of bed and looked around, but it was only a dream. Why had she let her baby leave? Because it was the only way to save her child's life.

Her house became too quiet. Without Blessing there were no chomping sounds and no "goo, goo, goo, goo, ha, ha, ha and ah, ah, ah" noises to greet Sandy each morning.

There was no one to hold, and no one to kiss, and no one to cuddle. No laughter. No happiness. No baby.

Lord, please keep Blessing safe.

***

Deep commanding words shook Sandy from her reverie. "Good morning, Miss Calbrin."

The Lieutenants had returned, but Blessing was gone. They could never hurt her baby now. She thanked God that she'd sent her child away. Sandy went outside and closed the door.

"Your baby should have returned from visiting her father by now."

"She has not come back."

Lieutenant Courteous eyed the front door. "Can we look inside your house?"

"Yes, of course. Go inside." Sandy moved aside and waited.

252

Hearing female voices on the opposite foot trail, Sandy turned to Phoebe and Eve as they approached her.

"Your front door is open." Eve stared at it.

Sandy whispered, "The officers are inside."

Lieutenants Courteous and Scarface came outside.

Sandy pointed to the big mango tree. "Would you like to sit under the shade?"

Lieutenant Courteous walked to the tree. "Miss Calbrin, we need to see the paper you have for your baby."

Lieutenant Scarface glared. "If a small baby goes on a trip to visit someone, she returns the next day."

"Her father came here several times, but I've never gone to his village. I don't know where she is." Sandy shrugged. "I'll go in the house and get the paper for Blessing."

"I'll go with you." Lieutenant Courteous started to follow her.

"The ladies are here to help, and they will collect the paper." Sandy sat down on a log and motioned Phoebe to come. "Will you please go inside and bring my small suitcase so I can show these officers a paper?"

Phoebe brought the carry-on bag outside and gave it to Sandy, who opened it. She pulled out the contract with Blessing's father and handed it to Lieutenant Courteous.

He gripped the paper in both hands and peered at the upside-down words. "I will take this document with me." He left with Scarface.

Sandy giggled, the first laugh she'd had in three days, since handing Blessing over to Mr. and Mrs. Dugumou. She made the right decision by sending her baby away. Blessing was safe. Maybe for the first time in her life she had put someone else's life ahead of her own.

"I am relieved those officers left." Eve smiled. "Where's Blessing?"

Sandy grinned. "Blessing is gone."

"Gone?" Phoebe raised her eyebrows. "Where?"

"She went home."

"That's good. Now we need to think of your safety."

253

Loud popping sounds erupted in the distance. Phoebe and Eve turned to the explosions.

Sandy frowned at Eve. "Was that gunfire?"

"Yes, more soldiers are taking a shortcut through Koala."

"Let's go inside." Sandy led the way.

After they were seated, she asked, "Phoebe, if you stay here to sweep and wash clothes, will you be safe? May I take Eve with me through the bush to the dispensary?"

"Yes." Phoebe picked up the broom. "My son is working on his farm nearby, and he promised to check on us. The pastor told Eve to work in Adam's place at the clinic."

"Thank you." Sandy turned to Eve. "Let's go."

Sandy walked behind Eve on the short-cut through the bush to the dispensary.

Eve said, "I do not know what I want to do at the university. I would like to follow you around and watch your treatments. Maybe then I can decide if I want to study medicine."

"That's a good idea."

When they reached the clinic, Eve swept and dusted as Sandy set out the bandages.

Colonel Big slammed open the door and stomped into the clinic. Sandy's hands shook. The bottle of pills slipped out of her hand and to the floor.

"Miss Calbrin, may I have a word alone with you?"

"Yes." Her heart beat like the African war drums calling warriors to fight. His frantic arrival and the concern etched on his face sent shivers down her spine.

She pointed to the bench under the shade of the baobab tree. "Please sit down." Sandy lifted a hand and pressed it on her forehead.

"There may soon be danger. I am very fond of you. I love you."

She whispered, "Love me?" She lost her breath and tried to take in air.

"Marry me, and I can save you."

For a full minute, her throat tightened. Sandy couldn't move her mouth. Her heart pounded. She tried to look away, anywhere, and

254

everywhere, except his eager face. His marriage proposal sounded sincere, but was it? She couldn't hurt his feelings, nor be unkind to him.

Sandy clasped her trembling hands together. "Sir, I couldn't marry you."

"I want you to be my wife. You are the strongest and most beautiful woman I have ever met. You are good, very good. I love you. I have three legal wives. You could be my fourth wife and under my protection. It is the only way for you to stay here and keep your baby."

His shining, excited eyes met hers. He was offering a way of escape, to save her and Blessing. But it wasn't the right way for her to keep her baby. Her breathing grew ragged. Could he really love her? He was no longer interested in having an affair or taking her away for the weekend. He proposed marriage. It was a serious offer, and she couldn't offend him.

"Sir, I am a Christian. It is forbidden for a believer to marry an unbeliever."

"You are a kind and loving woman. We could be happy together and have a wonderful family."

Her jaw dropped. She shivered and took a deep gulp of air. He sounded as if he might love her.

Lord, give me words.

A thunderous popping erupted. Colonel Big jumped up and yanked his gun out of the holster belted around his waist. His arm flew out, keeping Sandy in place, as if he were trying to protect her. Military men stormed out of the bushes and surrounded them, but something was wrong.

No one wore a complete military uniform, only a torn jacket or crumpled pair of trousers. Bits of straw and grass stuck out of the men's hair as if they had spent the night in the bush. All were barefoot. They were rogues, common renegades. A cold tremor coursed through her spine as she looked over the filthy dress of the rebels. Blood splatters on their hands and arms turned her throat to ice.

Colonel Big holstered his gun. "Leave this woman alone. She is under my protection."

The man wearing a torn lieutenant's jacket moved closer to Sandy. "What do you have for us?"

Sandy's voice quivered. "I give you the love of God."

"We must have money. We need funds for our soldiers."

Sandy put her hands in her skirt pockets and pulled out the linings, shaking her head. "I have no money."

Colonel Big extended his hand toward her. "I know this woman, and she has nothing for you. It is best if you move on."

The Lieutenant urged his men away. They scattered into the bushes.

Colonel Big turned to her. "I care for you, and I can protect you."

"Thank you, Colonel Tsaou. I appreciate you helping me. In view of what has happened, I must report to my superior, Mr. Jubilee in Hose, and seek his advice."

"I would never force you to do anything you didn't want to do. I love you and want to marry you. Maybe one day you could convince me to follow your Jesus God. You have my deepest respect. I have seen for myself you are a true Christian." Colonel Big nodded and dashed after the insurgents through the bush.

She tried to calm her shakes. Colonel Tsaou might love her in his own way, but she could never marry an unbeliever. Maybe through her witness, he would become a Christian.

Explosions. She jumped as they filled the air. A car engine grew louder. Her posture stiffened. She couldn't move.

What now?

CHAPTER THIRTY-NINE

A few minutes later, David and his father, Mr. Jubilee, drove up to the clinic in the Mercedes Benz. When the car stopped, they jumped out.

"Good morning, Sister Sandy," Mr. Jubilee said. "There is unrest everywhere in the country. Your Embassy is evacuating all the Americans. Prepare your baggage and come with us."

"What?" Her voice shook. "Right now?"

"Yes, we must leave immediately. There are military forces on all the major roads. Former insurgents have entered our country."

"I'll get ready."

"Do you have a camera?"

"No, I never brought one with me. Why do you ask?"

"We wanted to hide it for you. People taking pictures are being arrested. All cameras and films are being thrown away." Mr. Jubilee reached into his briefcase. "I was able to secure your passport, but due to the military confusion no one corrected the mistaken dates stamped in your initial visa. The soldiers at the airport might cause a problem."

"What will they do?"

"If God is with you they might only send you out of the country, but evil officers could take you to prison." Mr. Jubilee handed over the passport. "Most likely they will stamp deported in your passport. Then you would never be allowed to return."

I want to come back.

Sandy stood frozen to the spot. Maybe she shouldn't leave the country, if they'd never let her come back. She could stay in Koala and trust God for protection. No, she couldn't ask the local people to hide her and imperil their lives. If the soldiers restrained her, they might torture her to get information about Blessing or learn her whereabouts. Would she stand up under physical brutality, rape, and imprisonment?

Men, dressed in rumpled uniforms, burst out of the shrubs and clumps of grasses. They stumbled over roots and came closer. The leader screamed, "Stop. Halt. Get down on the ground."

The renegades pointed machine guns and pistols at Mr. Jubilee, David, and Sandy while they surrounded them.

Ice seared Sandy's veins and froze her in place.

The man in a captain's uniform aimed his rifle at her. "I ordered you to get down on the ground. Down! Now!"

Sandy, David, and Mr. Jubilee knelt on the ground, leaned forward, and pressed themselves flat. Seven of the warriors squeezed into Mr. Jubilee's Mercedes Benz.

The man in a sergeant's jacket snapped, "Toss the keys to me."

From the ground, David slid his hand into his pocket, pulled out the keys, and threw them to the one remaining renegade, who stood guard over them. The rebel soldier entered the car with the others and drove off.

Sandy struggled to her feet. Her heart pounded and limbs shook. Without transportation she would have to stay in Koala. It appeared God didn't want her to go anywhere.

Mr. Jubilee jiggled the coins in his pocket. "David, go to the taxi station and see if you can find a vehicle traveling to Hose."

After David departed, Phoebe arrived. "Sister Sandy, the radio said several hundred people were shot in the city."

The blood throbbed in Sandy's temples. "Phoebe, come inside and wait with Mr. Jubilee, Eve, and me."

Sandy went into the dispensary and shouted, "Eve, are you alright?"

Eve emerged from behind a stack of broken benches and a pile of firewood. "I hid to listen to the military officers. If they took you some place, I could report it to our church leaders."

Mr. Jubilee looked around the room. "Where is Blessing?"

"She has traveled home." Sandy's vacant heart thudded.

Mr. Jubilee sat down in one of the chairs. "I'm glad she is safe. I do not think we could protect such a famous baby."

Sandy would never get used to all the scars that ran up and down Mr. Jubilee's dark face. They made him look fiercer than the rebels who had held guns on them, but his smile made him appear friendlier.

Thirty minutes later, David returned from the taxi station. "There are no vehicles. The soldiers from the opposition party have confiscated all of them."

Mr. Jubilee stood and paced. "Sister Sandy, we are concerned for your safety. This is our home and country. We will be fine, but we drove here to take you to the airport."

Sandy took a deep breath. "Mr. Jubilee, why don't you and David go to the chief's house and ask about any transportation that may be available in the village? Eve, would you show them the way, please? Phoebe, let's go to my house and pack."

They all nodded, but Mr. Jubilee mumbled. "Say a prayer."

Phoebe and Sandy hiked through the bush to her house. They went inside and packed the bags.

Twenty minutes later David, Mr. Jubilee, and Eve drove up in a dilapidated burned-out van.

As they climbed out of it, David said, "This old van belongs to the chief's brother-in-law. It survived a fire. Even if it breaks down on the road it will get us away from Koala where most of the troops are taking a short cut south."

He lifted Sandy's bags and loaded them into the back. Sandy and Mr. Jubilee slid onto the second seat.

She waved. "Goodbye. Phoebe. Eve. Thank you."

David started the engine and turned down the dusty trail. Several miles outside the village of Koala, the road was blocked with logs. Thirty military rogues rushed out of the bushes and circled the vehicle. David locked the doors.

Sandy stared into the contorted faces and angry eyes of the renegades. Her heart thundered, and she screamed.

The rebels smacked the sides of the vehicle with the palms of their hands and shouted obscenities. The armed combatants beat the van with clubs and rifles, and then they smashed the back window. Glass shattered. In unison they ran to one side and shoved the van over onto its side. It dropped with a loud thud.

Raw terror consumed her, and she couldn't breathe. Her teary eyes blurred.

The leader yelled, "Get out, all of you!"

She couldn't move even if she wanted to for she was paralyzed with fear. Would they hack Mr. Jubilee, David, and her into pieces with their machetes?

Lord Jesus, please help.

Then a war cry sent shivers down her icy spine. The shriek came from another group on the opposite trail. The Koala chief led the village men, who were armed with cutlasses, hoes, and clubs as they dashed toward the renegades.

Tears raced down her cheeks for she had treated all of those men in the clinic.

God, help those brave, good men.

Their assault drove the rebels away.

David, Mr. Jubilee, and Sandy climbed out of the overturned vehicle. Sandy wanted to throw her arms around every man who came to her rescue, but that would have been another taboo. Through tears she clutched each man's hand in both of hers and bowed before each one. It was the highest respect she could think of.

The chief stuck his spear in the ground. "We heard evil men planned to steal your vehicle. Sister Sandy, you need this van to reach the airport and safety."

David stepped closer. "Let's all shove the vehicle back onto its wheels. I do not think it has been damaged." After the van was upright, David checked the engine over and started it.

Sandy didn't want to leave the villagers who had saved her. She closed her eyes for a moment. Then she hoped and prayed all of them would be alive after the tribal conflicts.

The pastor shook his head. "We do not want you to go, but we came so you could reach safety. Please come back to us when the fighting is over."

As the van drove off, Sandy turned back and waved.

The beaming chief held his staff high and raised his voice. "Come back, Sister Sandy. Please come back to us when it is safe. We will be waiting."

Sandy couldn't stop crying. It had been hard, but she belonged in Africa. Over the months she'd grown and learned to give up everything that she'd held dear, even her precious baby.

Her Blessing had been shaken out of her hands. No, her daughter hadn't been taken. Sandy had learned to surrender. She had no regrets. Obedience to God brought peace.

David drove fast. Each time he met military tankers or trucks, he swerved off the main road into the bushes. She closed her eyes and prayed they would reach the airport and safety.

Would they arrive unharmed?

CHAPTER FORTY

All the main roads to the airport in the capital were barricaded. Military officers halted the vehicle at every blocked road outside the national metropolis.

As David approached the airport, a police officer stopped the van and leaned inside. He shook hands with Mr. Jubilee.

The policeman nodded at Sandy. "All the Americans are hiding out in the abandoned embassy residence behind the airport. They are waiting for a government plane to fly them out of Norgia." He turned to Mr. Jubilee. "You can take Mommy Blessing there. Ask her to sit on the floor so no one will see her as you drive down the streets. It is not safe."

Mr. Jubilee asked, "Should I telephone to inform them we are coming?"

The officer took a deep breath. "The airport is closed. All government offices, post offices, and schools are shut down. The television networks, radios, telephone lines, and electric lines have all been severed to prevent opposition parties from gaining control."

After the vehicle pulled away, Sandy slid to the floor. "If the airport is closed, how will the Americans fly out of the country?"

"They have sanction." Mr. Jubilee removed his suit jacket and covered her.

As she scrunched on the floor under the garment, she tried to take slow deep breaths to remain calm. The vehicle braked. If she hadn't been squeezed in the tiny space, she'd have slammed into the front seat. Sensing the vehicle zoom faster down the road, she spread her palms on the floorboard to maintain her balance. After a sharp turn the van braked again.

"We have detoured around the closed international airport," Mr. Jubilee whispered. "There's an abandoned residence up ahead."

"I think that is it." David spoke to his father. "There appears to be no way to enter the yard. The gate is locked and the fence is thirty feet high. We cannot telephone and tell them we are here. I am not sure how to get Sister Sandy inside the building."

Sandy threw back the jacket and lifted herself to the seat. She handed the garment to Mr. Jubilee and nodded. "Thank you." She pulled her carry-on bag onto her lap. "Let me out right here."

Mr. Jubilee put his arm out to stop her. "No, do not get out of the car. If the Americans are hiding here, there could be snipers. They could shoot you before the gate is opened. We are not certain this is the right place. We cannot leave you here."

"There's only one way to find out." Sandy reached into her bag and grabbed her passport. "Wait here. I'll be fine."

She didn't feel fine, but God's courage filled her to step out of the vehicle. Sandy needed to get away from Mr. Jubilee and David so they could drive to safety. She had nothing more to lose, except her life, which would have been her gain.

David turned into the drive and slowly went down the short way. When he stopped, she opened the door and jumped out.

He yelled, "No, Sister Sandy, do not go out there! Let me see if it's the right place."

Sandy ran to the locked front gate.

Lord God, help me.

American marines dressed in military fatigues darted out of the building. They carried machine guns, rifles, and drawn pistols aimed at her and the vehicle.

Reaching the gate, she pressed up against it and held her passport out through the bars toward them.

A soldier took it. "Where are you from, ma'am?"

"Florida."

It seemed so long ago, but she'd only been in Norgia less than a year.

The lieutenant unlocked the gate. "Step inside quickly, ma'am. These men standing by the car cannot stay." He locked the gate.

"They drove me here."

David unloaded Sandy's luggage.

One of the marines said, "Ma'am, you will only be allowed to take one carry-on with you on the military plane, which will arrive tomorrow morning."

Since coming to Africa, she'd been slowly giving up career, money, home, car, shoes, and jeans, but in that process she'd been surrendering to the Lord. Was she leaving empty-handed, even without her Shea nuts? Had she sacrificed too much, including her baby? No, she was going out of the country much richer. She had satisfaction, peace of mind, fulfillment, and a little baby daughter. And God had taught her that her life was to be a living sacrifice.

An officer said, "Perhaps your friends could take the other bags back to your home and keep them for you."

Mr. Jubilee extended his hand through the bars and shook Sandy's hand while David put the bags back into the van. "Goodbye, Sister Sandy. We wish you a safe journey. Please come back to us when it is safe."

He climbed into the van with his son. David waved and started the engine. Then he turned the vehicle around to head out of the city.

"We are visible out here." A marine sergeant led the way. "Let's go in the building."

When Sandy stepped inside, she ran to Helen and hugged her.

An explosion erupted, and the ladies jumped. They turned their heads toward the front door, but it was securely barred with four marines standing by it.

Helen smiled. "Let me show you to the women's quarters."

Sandy followed her into a military barracks filled with cots. She couldn't keep her eyes open. "Helen, I'd like to lie down for a while."

"I'll save supper for you. Our colleagues outside are sending in big pots of food."

Sandy woke and found her supper in a covered bowl on top of the little table next to her bed. She lifted the plastic lid and chuckled. She never learned to eat fish heads, so she mixed a small spoon of tomato sauce into the rice and put the fish heads back in the bowl and covered them.

After she ate, Sandy pulled out her passport and alien's identity card to examine the entries. It was the middle of the night. Everyone was sound asleep.

In the commotion and rush to leave the village, she forgot to stop at the police station to have her alien's book stamped. There was no stamp in her card to give her permission to leave. Tears blurred her vision. The military officers at the airport would detain her for not having her alien's book stamped. Or they would haul her off to prison or deport her so she could never return to Norgia.

Either the unstamped alien's book or the invalid dates in her passport would cause her problems. Her heart pounded faster, and her hands shook as she studied the identification book, a cheap little card. It would be easy to change the zero to an eight, and then the dates would match.

She picked up her pen and pressed it on the number but threw the pen down. Christians shouldn't break the laws. She lifted the pen again and started to write, but lay it down. Raising it a third time, she pressed it on the page and altered the government alien's book.

Every possible scenario raced through her tortured mind. She became a criminal and would be deported and never allowed to return to Africa again, or the police would throw her into prison. Why had she done that? If she had to leave the country, she wanted to do it legally so she could come back.

She flipped over to the back of the alien's book and scanned the regulations. They declared it a government offense to change an entry in the book. The penalty was ten years in prison. Her heart pounded harder, and her limbs shook. She collapsed on the bed and sobbed.

On impulse, Sandy picked up her bottle of hair conditioner. She poured the slippery solution onto the offensive page and rubbed it. Turning that page over she read, "Anyone destroying government property would be sent to prison for twenty years."

She fell back on the bed and closed her eyes as she re-lived the military renegades who beat the van. She was condemned and going to prison for life with those rebels. She stretched out her hands to stop the swaying furniture as the walls swirled around her.

Sandy recalled the terror and harassment of the military officers over the past months. Without thinking of the consequences, she ripped the alien's book into hundreds of pieces. She took out a match from the tiny box next to the bush lantern, struck it, and torched the torn pages. With the burning papers in her hand, she raced into the bathroom to toss the flaming sheets into the sink. In a daze she watched the blaze soar higher, pressed her palms together, and bowed her head.

Guilty of destroying government property, she stared at the ashes. The officers would throw her in prison for one hundred years. Her heart exploded and chest hurt.

Lord, please forgive me.

She closed her eyes and saw the compassion in Colonel Big's eyes when he had asked her to marry him. He was a sinner, in need of the Savior, like she had been.

Lord, you've been so good to me. I'm a sinner. Forgive me, Lord. I can never be like Helen, a sweet dedicated Christian.

Be like my Son, Jesus. Imitate Him.

Yes, Lord, make me like your Son.

Sandy spent the rest of the night worrying about the years she'd spend in an African prison. God had forgiven her, but she had to face the consequences of her actions. She was guilty and deserved prison for destroying government property.

Early the following morning she trudged behind the others as they mounted the stairs to an airport bus. Her limbs shook and sweat dripped from her body as she traipsed toward a vacant seat. It was a slow short ride, about a half of a mile to the international airport. She forced one foot ahead of the other as she descended the steps and walked through the doors. Her eyes scanned the building for immigration officers who would demand her alien's book.

Sandy lifted her hand to her thumping heart. She headed toward the passport check point, visa inspection, and customs declaration. At every booth, she looked for military officers, but they weren't there. Then two military policemen headed toward her. She stopped and her heart rose to her throat. She tried to catch her breath as they closed in

267

to arrest her, but the officers laughed and walked right past her. Her thumping heart slowed.

She reached the booth labeled, "Alien's identity card control," where the officer with his giant ledger should sit. No immigration officers were on duty that morning.

Sandy searched for officers at every military checkpoint. They weren't there. She wasn't arrested.

She walked up to Helen. "I've done something terrible."

Helen stared at her. "What did you do, Sandy?"

"I burned my alien's book."

"Why?" Helen's jaw dropped open.

"I went crazy last night reliving all the times the immigration officers demanded I sleep with them or spend the weekend with them before they would stamp my book. I sat all day in their offices waiting for them to find the lost stamp, which was never lost."

"Why did you put up with it?"

"I'm not an African. I'm not a citizen. I'm not a missionary. I'm just a single, white woman who wanted to help. It's their country. They can say and do whatever they want to me. I was terrified of their power to send me out of the country. God always delivered me, but it was hard."

Lieutenant Scarface marched into the waiting room and stepped into the crowd of Americans. He reached out to take Sandy's elbow. "Come with me, Miss Calbrin."

Helen glared. "What do you want with her?"

"She is under investigation."

Helen snapped, "How can she be under investigation since you are evacuating all of us. Do you see all those American marines over there?" She pointed to them. "We are now under their authority."

Lieutenant Scarface glared at Sandy. "I will get you next time, Miss Calbrin." He stomped away.

She sniffed back tears. "No one asked to see our alien's books."

Helen furrowed her brow. "I heard they might no longer be required."

268

Sandy put her hand to her chest. "God is good. My sins are washed away and remembered no more."

Helen put her arm around Sandy. "You've done a lot of great work here. We had a noticeably higher number of mothers come this year to the hospital to vaccinate their children. They spoke of the helpful lessons you taught them."

She walked beside Helen across the airfield to the plane. Then Sandy dropped behind the older woman to take last place. At the bottom of the steps, she turned to see the land she had learned to love.

Hearing screams and then a shot, she sprinted up the ladder and into the aircraft. She dropped into a seat as a young man slammed the door behind her. She didn't have time to buckle her seatbelt before the plane started down the runway.

She glanced out the window. Colonel Big struggled to his feet. Two military men with machine guns ran away from him. Blood dribbled from his lip and forehead. Had Colonel Big tackled an officer who would have stopped her from getting on the plane? He lifted his hand and waved.

When he smiled, Sandy grinned at him and waved.

Africa had become her home. Would God let her come back?

THE END

Dear Reader,

The story of Blessing is true and taken from my journal nearly fifty years ago. Police officers' harassed me, military officials threatened me, and immigration officials propositioned me. Names of people, villages, and countries are fictitious.

Scenery, open African markets, housing, roads, dead man's alley, and the black market are descriptive of actual incidents from my diary.

I have old photographs with Blessing, one of which is on my back as I drove the motorcycle.

Treating the patients as I described was real, and their understanding and descriptions of diseases were precise.

Taboos within the culture and traditions were ones that I heard from the local people in various areas nearly fifty years ago, and may no longer be practiced.

I was stopped on the road by the television news crew. The interview took place as I described and was seen by thousands of people on the national, state, and local news stations. According to the dates and places from which people viewed the interview, it was shown numerous times.

I gave Blessing to a childless couple before the military coup started. I left the country with the initial wrong dates still in my passport before the violence started. Other missionaries experienced the shooting, dead bodies in the road, and rioting renegades. Their vehicle was smashed by rebels, but they escaped uninjured.

I submitted my diary about Blessing to publishers. They loved the story but recommended that I submit it to Christian publishers, or those who published journal-type stories or nonfiction. That didn't work out, so I self-published.

Celeste

I hope you enjoyed this book. Would you take a few minutes to leave a short review.
Thank you.

Made in the USA
Middletown, DE
05 March 2024

50288140R00156